S0-BOT-691

Lunar Encounter

by

Harold W.G. Allen

Perspective Books

By the same author:

Ye Shall Know the Truth
The Edge of the Universe
Higher Perspective
The Eternal Universe
The Face on Mars
Cosmic Perspective

First Edition

Perspective Books,
P.O. Box 6123,
Spring Hill, FL. 34611
U.S.A.

ISBN: 0-9624555-2-0
Library of Congress Card Number: 00-190493

Printed in the U.S.A.

Lunar Encounter

by

Harold W.G. Allen

The Universe

Through distant ages man has gazed, with reverence, into the sky;

Foremost in his mind, that momentous question: Why?

How far are yonder points of light?

Shining like tiny beacons on the darkest night?

Whence came the stars, our heavenly host,

Their soft light shimmering like a phantom ghost?

Born of countless suns our Milky Way doth shine,

An enigma to ancient theories, which man must now refine.

Beyond the reaches of our Galaxy, in the enveloping depths of space,

Unnumbered starry systems participate in a truly cosmic race.

For the very universe is expanding, at a most prodigious rate;

Motivated, one would deduce, by Principle: A synonym for Fate.

H.W.G.A.

INTRODUCTION

A great deal of what passes today for science fiction should really be classified as fantasy fiction. In point of fact, genuine science is often conspicuous by its absence. Other than serving as mere "escapist" literature, little else is offered the reader. Of superior worth is a book that is able to both entertain and impart knowledge. It is hereby contended that *Lunar Encounter* constitutes a most unique blend of legitimate science and philosophy, in close conjunction with what is a truly believable fiction plot— one affording an ample serving of such basic ingredients as mystery, drama and space adventure.

The revelations of modern science may well be described as phenomenal. Insight into our physical universe has increased at a rate far surpassing that of philosophy and religion. Not only has man walked the lunar surface, but he is poised to visit the planet Mars within the next few decades. Contact with extraterrestrial intelligence — via the radio telescope— is not out of the question in the foreseeable future. Much of what was once science fiction has already become a reality.

However, in the process of making many remarkable discoveries, science has also managed to undermine certain popular religious beliefs— producing a vacuum in the minds of large numbers of inquisitive souls. The very thought of other worlds and other civilizations must serve to raise issues of a theological nature — issues which simply cannot be avoided if one would truly seek to comprehend our evolving universe. For instance, are these myriad worlds blessed with a "Christ?" Or, on the other hand, do our theologians even know what they are talking about by upholding such a dogma?

In discussing a number of fundamental religious misconceptions (see Chapter Two), valuable insight is offered into a generally misunderstood body of literature: the Bible. Originally written for the prime purpose of expounding a moral or principle — often by means of symbolism— our churches have consistently ignored modern scholarship in their endeavor to thrust an outworn and naive literal interpretation upon an unthinking public. Moreover, their very suppression and withholding of vital new evidence— as revealed by the Dead Sea Scrolls— can only be regarded as inexcusable, if not criminal.

While the strength of the scientific method lies in willingness to subject theory to test, it is also a sad fact that there is usually little or no correlation of science with the premise of *Cause* or *Purpose*. In short, seemingly mundane physical phenomena may well have roots buried deep in the realm of philosophy. For this reason science has not always been free of error when it comes to interpreting available evidence. Indeed, one graphic example of this failure to recognize *Principle*, in attempting to reduce data to theory, has led to widespread acceptance of the Big Bang model of creation— a cosmology which is now shown to be false and without foundation, being the product of incomplete laws of gravitation and an erroneous concept of radiation propagation! (Essentials of this assertion are given in Chapter Six, where the reader is introduced to a truly revolutionary treatise — one which will be seen to link the scientific fact of evolution with the principle of reincarnation and Cosmic Destiny.)

Lunar Encounter

Given sufficient incentive, it is to be expected that many of nature's secrets could be made to yield to the probing of an unbiased and inquiring mind. Ultimately, an aroused curiosity— whether inspired by science fiction or a serious philosophical essay— is bound to be reflected in terms of a richer perspective.

It is the fervent hope of the author that *Lunar Encounter* will stimulate a personal search for insight into the wonders of the universe. If so, it shall have accomplished a primary function within the context of an intriguing science fiction novel— a story which might well depict the mixed reaction of present-day Earth society should it suddenly encounter a highly advanced alien race.

H.W.G.A.

Chapter 1

LOST CONTACT

A blue-white crescent Earth hung above the bleak lunar landscape, now clearly visible to both occupants of the *Antares*, as the vehicle crawled through an open hangar door. Designed to house up to twenty scientists in pressurized aluminum alloy structures, covered by a one-meter layer of soil as a safeguard against micrometeorites and cosmic rays, *Lunar Base* was an international venture. Completed some two years earlier, in 2093 A.D., it was situated near the northwest corner of Mare Imbrium (Sea of Rains), the largest of the Moon's maria with a width of over 1,200 kilometers. Man's first permanent lunar complex was constructed within 10 km of the crater Iridium-A, roughly 44 degrees north latitude and 27 degrees west longitude.

At the controls of the Antares was 31-year-old American pilot/geologist John Baldwin, his 5'-9" frame weighing a mere 24 lbs in the weak one-sixth lunar gravity. His companion was 35-year-old senior geologist Michael Frost, a native Australian who stood several inches taller and was about four Moon pounds heavier. Unencumbered by a bulky space suit in their pressurized cabin, Baldwin's long blond locks were in visible contrast to his colleague's dark brown receding hairline. Their mission was to explore a specific region of the Teneriffe Mountains, a small range of high cliffs projecting out of an extensive flat plain to the southwest of the large crater Plato.

Pride of the base's rather limited transport fleet, the *Antares* was a unique combination of tractor and rocket-powered hopper. This latter feature was a recent innovation in lunar mobility, in the sense that it offered a choice of travel by either sub-orbital space hops or by land. Subjected to successful field testing, during the past four months, it was deemed capable of making a round trip flight to a site some 800 km distant. In this instance, their intended objective was of the order of only 300 km. It was to be a brief hop which would save them many hours of otherwise tedious surface travel.

"Don't forget to close the garage door after us," quipped Baldwin, over his radio link with *Lunar Base*, as the vehicle cleared the hangar bay and emerged into full sunlight.

"See you guys in two Earth days," responded the voice of Canadian communications specialist Paul Cooper, over the craft's audio speaker. "Avoid littering the pristine landscape with empty food packets and other refuse."

"Closing the outer door now. Keep in touch," said Andrei Kovakov, an electronics technician and one of four Russian personnel currently stationed at the base.

As the big door slowly closed behind them, Baldwin eased the *Antares* to a stop about a hundred meters away and activated a button which would raise the vehicle onto four combination shock-absorbing launch pad/landing legs. "Ready to initiate our pre-flight check," he announced to his companion.

"Coordinates punched into the computer and all systems are green," Frost declared, after completing a scan of multiple instruments. "The runway is clear. Take her up, John."

"Ignition!" shouted Baldwin, as the *Antares* shuddered in response to the recoil action of hot gases spewing at high velocity through twin nozzles.

Lunar Encounter

Rising vertically amidst a cloud of lunar dust kicked up by rocket exhaust, the small craft climbed with increasing speed on tongues of orange flame, eventually pitching over to a 45 degree angle at an altitude of some 400 meters, as engine nozzles swivelled in response to computer command. Strapped into their well-cushioned reclining seats, the two geologist/astronauts were subjected to mounting but quite tolerable "G" forces. In due course, this intrusive thrust was abruptly terminated upon engine shutdown, and they experienced a state just short of the weightlessness which they had come to know on many previous occasions.

To their left the semi-circular ring of the Jura Mountains could be seen through a port side window of the *Antares*, its highest peaks rising some 20,000 feet above the depression of Sinus Iridium (Bay of Rainbows). The product of an asteroid impact, early in the Moon's history, it had left a huge scar that was close to 300 km wide near the northwest corner of Mare Imbrium. Molten matter had later merged with this impact to all but obliterate the crater's eastern wall. To their right and a little to the south two relatively small craters, Helicon and Le Verrier, were clearly visible as they protruded above the flat expanse of terrain which stretched far beyond the eastern horizon. Peering directly ahead they could see the outline of the crater Reese, a slightly smaller impact scar which lay immediately in front of their intended destination. The higher elevations of the Teneriffe Mountains could now be viewed in detail, along with a second line of steep cliffs to the left of this group known as the Straight Range. Beyond and to the northeast they could perceive the great circular rim of the large crater Plato, with its walls extending more than 7,000 feet above the floor of this primeval asteroid strike.

"Sure beats plodding over the surface in the *Hercules*," Frost remarked, referring to their base's most illustrious ground tractor.

"The view is also a lot better from on high," commented his

companion, just as the *Antares* reached the apex of a trajectory which would see the craft begin its descent in a long curving path.

"We're right on course," announced Frost, dutifully monitoring the screen before him. "The small crater Iridium-D is directly beneath us."

"Should soon be time for rotation," advised Baldwin, as they presently passed beyond the crater Reese.

As if on cue, the craft's computer automatically cut in to fire short bursts with tiny vernier jets, causing the vehicle to turn in space so that its main rocket nozzles were oriented in the direction of flight. Braking thrust would commence at an altitude of 2,000 meters, following which manual control would be used to direct the *Antares* to final approach and landing.

"Retro burn right on schedule," declared Frost, in response to an abrupt nudge which pushed them into their seats.

"Appears to be a level area just a little ahead and to the left," observed Baldwin, scanning the terrain below and initiating a brief burn designed to bring them directly over the chosen spot.

"Altitude 800 meters," declared Frost. "Only a few minor craters and the odd sizable boulder on my screen."

"What's our descent rate?"

"Dropping ten meters per second....Forward motion one meter per second....Altitude 200 meters....Still looking good," came the reply.

"Increasing thrust slightly," responded Baldwin.

"Four meters down per second....Altitude 150 meters.... Steer right to avoid a patch of rough ground."

“Acknowledged,” voiced Baldwin, hastening to make appropriate nozzle adjustments.

With a gentle lurch the *Antares* settled on the lunar surface amidst a cloud of dust thrown up by their propulsion system—dust which had lain undisturbed for aeons in the absence of an atmosphere with which to produce weather.

"The *Antares* has landed and all systems are green," Frost notified Paul Cooper at Lunar Mission Control, via one of two communications satellites placed into staggered orbits so as to facilitate constant monitoring of the Moon's perpetually facing Earthside.

"What's your exact position?" inquired Cooper.

"We managed to touch down close to our planned location," Frost responded. "Coordinates are as follows," he added, proceeding to transmit the requested data.

"Coordinates received loud and clear. Don't forget to keep us informed of events....Cooper, over and out."

Some forty minutes later the two astronauts— now transformed into geologists — exited through the air lock of the *Antares*. Clad in their protective space suits, they carried an assortment of implements that were clipped to a utility belt. Strapped to each back was a rather sophisticated jet pack resembling, in effect, a Buck Rogers flying belt. Not only would this device enable them to leap over annoying obstacles, but it was capable of permitting the explorers to reach elevated regions that would otherwise be inaccessible.

"Too bad we couldn't have tractored the *Antares* closer to the southern face," opined Frost, as the two trudged steadily toward a distant cliff.

"It simply wasn't feasible. The terrain gets rapidly worse as you approach the mountains, and it would not have been wise to risk damage to our vehicle for the sake of a few kilometers," Baldwin replied, carefully picking his way around boulders and up a steep incline.

"Oh well, just another couple of kilometers more to go," said Frost, resigned to the role of a pedestrian.

"Tell me, Mike, what do you think about the prospects of our radio astronomers contacting an extraterrestrial civilization during the span of the next century or so?"

"Good question. I'm sure there must be large numbers of advanced worlds out amongst the billions of solar systems that are bound to exist within the confines of our Milky Way galaxy. But I am forced to concede that it is more than a little discouraging that efforts to date have produced only negative results."

"Perhaps most have evolved beyond the point where we would be of interest to them."

"You mean, John, that we might be looked upon as primitive savages unworthy of communion with a truly exalted race?"

"Possibly, although it is conceivable that many would prefer to check us out first before revealing their presence."

"In other words, they could be reluctant to share their superior science and technology with a world which might pose a threat to other galactic societies."

"Exactly," answered Baldwin. "You must admit that mankind's past track record is far from satisfactory — what with all the foolish wars and atrocities that have been perpetrated in the name of religion. Nor would an ubiquitous selfish greed for personal wealth and power tend to endear us to an alien race that had developed a really high sense of moral principles."

“I see what you are implying — namely, that any civilization of sufficient maturity as to actively search for intelligent life forms on other solar systems would almost invariably be more highly advanced than ourselves, both morally and scientifically."

"My point, indeed, Mike. Considering the vast interval of time required to evolve to our present level — which has come to feature the radio telescope only in comparatively recent times — it is highly unlikely that our first extraterrestrial contact would occur with beings no more advanced than ourselves. Furthermore, I just have to believe that moral integrity cannot be permitted to lag too far behind science — without the very grave danger of such a society destroying itself!"

"I must concur with you on that statement. I have often felt that the human race has placed itself on the brink of global suicide through failure to achieve a total ban on nuclear weapons."

"There is also the frightening prospect of germ and chemical warfare to consider," Baldwin was quick to add. "As matters currently stand, almost every minor nation on Earth — including many run by tyrannical petty dictators — now possess nuclear capability and/or stockpiles of chemical/germ agents."

"We are unquestionably citizens of a very sick world," Frost was forced to concede. "There are times when I wish some divine deity would intervene and bang certain heads together. In spite of frequent attempts to convey a sense of security — under the auspices of a so-called United Nations — it is largely a political facade. Only on the Moon or an orbiting station, where the deadly vacuum of space poses an ever-present threat and serves as a unifying factor, is there genuine spirit of cooperation."

"Likewise, the overpowering majesty of the heavens — along with the incredible complexity of the simplest cell — has managed to convince many scientists as to the reality of some universal *God/ Principle* behind creation," philosophized Baldwin. "In the face of such, any vain loyalty to individual nations and naive religious concepts tends to fade into obscurity."

"To return to our weak and inept United Nations, it is a most unfortunate fact of history that, from its very inception, it has done precious little to abolish armies and rectify a host of injustices," Frost continued. "Since the dawn of the 21st century this ineffective organization has failed to prevent the explosion of no less than six nuclear bombs, obliterating six cities in the Middle East and Asia — to say nothing of allowing crazed leaders to remain in power long after they had unleashed diabolical infectious diseases against their enemies in blatant acts of terrorism."

"Your criticism of our United Nations is certainly well founded, Mike. Clearly, the problem lies with a widespread reluctance to adopt a charter of fundamental human rights— and to back this charter with a World Army ready and capable of deposing any government which would flaunt these rights."

"That would definitely be a big step toward sanity."

"All we need is your magical deity to knock appropriate heads together," commented Baldwin, as he came to a halt and gazed up at the rugged cliff face which lay before them.

"I only wish I knew where to find the proprietor of this valuable service. However, I suppose we had better put business ahead of any missionary venture and concentrate upon a mountain of work which awaits us," Frost quipped, likewise pausing to take in the scenery.

For the next ten minutes the two geologists busied themselves chipping and collecting rock samples, which they carefully deposited into tagged plastic bags for subsequent analysis. Presently, their attention shifted to a section of the cliff wall high above them. Glistening in the bright sunshine was a narrow band of peculiar rock strata which begged investigation.

"Shall we flip a coin to see who makes a hop up the cliff face? There's a handy ledge to our right where one might perch to obtain a sample," Baldwin suggested.

"I'm afraid a coin is quite out of the question. But how about guessing which hand holds this small rock," Frost proposed, reaching down and picking up same. Putting his gloved hands behind his back, he then held them before Baldwin and urged him to choose.

A few minutes later the winner launched himself from the lunar surface with his jet pack. Hovering overhead while his companion watched in silence, it was not long before Frost succeeded in reaching the intended ledge. Gaining a foothold, he proceeded to collect the desired sample. However, instead of descending with his prize, he decided upon a different plan. "I'm going to take a quick look at the top of this mesa," he informed his colleague over their helmet radio link.

"If you encounter any little green men, be sure to request an audience with their leader," Baldwin responded in jest.

With a burst of exhaust gases from his jet pack, it was not long before Frost reached the top of the cliff, some 400 meters above the plain below. Finding a sizable level spot he eased himself to a soft landing and began to survey his surroundings. The view was quite impressive. Several kilometers to the south the Antares glistened with reflected sunlight; while to the north and east a number of scattered mountain peaks dominated the scene. On the western horizon the more distant projections of the Straight Range lay just out of sight due to the Moon's curvature. Moving away from the cliff edge, he turned his attention to the task of obtaining rock specimens.

"You know, John, I bet this small boulder was ejected from Plato when it was formed as a result of a primeval asteroid strike," voiced Frost, before he suddenly realized that his companion would be unable to hear him. (Now out of line of sight with Baldwin, in the lunar atmospheric vacuum there was no way in which the weak electromagnetic radiation of his helmet radio would be deflected so as to reach his colleague's receiver.)

Resuming his quest for specimens, Frost eventually found himself wandering eastward toward a steep 30-meter cliff which protruded most conspicuously out of an otherwise flat mesa. Situated less than a kilometer away, it was only a short while until he had approached to within a few hundred meters. Uncertain as to whether or not he should return to his waiting comrade, out of the corner of his eye he thought he saw a brief flash of light reflecting off something at the top of this cliff formation. Promptly dismissing the notion as imagination, he was fully prepared to turn and head back— until there was a repeat of the same illusion....Or was it an illusion? Succumbing to his curiosity, he decided to move closer for a better look.

Meanwhile, down at the base of the 400-meter mesa, Baldwin

had become preoccupied with a vein of rather interesting rock strata some distance to the west of their original starting point at the cliff face. With his geologist's hammer he had been busy chipping off several samples, one of which extended below ground level and had necessitated the excavation of a small amount of lunar soil. Almost oblivious to the passage of time, close to forty minutes had elapsed before it occurred to him that Frost had not returned.

"Mike! Can you hear me?" he shouted into the radio transmitter embedded in his helmet, not really expecting a reply as his fellow scientist was nowhere to be seen.

Receiving no answer, Baldwin began to retrace his steps, soon arriving at the very spot where Frost had commenced his jet propelled flight. Failing to obtain a response to yet another attempt at radio contact, he prepared to launch himself to the top of the mesa in search of his overdue comrade. Mentally recalling his previous jet pack training exercises, it was not long before he had risen well above the lunar surface. Looking downward, he could see the plume of dust which had been kicked up by his rocket exhaust. In the opposite direction, the top of the cliff face was rapidly approaching, causing him to reduce the throttle setting on the control box around his waist. In due course, he managed to effect a safe descent not far from the vicinity of Frost's earlier landing. However, the senior geologist was not to be seen.

"Mike! Where the devil are you?" Baldwin shouted into his helmet microphone, much perplexed over this unexpected turn of events. Once again, total radio silence prevailed.

Commencing a systematic search for any telltale footprints, impressed upon a covering layer of dust/sand, he was finally rewarded. As he peered down at what was indubitably Frost's tracks, it was noted that they extended toward a prominent cliff to the east. Wasting no time, Baldwin set off at a loping gait in pursuit of his missing colleague. The tracks led directly toward the base of a near vertical cliff wall, before vanishing altogether in a jumble of surface markings which suggested the use of a jet pack. He gazed upward, half expecting to see Frost waving to him from the top of the escarpment.

There was little choice but to jet up to the summit of this second and much smaller mesa. In any case, it was clear that he had to climb above the surrounding terrain in order to establish radio contact. With such a thought in mind, Baldwin again proceeded to activate his jet pack for what would be a relatively short hop. Rising once more in the weak lunar gravity, he quickly reached the top and received a great shock: *Frost was nowhere to be found*! Recovering, he arched his back and sailed over the brow of the cliff....Nothing! Settling to the ground, he began to search for evidence that his companion had indeed visited this mini-mesa. Roughly 300 meters wide by 400 meters long, at first glance this essentially flat ridge — permeated by an occasional boulder— seemed devoid of interest. His initial thought was that Frost must have jetted elsewhere — or, perish the thought, he could have experienced mechanical failure and crashed somewhere on the lunar surface. It looked as if he would have to search the entire perimeter of the escarpment. But then, quite abruptly, he made a discovery which caused him to change his mind.

Noticing an area where the covering veneer of dust appeared to be disturbed, as if from jet pack exhaust, he bent over to investigate. A set of footprints could be discerned that led toward the center of the mesa. After following the tracks for a distance, his search came to an impasse when the trail terminated in a chaotic jumble of faint and mysterious impressions. Studying the confusing scene before him, Baldwin observed that they ended at the brink of a distinctive one-meter deep circular depression, which he estimated to be about 20 meters or so in diameter. Examining the flattened surface, he could not resist a temptation to brush away a thin coating of dust and chip off a tiny portion of the underlying rock. Somehow, it seemed quite different from any of the other lunar samples.

Baldwin was still pondering the significance of this latest peculiarity when his attention was diverted by a shadow that seemed to appear from nowhere. Turning, he was suddenly blinded by a strange purple light which acted to drain him of all strength. Helpless, he could feel himself drifting....falling....falling into total oblivion.

....

Some twelve hours later Colin Bergman, newly appointed commander of Lunar Base, was awakened from a deep sleep and summoned to an urgent meeting in the Operations Center of the base.

"I'm afraid I have some bad news to report," Paul Cooper informed him as he entered the room.

"What is it, Paul?" Bergman asked, noting concern written on the faces of all who were present.

"We've lost contact with the *Antares*," replied the base's chief communications specialist. "They were scheduled to make a broadcast hours ago, and we have been unsuccessful in achieving any response in spite of repeated attempts."

"What really concerns us is that their suits would have run out of oxygen more than an hour ago. Unless they had already returned to the hopper by then they are not likely to ever do so," elaborated Dr. Lin Chang, a Chinese physician who had been assigned to the base for the past four months.

"Could it be just a simple case of transmission breakdown?" Bergman wanted to know. "What about the *Antares*' radio transponder?"

"Everything is fine, both at this end and with respect to our satellite relay station," Cooper assured his superior. "As for the vehicle's transponder, all attempts to activate it have drawn a blank and it is a complete mystery to us."

"If we assume that transmitter failure aboard the *Antares* is at the root of the problem, it is conceivable that they might just decide to abort their expedition and return to base, so as not to alarm us," theorized Bergman, tugging at the impressive beard which he had sported since his days as a U.S. Air Force colonel. Now a civilian at age 38, he was not one to take this new responsibility lightly.

"We have thought of that possibility — even to the extent of initiating a radar scan," enjoined Vladimir Petrov, the chief Russian scientist. "At this moment I have Marie Bouchard monitoring the situation; but the results so far have been negative. Wherever they may be, they have yet to leave the surface."

"Let's confirm that they're still at the original landing site," reasoned Bergman. "We can program our lunar telescopic satellite to perform a high resolution search of the *Antares*' coordinates with its 24-inch instrument."

"It will take a little while, but it should be feasible to obtain video telemetry pinpointing the hopper," agreed David Carpenter, the base's senior optical astronomer. Having almost finished a six-month tour of duty on the Moon, the likeable scientist was due to return shortly to his native England.

"How long are we talking about?" asked Bergman, starting to pace the room.

"Give me an hour," requested Carpenter. "I'll get Amy Wilson, our best computer expert, to assist me."

"Better jump on it right away, David. Let me know the minute you come up with anything," responded Bergman.

"Shall do," said Carpenter, opening an airtight door which gave access to an outer corridor.

....

Some two hours later all five participants had reconvened to discuss options following a rather unexpected disclosure from the astronomer.

"You mean to tell me that the *Antares* is not at their reported location?" Bergman questioned.

"That's right. Either the coordinates were wrong or the hopper has since departed for regions quite unknown," Carpenter stated. "We thoroughly searched a radius of four kilometers, with a resolution which should have revealed its presence."

"Then we have to hope that they are currently en route to us by surface. It must be that their rocket propulsion system is somehow inoperable, and they have been forced to resort to tractor mode," concluded Bergman.

"Sounds like a plausible interpretation of the facts — unless, of course, they took off and subsequently crashed," opined Petrov.

"I think we should proceed upon the basis of the first and most favorable assumption," Bergman decided. "David, I want you to check with Hans Mueller, in cartography, with the idea of plotting the most probable return route. We could then program the orbiting telescope to make a detailed scan of this narrow path."

"How wide of a search band would you suggest?" Carpenter asked, glancing at a projection of the area on a large video screen set in the wall before him.

"Offhand, I would say that a width of some four kilometers should be adequate for the purpose. Such a swath might even suffice to check out the second possibility of — heaven forbid— a crash landing," answered Bergman, peering intently at the same video image.

Receiving no further commentary or suggestions, the meeting was adjourned and Carpenter once more undertook the task of programming their lone satellite telescope—this time for a considerably more ambitious search.

Unfortunately, the endeavor would serve only to compound the mystery of the missing *Antares*, when it proved to be no more fruitful in supplying an answer.

"You're sure the resolution is sufficient to detect such a small target?" questioned Bergman, more than a little frustrated by the lack of progress in their search.

"Absolutely!" insisted Carpenter, quite adamant in making his pronouncement. "Not only would the highly reflective orange paint of the *Antares* be in strong contrast to the dull gray color of the lunar surface, but a moving tractor is bound to churn up a noticeable trail of dust in the weak gravity of the Moon."

"I'm afraid there's one unpleasant scenario that could account for all the known facts," voiced Cooper.

"What's that?" Bergman asked.

"If they had taken off, and later crashed, the wreckage might be so distributed — or even covered with dust— as to preclude detection with our modest telescope," came the reply.

"I would have to acknowledge this possibility," Carpenter was forced to admit.

"The remaining alternative is to presume that our search pattern has been too narrow, and that they have somehow wandered outside the ideal path which we had plotted," Petrov hastened to suggest.

"Let's proceed upon the premise of this far more optimistic outlook," Bergman decided. "We'll increase the width of our scan from their landing site to *Lunar Base*. Surely, a corridor of 10 km will be adequate. If not, then we'll double it to 20 km."

"What if the results are still negative?" Carpenter asked.

"Then I suppose our next step should be to focus attention upon their landing site. We'll start with a 20 km radius and gradually increase the search area in stages up to a maximum of 50 km," Bergman announced. "If this fails, I'm open to suggestions involving the supernatural."

However, as time passed without any trace of the *Antares*, anxious concern turned to a strong foreboding of disaster. Such fears seemed even more justified after completing their scan of the 20-kilometer-wide corridor. To their consternation, negative results were still forthcoming.

Reduced to a final option, Bergman ordered a high magnification scan to be centered upon the landing coordinates given by the *Antares*' crew. But after a radius of 20 km had been searched in vain, it was with much regret that he felt resigned to draft a news report for the outside world— a report which he would delay for another hour in the slim hope that a near miracle would intervene.

Chapter 2
SPACE STATION ORION

It seemed as if the black sky held a million delicate points of light. To the extreme left of two appreciative viewers a crescent Moon became clearly visible through a window in the lounge of *Space Station Orion*, as it orbited some 1,200 kilometers above Earth. As the pair watched in fascination, the slowly rotating wheel-like structure soon turned sufficiently to permit them a night side glimpse of the planet below. A number of scattered glows, representing entire cities, could be seen with the naked eye. Somehow, the world of their birth appeared rather insignificant in comparison to the rest of the universe.

"What are you thinking?" asked Mark Hamilton, focusing attention on his attractive feminine colleague.

"Just wondering what it will be like to go cavorting about on the lunar surface," replied Susan Baldwin, as she continued to gaze out of the oval window. "I'm also looking forward to seeing my brother, John. It has been quite a while since we saw him lift off at Florida's Cape Canaveral." (At this point in time the two had no knowledge of the missing *Antares* and its crew. Nor did they have any idea as to the role which both would soon play in the course of Earth history.)

Lovers for the past several months, the couple was scheduled to depart shortly to begin a four-month tour of duty at *Lunar Base*.

A 33-year-old American astronomy professor, Hamilton was also a noted philosopher and author who would replace England's David Carpenter. His 27-year-old shapely blonde companion, likewise an astronomer by profession, was to be an American replacement for another returning astronomer. Both had received astronaut training, including the operation of jet packs. However, only Hamilton could boast of previous lunar experience. This latest stint would be his third visit to *Lunar Base*.

"You're bound to like the one-sixth gravity on the Moon. It's even better than the one-half "G" of *Space Station Orion* in which to make love," said Hamilton, grinning as he put an arm around Susan's slender waist.

"And just how would you know this for a certainty?" she asked, attempting to elicit an answer to what promised to be a revelation of sorts.

"I'm afraid that hearsay evidence has been allowed to confuse the issue in this instance," Mark hastened to reply.

"In such an event, I suppose that I must give you the benefit of any doubt," said Susan, turning to embrace her willing companion.

Responding to the occasion, in the highly subdued lighting of the lounge, Mark proceeded to kiss her passionately on the lips. "You know, I've always wanted to propose marriage to a prospective mate on the Moon, or while she is vulnerable in space," he said at last.

"Then what's stopping you?" she found herself saying in words that were barely audible.

Pondering exactly what to say next, he was prevented from answering by the entry of a third person into the lounge compartment. It was Adam Wentworth, a free-lance journalist/reporter who was one of four passengers due to board the *Moonbeam* in little more than an hour. It was expected to be a routine three-day flight in the shuttle to *Lunar Base*.

Closing an airtight door behind him, the newcomer spoke: "I

do hope I'm not interrupting anything," he said.

"Saved by the bell, my dear," Susan muttered under her breath, moving slowly away from the viewport and depositing her curvaceous 5'-4" frame (117 lbs Earth weight) onto a nearby sofa.

With the magic of the moment lost, Mark sat down beside Susan and gave her hand a gentle squeeze. Then, turning to face Wentworth, he said: "Tell me, Adam, is it true that you plan to write a book detailing all of man's lunar exploits?"

"My intention is to compile a history of lunar exploration, from the Apollo missions of the late 1960s and early 1970s to the present day," answered Wentworth, seating himself in a reclining chair which afforded an unobstructed view through the lounge window.

"Exactly how long do you expect to stay on the Moon?" Susan inquired of Adam.

"Probably about a month," came the reply. "I say, Mark, I understand that you have several published works to your credit. Are they all on the topic of astronomy?"

"Actually, cosmology and philosophy would be a much more accurate description. I consider the science of astronomy to be merely the means toward an end," responded Hamilton.

"The rather profound enigma of creation is at the forefront of current scientific research," Susan informed the journalist.

"To my mind, the issue of creation is one which is covered quite adequately by the Bible," Wentworth stated, looking out the window at a multitude of stars adorning the night sky.

"Have you really examined the scientific evidence behind a modern picture of our universe?" Hamilton asked.

"Are you aware of the fact that our Milky Way galaxy contains no less than several hundred billion stars, and that there are literally hundreds of millions of galaxies within range of our telescopes?" questioned Susan. "What is their purpose?"

"Indeed," continued Hamilton, "since it has long been a well established fact of science that the formation of solar systems is a natural byproduct of stellar birth, one simply has to wonder if a reasonable proportion of them might not feature biological life forms equivalent— or superior — to that of man. To deny such a scenario is to rashly assume that the vast bulk of the universe is merely window dressing for a single obscure planet called Earth."

"It would be tantamount to taking one drop of water out of a great lake and thinking that it is unique— that the overwhelmingly large number of other drops have absolutely no significance," said Susan.

"The Lord moves in mysterious ways, His wonders to perform," said Wentworth. "Until I personally meet with an inhabitant of one of these hypothetical civilizations I shall continue to believe in Jesus Christ the Saviour."

"Assuming the reality of all these other worlds, Adam, would you be willing to concede that they also have a Christ?" asked Hamilton. "As a matter of fact, do our esteemed theologians even know what they are talking about when they use the term of Christ?"

"One must have faith," replied Wentworth, still adamant in his beliefs, but nevertheless fascinated by the large number of stars that could be viewed above the clouds and smog of Earth's atmosphere.

"Blind faith is the folly of fools, I'm afraid," remarked Susan. "It is to accept— without thought— the concepts of others, quite regardless of justification. Moreover, it is to ignore one's own faculty of reasoning, reducing man to the status of a puppet."

"Have either of you ever studied the Bible in depth?" Wentworth asked, hoping to avoid further entanglement in a debate which he felt likely to lose.

"It just so happens that I have spent a great deal of time and effort into researching this very body of literature," Hamilton was quick to respond. "May I ask upon what foundation your own biblical studies are based?"

"Until his death, three years ago, my father was a prominent Roman Catholic bishop in the city of Boston. Being an only child, you may correctly surmise that I received a thorough religious education," declared Wentworth.

"I thought Catholic priests were forbidden to marry," Susan could not resist mentioning.

"It was only after my mother died that my father decided to become a priest," Wentworth explained.

"I'm sorry to hear that you lost your mother so early in life,"said Susan. "It must have been a very difficult time for you."

"Actually, it turned out to be a blessing in disguise, since it induced my father to become devoutly religious, and to later rise to leadership in the church," Wentworth replied.

"Unfortunately, our church leaders are highly reluctant to examine opposing points of view— presupposing that any other interpretation is erroneous simply because it is contrary to immutable tradition," stated Hamilton.

"Would I be intruding if I were to ask exactly what is contrary to tradition?" inquired Dr. Rita Mitchell, an attractive 28-year-old brunette who had just entered the *Orion's* lounge. A noted Canadian physician, specializing in space medicine, she constituted the fourth passenger scheduled for embarkation on the Moonbeam.

"By all means, please join us," said Susan, motioning to an empty chair beside them. "We were about to commence a discussion involving biblical credibility — a subject in which Mark is somewhat of an authority. His last book presented a highly illuminating picture of authorship, along with an intriguing system of symbolism which has been incorporated into both the Old and New Testaments. It also features a chapter dealing with the

Dead Sea Scrolls, revealing a cover-up of evidence sufficient to make one's blood boil."

"Tell me more," responded the new arrival. "It sounds most intriguing. I have always thought there was a great deal that our churches were reluctant to disclose regarding the translation and publication of these ancient scrolls."

Unable to fabricate an immediate and plausible excuse to leave, Wentworth resigned himself to having to listen to dialogue which would almost certainly not be of his choosing. What he was unprepared to hear was evidence that threatened to undermine faith in the very concept of organized religion.

Professor Hamilton began his discourse as follows:

"All too often tradition serves to leave deep mental scars. Erroneous biblical concepts, implanted in childhood, tend to persist throughout one's lifetime— effectively precluding acceptance of logic and the revelations of science. It is really quite incredible that widespread ignorance of this corpus of literature should prevail well into the 21st century, in open conflict with both science and reason.

"First and foremost, it is essential to realize that the various biblical documents are not the product of any divine revelation, stemming from God, and bestowed rather suspiciously upon a handful of chosen individuals. Is it not obvious that the views of the ancient scriptural writers must be considered inferior to those of modern man, with his vastly superior knowledge of the universe?

"On the whole, the extensive collection of Old Testament writings merely depict a lengthy and frequently painful struggle of the Jewish race to develop a monotheistic theology, in the face of many hostile neighbors embracing multiple deities. In a frequently trying endeavor to impart enlightenment to their largely ignorant flocks, the biblical prophets chose to express —by means of a unique system of symbolism— certain events and ideas which they wished to convey. Also, in order to obtain credibility for their views, it was common practice to sign God's name to such writings. Thus, in an era where the masses were prone to accept authority without question, a host of bizarre beliefs were bound to prevail.

"Unfortunately, this highly unethical policy was to lead to later problems; for once a false and provisionary philosophy ever becomes popular, tradition acts to defer recognition of a superior viewpoint. Invariably, we of a more enlightened age must learn to respect our own conscience in preference to the restricting influence of tradition. It is hardly a credit to mankind that the vast majority of us end up accepting— more or less— the particular religion or philosophy to which we have been most strongly exposed during our lifetime. In essence, individuals brought up as a Christian, Moslem, Jew, Buddhist, Hindu, etc., will generally retain the beliefs of their parents. Such persons fail to ask themselves what their faith would have been had they been born into an environment featuring a different religion. How, then, can they possibly consider their cherished beliefs to be true?

"In structure, the Old Testament is a mixture of actual and highly biased history, folklore and myth. Handed down by word of mouth and in the form of scattered writings for centuries, it was not until the Prophetic Era— from roughly 900 B.C. to 300 B.C.— that an assortment of editors gathered much of this material together to produce a series of documents or books.

"Composed some time prior to the writing of the seven-day creation story, we have the Adam and Eve narrative. Clearly, any thought of a literal translation of this text is so ridiculous that one would surely expect it to bring even the most imaginative theologian back to reality. Ostensibly written as an explanation for our imperfect world, such an interpretation actually denies the principle of free will and conscience. For if we accept the traditional church doctrine of original sin, it becomes tantamount to insinuating that we are responsible for the sins and actions of ancestors whom we have never seen! The very integrity of the spiritual cosmos would be threatened by a state of utter chaos.

"In direct contrast to this totally unacceptable dogma, the true objective of this purely fictitious narrative was to signify that man's sense of spiritual awareness (or conscience) was now much higher than other surrounding life forms. In reality, the Adam and Eve story was composed for the express purpose of upholding the principle of conscience and free will. Is it not perfectly clear that this is so when we read that one partaking of the fruit of this magical tree (called the *tree of knowledge of good and evil*) will be able to discern good from evil? Thus the reason why Adam — *a fictitious symbol depicting mortal man*— is caused to suffer as a result of his actions becomes quite apparent, since he is bound to be persecuted by his fellow beings who are less spiritually evolved and who continue to worship material values. This very point, incidentally, is promptly illustrated in the following allegory of Cain and Abel, where the mere physical sense slays one of higher principles.

"Likewise, the seven days of creation story is simply another symbolic parable designed to convey a moral or principle. In fact, upon close study, it is revealed to contain a sevenfold process describing spiritual evolution. Such stages of enlightenment may be depicted as follows: (1) The first recognition of *conscience*, of an Intelligence controlling the universe (i.e. the light of the first day of creation, since the Sun, Moon, and stars have yet to be introduced into the story), is expanded in systematic fashion through: (2) an understanding of the virtues of conscience and sensing that it can separate good from evil (i.e. the firmament or *separation* of the second day); (3) a spiritual uplifting as a result of following conscience must bring forth fruit and a firm sense of reality which can be depended upon (i.e. the *dry land and vegetation* of the third day; (4) the realization that the revelations of conscience arise from a divine *System* or *Principle* (i.e. the vast system of the *celestial universe* epitomized by the Sun, Moon, and stars of the fourth day); (5) a sense of *exalted thought* and *abundance of life* arising from the progressive revelations of conscience (i.e. the fifth day where the *birds of the air* are used as a symbol of exalted thought, and in which the *fish of the sea* symbolize abundance); (6) the recognition that man is to have dominion and be the ultimate earthly creation, and that his soul is actually of an *immortal* nature, since he is now capable of communion and identification with God; (7) and finally, realization of man's great potential must bring to him a sense of peace and rest, since the attributes of *immortality* and *harmony* with God are all that might be desired (i.e. the *fulfillment* and state of rest depicted by the seventh day).

"Recognition of these seven messages, or stages of spiritual thought, constitutes a valuable key capable of unlocking the real meaning behind much otherwise obscure biblical literature."

"Tell me, Mark, is it just a coincidence that both Old and New Testament stories are permeated with a repetition of certain numbers? Is there some hidden symbolic meaning behind this pattern?" Rita wanted to know.

"Indeed there is," responded the lecturer, taking several long sips of fruit juice from a container which Susan had placed before him.

"We still have plenty of time left. Why don't you tell us more?" said Rita, oblivious to the look of utter dismay which had now appeared on Wentworth's face.

Again, Professor Hamilton undertook to elucidate:

"Early in the composition of what has come to be referred to as the Old Testament, the scriptural writers adopted a unique system of numerical symbolism. Although various combinations hold significance, the general plan embraced the basic numbers: 1,3,4,7,10,12. Each of these selected numerals was used to impart a specific message, either individually or in combination with one or more of these special numbers. A brief measure of insight, along with examples of their usage, follows:

"The number *one* was used to symbolize that there is but a solitary *Supreme Being*, of but one God ruling the universe. An example would be Jesus' reprimand to Peter for failing to *watch with me one hour.*

"The figure *three* posed an important symbol depicting *insight into spiritual matters*, of success in attaining some degree of the truth. It was most likely suggested by the sum of the conspicuous types of heavenly bodies— namely, the Sun, Moon, and stars. Examples of the numerous instances of its usage would be Jonah in the whale's belly for *three* days and *three* nights, the rising of Christ on the *third* day, and the episode of Saul (later renamed Paul) being blinded for *three* days while on the road to Damascus.

"Selection of the symbol *four* may well be traced to the four cardinal points of the compass, and perhaps also to the four basic processes of mathematics: addition, subtraction, multiplication and division. This number is often used to signify a *sense of direction — the act of seeking the truth*. Some examples of this would be the *four* thousand fed by Jesus, the raising of Lazarus who was dead for *four* days, and Jesus' walking on the sea in the *fourth* watch of the night.

"The number *seven* was evidently derived from the sum total of all celestial bodies known to exhibit motion across the heavens in ancient times. As a result, it came to epitomize completeness of the heavenly system, being adopted as a symbol of *spiritual fulfillment and sense of perfection*. A few Old Testament examples of the frequent use of this numeral would be the *seven* days of creation story, the *seven* ascents of Mount Sinai by Moses, the numerous *sevens* appearing in Joshua and concerning the fall of the walls of Jericho. In the New Testament, Jesus is depicted as the 77th personage; while in the Book of Revelation we have the *seven* messages, *seven* seals, *seven* trumpets and *seven* vials, etc.

"Adoption of the figure *ten* as a symbol is believed to stem from the total number of fingers upon which we depend to perform so many human tasks. Hence, this number was selected to depict *application* of human resources to affairs of a spiritual nature. Examples of this would be the *Ten* Commandments, Jacob's statement of giving the *tenth* to God, and Jesus' parable of the *ten* maidens.

"The numeral *twelve* is invariably linked to the twelve signs of the zodiac, which at the time were held by many to influence the actions and policies of man. Accordingly, this number was used as a symbol of the *universal extent* and validity of *divine authority*. Examples would be the *twelve* sons of Jacob, the *twelve* stones carried across the River Jordan, the *twelve* apostles of Jesus, etc.

"While such basic numerals constitute the primary mechanism of biblical symbolism, and are generally used in the sense described, there are notable exceptions and additions that must be mentioned. For instance, *six* is often used to express imperfect mortal thought; while the various days of creation may convey the essence of a particular number. Also, it should be pointed out that there are times when the symbolic role of these esteemed numbers is reversed and used in the *opposite* sense! Examples of this would be the *three* temptations of Jesus by the devil (a symbol of ignorance), Peter's *three* denials, and Judas betraying his master for *three* times *ten* or thirty pieces of silver, etc. Still other biblical symbols include the *stone*, which is often used to portray the *appearance of truth*; while *wine* and *mountains* symbolize *inspiration* and *exalted thought*, respectively. Moreover, angels are used throughout the Bible as *messengers of God, or conscience.*

"Once it is realized that the Scriptures were constructed for the prime purpose of imparting a decidedly spiritual message, rather than to record mere physical and historical occurrences, the picture at last begins to make sense. That this highly conspicuous feature of the Bible has been largely ignored is quite surprising when we ponder the obvious and extensive usage of symbolism. Much more astonishing is the fact that so many religious leaders still fail to realize, even today, that none of the supposed miracles really occurred, but were devised for the purpose of conveying a specific moral or principle. (In assessing the overall structure of the Bible, it is to be noted that many passages were written so as to lend themselves to a literal interpretation— if simple minds were willing to give them such a degree of credibility.)

"We can perhaps understand and partly forgive the actions of the ancient scriptural writers, since they must have had strong incentive to provide inquisitive souls with some tangible idea of how, for example, the universe came into being. However, this excuse is hardly valid in our present age of enlightenment, and those who would preach a literal interpretation in the face of reason are in reality false prophets doing much to hinder the advance of knowledge."

"What I would like to know is how the strange belief of Jesus, as being an incarnation of God, ever came to be so widely accepted," remarked Rita, following a pause in the professor's discourse.

"I would have to say that it necessitated an unusual combination of events," responded Hamilton. "But a far greater mystery is why this bizarre idea, in open defiance of both modern science and common sense, has not been overthrown."

"I suppose it just goes to show you that fear of the unknown can act to prevent many from thinking for themselves," said Susan, casting a discrete glance toward Wentworth, who remained silent.

"Indeed, it is human nature to require a philosophy of some sort upon which to base one's life— even if it should be unfounded and illogical," commented Rita.

"I believe a scientist would equate such a state of affairs with the statement that nature abhors a vacuum," philosophized Susan.

"Although I most certainly don't have all the answers, as an astronomer I am convinced that we live in a universe ruled by laws of *Principle*— a universe in which the actual driving mechanism is acknowledged to be evolution," opined Hamilton. "I also feel that existence is rooted in some form of cosmic reincarnation."

"You may very well be on the right track," agreed Rita. "But I still have unanswered questions regarding Christian origins and the Dead Sea Scrolls."

The professor undertook to oblige by continuing as follows:

"Just as our church leaders have steadfastly refused to properly recognize the symbolic structure of the Bible, so they have been guilty of propagating a greatly distorted picture of a Jesus Christ personage. What they have failed to grasp (or admit) is that a *Christ* is really a *symbolic title or goal*— in the sense that it refers to a *hypothetical* being who has achieved a state of Perfection. In their endeavor to expound a moral, the gospel authors elected to portray Jesus (in symbolic terms) as though he were actually of a divine nature— if naive minds would be willing to give the idea credence. This logical interpretation will be seen to resolve a long-standing paradox with regard to contradictory biblical passages — namely, occasions in which some passages infer that God and Jesus are one, while others clearly state that the Father is greater than the son.

"Of the four biblical gospels, all were written decades after the crucifixion. The Gospel of Mark (about 70 A.D.) is widely regarded by scholars as being the oldest; while Matthew is presumed to be next at roughly 80 A.D. A date of approximately 85 A.D. is generally assigned to Luke. John would seem to be the more recent document, appearing on the scene about the year 100 A.D., which is long after the apostle by this name would have passed away. Since Mark was not one of the original disciples, and both Matthew and Luke are widely conceded to have been derived — at least in part— from Mark, it follows that such biblical accounts were written by persons who had no first-hand knowledge of their subject. Thus it is clear that ample time and opportunity existed for a host of extraneous ideas to have arisen before the teachings of Jesus were committed to scripture. During this interval there is good reason to suspect that interpolations and changes in doctrine have served to distort the philosophy taught by Jesus, the alleged founder of Christianity— changes so drastic that Jesus himself would have been shocked by the end result!

"To really understand the sequence of events, which served to transform the simple teachings of Jesus into a God/Redeemer deity, it is necessary to delve into one aspect of ancient history that Christian theologians tend to avoid like the plague. There is absolutely no question but what the weird concept of a Redeemer — which was never a dogma of the early church— owes much to pagan beliefs of the time, as is evidenced by the fact that this false redemptionist doctrine did not develop until the new religion had spread out from Palestine into the foreign world.

"Mithraism, in particular, definitely imposed a very considerable influence upon developing Christian theology. Originating in Persia, it had reached Rome at least a century before the crucifixion, where it flourished until the 4th century A.D. However, rather than merely falling by the wayside, many of its more fundamental tenets were clearly absorbed into the structure of an emerging sect which we now call Christianity— including the very practice of observing Christmas upon the 25th day of December, the acknowledged birthday of Mithras! (Nowhere, in the entire corpus of New Testament literature, is there any hint as to the birthday of Jesus.) Other supposed Christian practices which may be linked to Mithraism include the barbaric notion of blood redemption, the ideas of baptism, confirmation, and a truly mystical salvation from a eucharistic Last Supper. It was also at this time that the Jewish Sabbath was switched to Sunday, the holy day of Mithraics.

"With regard to the deification of Jesus, it is an established fact that the apostle Paul was the initial and chief driving force behind this revolutionary idea. What our church leaders are reluctant to disclose is Paul's connection with certain of the Dead Sea Scrolls. In order to more properly assess this aspect of early New Testament history, it is perhaps desirable to make brief mention of one of several key scroll— specifically, a scroll known as the Damascus Document. This writing has allowed scholars to resolve a number of mysteries and to set the stage for a much needed overhaul of basic Christian theology.

"Well hidden from an advancing Roman army in sealed caves, among the cliffs of the region (most probably in the year 68 A.D.), the first scrolls were found in 1947 near the ruins of Khirbet Qumran. Located some 20 miles east of Jerusalem, and close to the northwest shore of the Dead Sea, Qumran served as a combination religious settlement and fortress at the time of Jesus. With the find sparking an extensive search for other nearby caves, by the early 1950s no less than 11 caves were discovered, yielding over 800 documents. While some were in a surprisingly good state of preservation, most were fragments which encompassed virtually every Old Testament book.

"What held great significance, however, was the finding of certain scrolls of a contemporary nature— scrolls which were composed in a period dating from the crucifixion until the eventual destruction of Qumran in 68 A.D. Several of these later scrolls (including the Damascus Document) told of a Wicked Priest, a Liar, and a Teacher of Righteousness. All three of these nameless individuals lived at the same time and were described as being antagonistic toward each other. Inasmuch as the Teacher of Righteousness was clearly depicted in terms of mortal man, in the eyes of orthodox Christians any notion of this personage being Jesus was obviously precluded. It was not until the identity of the Liar was uncovered that many pieces of the puzzle began to fall into place.

"First discovered in 1896, in the loft of an old synagogue in

Cairo, Egypt, for half a century the Damascus Document posed an enigma to scholars who were quite unable to relate it to any other body of literature. But with the finding of the Dead Sea Scrolls, it was immediately apparent where it had originated, since no less than ten copies of this same document had been uncovered in the Qumran caves by the mid 1950s. So named by reason of a place which it had called Damascus, scholars were eventually able to solve a long-standing mystery with regard to Acts 9, of the New Testament. In this story the apostle Paul is reportedly blinded for three days while on the road to Damascus, ostensibly with an armed band intent upon arresting a group of Zealots who were deemed rebellious against Rome and their puppet Temple high priest. Hitherto, it had been erroneously presumed that Damascus in Syria was the intended destination. But this had always posed an annoying problem, since an arrest warrant issued in Jerusalem would have been quite useless in a foreign country with a different governor. What now became evident was that the Qumran community was the place in the wilderness that was called Damascus at the time of Paul's escapade.

"Having made such a deduction, it was only a short step for astute scholars to deduce the identity of the Liar, who was described as a former persecutor who had been taken into their society for a period of three years, converted, and then sent out to preach their version of Mosaic law. Unfortunately, for their cause, he was subsequently accused of preaching lies. To an unbiased mind, there could now be little doubt but what the apostle Paul was the one referred to as the Liar. Why was this esteemed Christian personage considered to be a liar? Quite simply, he was the first to claim that Jesus had risen from the dead and was of a divine nature. In the eyes of those whose faith was firmly rooted in Jewish tradition, he had chosen to preach utter blasphemy!

"With knowledge of the Liar's identity, it soon became possible to adduce the names of the other two adversaries that were mentioned in the scrolls. The Wicked Priest was almost certainly Ananas, the Temple high priest at the time, and a man considered to be a puppet of Roman authorities. His opponent had to be James, the stated brother of Jesus, who was a staunch proponent of Mosaic law and a high ranking member of the sect who inhabited the Qumran/Damascus community. This interpretation fits exactly the events described in Acts, in which Ananas' minions are said to have beaten James to death (about the year 62 A.D.). By way of retaliation, James' followers later assassinate Ananas. In due course, much of Jerusalem explodes into violence, eventually culminating in a general uprising against Rome and the Jewish armed revolt of 66 A.D.

"Why, one might ask, did Paul ever concoct the idea of a Jesus deity? The irony of it all is that it may actually have been quite unintentional. Being an educated man who was fluent in multiple languages, upon his conversion Paul was sent out of the country by James to do his preaching. Thrust into close contact with people who embraced a variety of pagan religions— including semi-gods endowed with magical powers — it is conceivable that he succumbed to a strong temptation to fabricate his account of Jesus in order to be more competitive. The masses just love his promises of a heavenly life, and Paul soon begins to make large numbers of converts — the only problem is that they believe in a Jesus/God deity.

"Hearing of these unfounded claims, James summoned Paul back to Jerusalem, where he is rebuked for his actions and then dismissed after a compromise of sorts is reached. Following a second and rather extended missionary venture, in which Paul persists in his fabricated account of Jesus, he is again recalled to Jerusalem by James to face renewed charges. Unfortunately for Paul, he is promptly attacked by a group of James' followers and would surely have been killed were it not for a timely intervention by Roman soldiers. According to the report in Acts, he is finally shipped off to Rome to await some kind of trial, where he subsequently vanishes into historical obscurity.

"But the die had already been cast, and the new Christ-Jesus religion quickly spread to surrounding nations, where it was soon further embellished by a succession of deceived and over-zealous theologians. In short order it came to bear little resemblance to the simple philosophy expounded by its alleged founder!"

"I must say that your brief lecture has been most informative, professor," commented Rita, casting a somewhat furtive glance at a seemingly dazed Wentworth. "But what I don't quite understand is why this account of Christian origins has not received greater publicity."

"I'm afraid that tradition tends to die hard," answered Susan. "Not only have our churches done their best to suppress pertinent information, but there is an inherent reluctance of man to listen to anything which would serve to jeopardize his faith, and thereby create an intolerable vacuum."

"This was indeed the case following discovery of the large corpus of Dead Sea Scrolls, back in the middle of the 20th century. In fact, attempts at suppression were little short of criminal," Hamilton went on. "Of the original seven-member team set up to translate and publish the scrolls, within a relatively short period of time all but one was a devout Roman Catholic priest/scholar, whose chief aim was to uphold the faith at any cost. Within a few years even this one and only open-minded scholar had been phased out and replaced by yet another pious supporter of catholic dogma. (It seems that he elected to blow the whistle on the others for their concealment of sensitive documents and biased reporting.) Incredibly, for almost forty years, not one Jewish scholar was allowed to participate in translating this priceless body of literature — literature produced by their very own ancestors!"

"Posterity will always wonder how, in this supposedly advanced age, such a deplorable situation could ever have been permitted to develop," remarked Susan, also casting a surreptitious glance toward a still silent Wentworth.

"What has always been a disturbing thought, in the minds of most unbiased biblical scholars, is just how many Dead Sea documents were actually destroyed on the grounds that they posed a serious threat to the Christian faith. Certainly, there was ample opportunity and ample motive. But, alas, there would seem to be no way of knowing the truth at this late date," sighed Professor Hamilton.

No sooner had Mark finished his discourse than the door to the lounge opened to reveal the presence of Peter Hawkins, a 45-year-old former U.S. Air Force general, who had recently been appointed as commander of *Space Station Orion*. "I'm afraid that I have some bad news, Susan, concerning your brother," he said, as the door closed automatically behind him.

"What is it?" she asked, immediately fearing the worst in an environment where the vacuum of space posed a constant and deadly hazard.

"He's missing and presumed to have come to an untimely end, along with Frost and the *Antares*," said Hawkins. "I'm so sorry."

Chapter 3
THE ENIGMA DEEPENS

The airtight door closed automatically behind Bergman, as he stepped briskly into the Operations Center of *Lunar Base*. Peering intently at a video screen, set into the wall directly in front of him, were David Carpenter and Paul Cooper. Hans Mueller and Vladimir Petrov sat at a nearby table, deeply engrossed in studying a number of photos and a large map of Mare Imbrium.

"We've found the *Antares*," said Carpenter, turning to face the new arrival. "But it's some distance from where it was supposed to have landed."

"Where the devil is it?" Bergman asked, moving toward the screen as quickly as he could.

"Right here," responded Cooper, pointing to a tiny orange blip at the center of the screen. "Funny thing is, the craft's transponder began to function normally shortly before we were able to zero in on its position."

"It's close to 40 kilometers from their reported coordinates," elaborated Carpenter.

"Almost due west, in fact," voiced Mueller, rising from his chair and addressing Bergman directly. "This would seem to preclude the possibility of a forced landing while en route back to *Lunar*

Base," he pointed out.

"What the devil could they have been doing so far off the mark?" Bergman demanded to know.

"Either they could benefit from a good refresher course in basic navigation, or else they moved the *Antares* once it set down," opined Petrov, entering into the conversation.

"I'll place my bet on the latter," said Cooper. "I find it hard to believe that they could have made an error of this magnitude."

"I definitely agree," stated Carpenter. "But why didn't they inform us of their intention to shift the *Antares* to a different location?"

"Unless, of course, their radio gave up the ghost," suggested Cooper. "But it still doesn't explain the temperamental operation of their transponder unit."

"Suppose we assume that they did indeed land at the intended site," Bergman began. "They return from their initial field trip, only to find that communications had short-circuited or was in some way inoperable. In this case, one big question immediately comes to mind: What did they find during this excursion that could possibly induce them to want to take the *Antares* to this new location?"

"It would make far more sense to believe that they simply made an error and landed where we now find their craft," remarked Petrov. "I'm at a complete loss as to why they should suddenly decide to move to this other site."

"Either way, this would seem to leave us with two scenarios. The first is to infer that some mechanical malfunction has since prevented them from returning; while the second is to presume that they again donned their space suits and subsequently met with misfortune," Cooper suggested.

"If we accept the first alternative, then there's still a chance that they could be alive, trapped inside a craft with no propulsion and no means of communication," Petrov reasoned.

"I think we'd better plan on dispatching an immediate rescue mission," said Bergman. "How soon can we get started?"

"I've got a detailed route to the *Antares* already prepared for the *Hercules*," Mueller announced, referring to their large nuclear-powered ground tractor.

Picking up a microphone, Bergman spoke into the base's intercom system, wasting no time in summoning four additional members of his staff to a hasty meeting. It was now well over a day since they had last heard from the *Antares*.

....

Some two hours later the *Hercules* emerged from the shadow of its underground hangar. Glistening a luminous yellow, in the intensely bright sunlight, the tracked vehicle moved forward at a slow but steady pace. Capable of a top speed of some 40 km per hour, it was expected to average little more than one-half of this figure during the course of the 300 km trip, as there would be a constant need to dodge small craters and numerous obstructions in the form of large rocks and boulders. Following close behind and linked to the tractor was a four-wheeled trailer. It contained a small nuclear reactor and a generator that would supply them with much needed electrical power. This time there was no exchange of good-humored banter over their radio link with *Lunar Base*, as worried concern for the safety of two missing comrades served to produce a rather somber atmosphere.

"Gyrocompass bearing locked on to our prescribed heading," announced Gustov Stromberg, a talented electronics specialist from Stockholm, Sweden. Some 6'-3" tall, the likeable 29-year-old was the tallest of the crew and a veteran of sorts when it came to travel aboard the *Hercules*, having logged a record number of hours during his previous lunar stint. It was reported that, some years ago, the handsome blond bachelor had turned down a promising tennis career in order to pursue his dream of reaching for the Moon.

At the controls of the vehicle was Jerry Butler, a 34-year-old American from Tampa, Florida. Experienced in piloting the *Antares*, he was reputed to be the best rocket propulsion specialist at *Lunar Base*. Married, with two small children, the dark-haired 5'-11" astronaut was currently serving his second tour of duty on the Moon, having earlier piloted two shuttle flights from *Space Station Orion*. "Maintaining a steady 25 kph," he informed Cooper, over a radio link via a lunar communications satellite.

"The reactor is functioning perfectly," declared Brian Erskine, studying a cluster of instruments before him. A 35-year-old American physicist from Los Angeles, he had assisted in construction of the much larger nuclear unit now powering *Luna Base*. Married, with one child, he was scheduled to return to Earth during the following month.

Constituting the fourth crew member of the *Hercules* was 31-year-old Boris Yashin, a former Russian Air Force pilot who had since become a versatile and accomplished astronaut who was quite capable of operating the *Antares*. Currently in the process of obtaining a messy divorce, he was not due for replacement for another two months, at which time he was fully prepared to seek a second lunar stint. He did not relish returning to an Earth beset by strife and widespread acts of terrorism — to say nothing of being confronted by an irate ex-wife. "We've covered a little over 20 kilometers. Let me know when you want me to take over, Jerry," he said.

"Will do. You're welcome to the controls just as soon as we reach the stretch of rough ground that Mueller cautioned us about," Butler replied, with a grin. "It should be another 20 kilometers or so down the road."

"When do I get to drive?" asked Stromberg, not to be upstaged by any of his fellow crew members.

"Just as soon as I get us stuck in one of those deep tank traps that our geologists refer to as craters," said Yashin, likewise endeavoring to raise spirits by injecting a little humor into the conversation.

"You back seat drivers are a riot," voiced Erskine. "Wake me up when we get there, or if anything exciting occurs, whichever comes first. I'm going to take a short nap, since I only had two hours of sleep before being drafted for this expedition."

"I'll watch your instruments," offered Stromberg. "Just don't snore so loud that you wake up the driver."

"We'll try not to hit any large potholes," said Butler, swerving to avoid a sizable depression.

As events transpired, the outbound journey was to prove more tedious than eventful. The constant need to dodge scattered boulders and crater pits required a great deal of diligence and concentration. Although their course had been plotted to minimize passage over rough terrain, there were still numerous hills and undulations which could conceal a potential danger lurking beyond the next rise. Caution, under such circumstances, quickly came to be the order of the day. Nevertheless, after more than 14 hours of exhausting travel, they were able to catch their first glimpse of the *Antares* from the crest of a hill.

"Steer four degrees to the left," advised Erskine, now fully rested and encouraged by the fact that the missing craft appeared to be standing in an upright position.

"I would estimate it to be about two kilometers away," responded Stromberg, currently at the controls of the *Hercules*.

"Let's get ready for our grand exit, Boris," advised Butler, opening a locker which held four space suits and two jet packs.

By the time Stromberg had pulled alongside the *Antares* his two fellow crew members had almost finished the task of donning their suits. Assisted by Erskine, they were already in the process of clamping on their helmets.

"Doesn't seem to be any visible sign of external damage," remarked Stromberg, as he completed a circle of the other craft and came to a full stop some ten meters away.

"I didn't notice anything amiss, either," agreed Erskine, just as Butler and Yashin closed the inner air lock door behind them.

Within a few minutes the two space-suited figures emerged from the *Hercules* and made their way directly to the *Antares*. They could not help noticing that footprints, conspicuous in the soft lunar soil, led away from the craft. What was highly disconcerting, however, was that none could be seen returning! Stopping momentarily to examine the depressions, before their own footsteps obscured matters, they began to suspect the worst.

"Sure looks like they went out and failed to come back," observed Butler, noting that two distinct sets of tracks led off toward the north.

"I guess we'd better check inside," said Yashin, opening the outer air lock door.

Cycling through to the interior, it was at once apparent that their worst fears had been realized. An empty cabin clearly foretold a story in which two fellow explorers had perished somewhere in the vacuum of the lunar surface. Most assuredly, there was absolutely no possibility that the limited oxygen supply of their suits could have lasted this long. It remained only to discover their bodies and try to piece together the sequence of events as they must have happened. With this somber thought in mind, they began a systematic search for evidence which might shed some light on the final actions of the crew of the *Antares*.

"The cabin air support system is in good shape," noted Butler, after removing his helmet. "In fact, readouts on the status of the oxygen supply and carbon dioxide filters tend to indicate that Frost and Baldwin could not have spent more than an hour or so aboard the hopper before their misadventure."

A hasty check of the craft's remaining rocket fuel disclosed that an inordinate amount had been expended for just a single ascent and descent. "I doubt if there's enough left for a safe return to

Lunar Base," said Yashin, upon running some figures through a computer which he had managed to activate.

"Would it be consistent with the supposition of a second flight from their intended landing site coordinates?" asked Butler, suddenly recalling that they had not noticed any tractor marks which would indicate an overland transit.

"Offhand, I would have to say that more than enough fuel has been expended to account for the short hop," replied Yashin.

"But why the devil wouldn't they have used the tractor mode, instead of jeopardizing their limited supply of return rocket fuel?" Butler wondered aloud.

"Beats me!"

"I'm certain that the intervening 40-kilometer stretch poses no great challenge to overland travel," said Butler, endeavoring to mentally review the terrain that he had recently studied on Mueller's detailed maps.

"I fully concur," agreed Yashin. "They could have easily covered the distance in two or three hours at most."

It seemed that with every answer to a question came even more unresolved mysteries. Whatever had induced the geologists to up and move the *Antares* to this particular site? Why had the craft's radio transponder gone dead for a period— before strangely resurrecting itself?

A definite course of action seemed clear to both Butler and Yashin. First, they would proceed to follow the tracks of their two missing comrades, in an attempt to learn their fate and possibly recover their bodies. Second, having already failed to establish any contact with the *Antares*' radio, they would have Stromberg give it a more thorough examination. If it could be made operational, by any member of the *Hercules*' crew, he was certainly the most qualified.

Exiting the *Antares*, the two carefully examined the exterior of the craft, paying particular attention to the dish antenna. They could find nothing wrong. Moreover, a study of the ground under the rocket nozzles, combined with the absence of any tread impressions, definitely confirmed their original conviction that the tractor mode had never been used.

"I think it might be wise to equip ourselves with jet packs before we attempt to follow their trail," said Butler, noting that the footprints led straight toward a nearby line of steep cliffs. "Do you suppose it was just such an equipment malfunction that did them in?" asked Yashin.

"Since their jet packs were nowhere to be found aboard the *Antares*, I would have to say that this may indeed prove to be the case," replied Butler, at a loss for any better explanation that would fit the facts.

Some twenty minutes later three space-suited figures emerged from the air lock of the *Hercules*. While Stromberg made directly for the *Antares*, Butler and Yashin began to follow the tracks of their long overdue colleagues. With jet packs strapped to their backs, they were prepared for a search which might well involve flight into a third dimension.

After following the trail for approximately two kilometers, they came to the base of an escarpment where, amidst a patch of disturbed lunar soil, they ended rather abruptly.

"Looks like they activated their jet packs at this point," opined Yashin, studying the ground beneath them.

"The big question, as I see it, is whether we should first go up to heaven only knows where, or spread out and search for signs of their return along the perimeter of this cliff," said Butler. "Any preference, Boris?"

"Why not go with the old adage of what goes up must also come down?" suggested Yashin. "This way, we might not have to risk life and limb on any cheap copy of a Buck Rogers flying belt."

"You know about Buck Rogers in Russia?" asked Butler, mildly surprised at his companion's knowledge of an archaic American comic strip.

"Of course! He was my childhood hero who probably influenced me more than anyone else to become an astronaut."

"I learn something new every day," responded Butler. "However, to answer your question, I must agree that it does make sense to check out the easiest alternative first. Do you prefer to go to the left or to the right?"

"To the left, naturally."

"It figures," said Butler, recalling that Russia had long since gone back to a communistic economy.

"Some day we must have a discussion on the economic system. We might both learn a great deal from each other."

"Agreed," said Butler, wondering just who was responsible for coining such words as left and right to depict the opposing economies of communism and capitalism, respectively. He suspected that it most likely originated in some capitalist society.

"How far shall we go?"

"Let's try about 400 meters in either direction. It would be unwise to proceed beyond radio contact, in any event," suggested Butler.

"We should also check for ledges on the cliff face as we go," said Yashin. "There's always a chance that they could have crashed and be hung up on the face itself."

"Good idea, Boris. See you shortly," said Butler, as he began his trek to the east along the base of the steep escarpment.

It was to be a search that would prove fruitless. By the time the two returned to their starting point it had become apparent that they would have to jet up to the top of this high ridge. Wherever their missing comrades might be, the key to finding them lay in picking up the trail where they had touched down.

"I would judge the height to be approximately 500 meters," said Yashin, staring up at the almost vertical rock face.

"I'll go first," Butler volunteered, activating the control box around his waist.

"Keep me informed of events," said Yashin, as his companion lifted off with a blast of exhaust gas.

Reaching the summit of the escarpment, it was immediately observed that the plateau consisted of a series of rugged steps and sharp peaks, each one rising higher than the other the further one got from the floor of Mare Imbrium. There was only a solitary level spot as far as the eye could see— and that was precisely above the point where the footprints of his missing colleagues had ended! Butler could not help wondering how (or why) this particular spot had been deemed to hold special geological interest. The odds of selecting this one flat region (about 40 meters across), by mere chance, seemed somewhat remote— especially when it was noted that the escarpment extended for many kilometers.

Urging his waiting comrade to launch himself to the top of the cliff, Butler proceeded to effect a soft landing in the middle of this favored location. To his utter astonishment, he could not find any trace of the geologist's footprints. What was visible to him was a large area that appeared to have been disturbed, as though from a great blast of rocket exhaust— considerably more, in fact, than what might have been expected from two jet packs. Still puzzled, he turned to greet Yashin as he rose into view above the cliff wall. "The airport runway is clear to land," he said, waving to his fellow astronaut.

Search as they might, neither Butler nor Yashin could find any indication that their missing colleagues had ever set foot in the immediate vicinity of where they presently stood.

"Do you suppose they continued their flight beyond this spot and landed on the second plateau?" asked the Russian.

"It would only be at the expense of risking insufficient fuel for a safe descent to the floor of Mare Imbrium," responded Butler, now staring at the nearest cliff wall which lay some distance away and was even higher than the first.

"I'm inclined to agree," Yashin finally conceded, upon giving the matter further thought. "I definitely wouldn't want to chance it."

"Perhaps a throttle got stuck and the flight could no longer be controlled," suggested Butler.

"Both throttles?"

"It could be that the other attempted a rescue, and neither was able to make it down safely," Butler surmised.

"I must agree that such a scenario does seem to be the most plausible. In fact, I don't know what else could have happened," said Yashin, casting a gaze at the expanse of jumbled terrain, which was seen to extend at least as far as the next plateau.

"Then I fear that we are left with little choice but to search amongst a rock jungle for their bodies," Butler reasoned.

"How far do you think they could have traveled before crashing once their fuel ran out?" asked Yashin.

"Good question. Why don't we continue to widen our search pattern until compelled to return to the *Hercules*?"

"I guess that's about all we can do," agreed Yashin. "As per usual, I'll start my search to the left while you explore to the right."

"Sounds reasonable to me."

Unfortunately, after a weary four hours spent searching in vain for their missing colleagues, both Butler and Yashin were ready to concede defeat. They could only conclude that Frost and Baldwin must have rocketed off into oblivion as a result of mechanical malfunction. Inasmuch as there was still a little matter of descending from their present 500-meter-high perch, the thought foremost in mind was whether their own equipment might give them trouble— especially since it was of the same manufacture.

"I don't suppose there are any footpaths off this accursed cliff," remarked Yashin, looking down with a measure of apprehension at the ground below. Somehow, the lunar plain seemed much further away than it did when they began their upward flight.

"I'm afraid not, Boris. But if it would make you feel any better I'll go first. Just don't come after me if my throttle should jam."

"Why not?"

"Simply because somebody has to survive in order to take the defective merchandise back for a refund."

"Your unique philosophy reminds me of the classical parachute guarantee," said Yashin.

"You mean, if it fails to open one has merely to return it for a free replacement?"

"Exactly!"

"If worst should come to worst you have my permission to sue the manufacturer," said Butler, firing up his jet pack and launching himself over the cliff.

Fortunately, all went well and before long both dejected searchers had landed safely at the base of the escarpment. By comparison, the two-kilometer trek back to the *Hercules* turned out to be a "piece of cake." Needless to say, they did not look forward to their role as bearers of bad news.

While the news from Stromberg was far from bad, it was also most puzzling. Other than a blown fuse and a loose connection, there was nothing wrong with the radio. It had taken him only a matter of minutes to find and remedy the problem.

“You’re telling me it was really that simple to repair?” questioned Butler, hungrily devouring a food packet of concentrated turkey, sweet potatoes and broccoli.

"That's the strange part of it," replied Stromberg. "Not only could I find no reason for the fuse to have blown, but the loose wire made even less sense. It was almost as if somebody had deliberately disconnected it!"

"Why, in heaven's name, would anyone do such a thing?" asked Yashin, similarly mystified by Stromberg's disclosure.

"I can't honestly believe that the loose wire was a deliberate act; but an explanation simply eludes me," voiced the Swede. "With regard to the blown fuse, I suppose it could be ascribed to a manufacturing defect. However, it still doesn't alter the fact that both of these problems should have been readily diagnosed and corrected. As for the radio transponder, I must confess that I have no idea as to why it was so temperamental."

"Didn't Frost take a short crash course in basic electronics?" inquired Butler.

"I'm quite certain they both did," said Erskine, recalling previous conversations with the two missing geologists.

The more the crew of the *Hercules* thought about it all the less sense it made. With a report of events already transmitted to *Lunar Base*, there was really little else that could be done and they soon began to make plans for a return.

"I wouldn't advise an attempt to fly the *Antares* back," said Butler. "It's questionable whether sufficient fuel remains to make a safe landing."

"I agree that it's much too risky," Yashin concurred. "There would be absolutely no margin for error."

"What about the vehicle's tractor mode? Does it have an adequate supply of electrical power for such a long trip?" Erskine asked.

"It could take us several days, since it would be necessary to make periodic stops in order to recharge batteries with its solar panels," Butler announced, after a brief computer session.

"It should be possible for the *Hercules* to tow the *Antares*," declared Erskine. "Our reactor is capable of providing the power, and it would only reduce our cruising speed by a few kilometers per hour."

"We could easily rig up a towing harness," said Yashin. "But it would require a driver aboard the *Antares* for steering purposes."

"Then let's do it," suggested Butler "But first, we should all catch a few hours of badly needed sleep."

With no dissenting voice heard, the four crew members of the

Hercules rested in preparation for the long journey back to *Lunar Base*. While they thus stood to retrieve a much prized machine, in the form of the *Antares*, it seemed small consolation for the loss of two valued colleagues.

Some seven hours later, after having successfully retracted the *Antares*' four shock-absorbing landing legs, the two vehicles were rolling over the bleak lunar surface. While Stromberg and Erskine shared the controls of the *Hercules*, Butler and Yashin took turns guiding the *Antares* at the end of a long nylon towrope. It was to be a journey which would take close to 24 hours and leave them all quite fatigued. But aside from a few minor dents and paint scratches, due to encounters with obstinate boulders, the expedition managed to recover and return the *Antares* in one piece.

However, while their fate seemed a foregone conclusion, the exact whereabouts of Frost and Baldwin still posed an unsolved mystery. There was, in fact, much that remained unanswered — not the least of which was the riddle of why they had moved the *Antares* to a different location which, as far as anyone could tell, was totally devoid of interest!

Chapter 4
IN SEARCH OF AN ANSWER

Within three days of departing *Space Station Orion* the *Moonbeam* entered lunar orbit. After an uneventful and routine flight the shuttle was now preparing to land. Aboard were four passengers, two crew members, and a large quantity of supplies. In another four days it was scheduled to return with an equal number of scientists and technicians who had completed the traditional four-month tour of service.

At the controls was Frank Wallace, a 38-year-old veteran American pilot from Atlanta, Georgia. His copilot was 35-year-old Alexei Belinsky, a talented Russian astronaut who was being groomed for the command of a new sister ship to the *Moonbeam*. Currently in the final stages of construction, alongside one of *Orion's* docking bays, it was expected to become operational in a few short weeks.

"Orientation confirmed," Belinsky informed his colleague, as he monitored a combination video/computer screen.

"Retro burn sequence initiated," responded Wallace, pushing a series of buttons.

Precisely ten seconds later twin tongues of flame spurted from exhaust nozzles, facing the direction of flight. In response, the shuttle began to arc downward toward the lunar surface. As their forward motion dropped, the Moon's gravitational pull acted to increase the rate and angle of descent. In turn, this necessitated renewed orientation of the craft's rocket thrusters. It was not long before *Lunar Base* came into view over the horizon.

"Target two degrees to the left," said Belinsky, as he made a slight attitude adjustment. Several short low-thrust burns put them directly over their objective. With all forward motion negated, the *Moonbeam* was allowed to slowly settle to a prescribed landing area amidst a cloud of dust kicked up by rocket exhaust.

"The *Moonbeam* shuttle has just landed," announced Wallace, as sensors automatically shut down the craft's engines the instant its four shock-absorbing legs touched ground.

Not designed for atmospheric flight, the lunar craft was devoid of sleek streamlining— a feature which had long characterized so many artists' impressions of what a spaceship should look like. Function, rather than appearance, dictated the external structure and silhouette of the *Moonbeam*. With clusters of spherical fuel tanks strapped to a somewhat cylindrical cabin fuselage, perched high above four spindly leg appendages, the craft was far from graceful in outline. A large disk-shaped antenna protruded above the hull, which was painted a brilliant red for the purpose of enhancing visibility.

As both the crew and passengers watched, a glistening silver vehicle emerged from a nearby hangar bay and made its way toward the shuttle. Quickly covering the intervening distance, it stopped and proceeded to extend an accordion-style docking tube. After some maneuvering, the operator managed to effect a positive seal with the *Moonbeam's* air lock, permitting a transfer of personnel without recourse to the use of bulky pressure suits.

While there was to be no blaring trumpets on hand to greet the new arrivals, as they entered the lunar ground shuttle, Mark Hamilton was pleased to be met by a fellow associate. "Welcome back to *Lunar Base*," said Carlos Bial, a Brazilian radio astronomer whom he had known for several years.

"It's good to see you again, Carlos," responded Hamilton, as he finished helping Susan clamber through the narrow passageway which connected the two craft.

"I'm so sorry about your brother," said Bial to Susan. "We're all deeply shocked by his loss."

"Anything new to report?" she asked, not really expecting much in the way of miracles.

"Bergman's holding a briefing session at 14.00 hours today. I do believe he's planning to send out an expedition to try and find out why the *Antares* was moved from the original landing site," said Elena Malovich, an attractive blonde Russian optical astronomer. Presently doubling as a shuttle operator, she was scheduled to return to Earth when the *Moonbeam* departed some four days hence.

"We shall both look forward to attending the meeting," responded Hamilton, as the air lock door was closed in preparation for severing their umbilical connection with the *Moonbeam*.

....

With the entire population of *Lunar Base* present, Bergman began his discussion before an attentive but somber audience. Highlights of his brief address follows:

"As you all know, the fate of Frost and Baldwin seems only too evident. What is not clear is the circumstances which led up to this great tragedy. While we strongly suspect jet pack malfunction to be at the root of their demise, there are many unanswered questions. To be specific, there are four major mysteries which may be cited.

"First, no plausible explanation has been forthcoming for the *Antares* to have experienced radio failure. Both the blown fuse and loose wire should have been easily detected and remedied. As for the craft's radio transponder, it is still unknown why it behaved in such a temperamental fashion.

"Second, although mechanical trouble with their jet packs is thought to have occurred, extensive testing of identical units has failed to reveal any manufacturing or design flaw. In particular, all throttle valves and fuel gauges— the two most likely components which might fail and cause a crash— checked out perfectly.

"Third, it is a complete mystery as to why they should have wanted to move the *Antares* to a new location— especially to one that would appear to possess no obvious geological appeal. Incidentally, there is now conclusive proof that the *Antares* did indeed land at precisely the intended location. By good fortune, it seems that our second lunar satellite just happened to be in a favorable position to permit triangulation of their last radio report. This has since allowed us to pinpoint its location with sufficient accuracy as to preclude any doubt

"Fourth, it is extremely puzzling why they would choose to fly the *Antares* a short distance of only 40 kilometers— thereby depleting their supply of rocket fuel needed for a return flight. It would have made far more sense to simply use the craft's tractor mode. Not only was there no difficult terrain to cover, but the time saved would surely be negligible.

"After much deliberation with both Earth authorities and staff members, it has been decided to dispatch a second expedition to the region of their original landing site. The chief objective of this mission will be to determine why Frost and Baldwin were induced to move the *Antares*— with such great haste — to the coordinates where it was later found. It is logical to presume that whatever they discovered to motivate this action is still there awaiting rediscovery. With this thought in mind, it has been agreed that a geologist should be included among the crew of this proposed quest.

"Needless to say, just about everyone on the station has expressed a desire to participate in the mission. It has therefore fallen upon me to arbitrarily appoint Butler as commander and chief pilot for the expedition. Petrov will be our geologist. The other two crew members that I have chosen are Hamilton and Baldwin's sister, Susan. Although Susan is primarily an astronomer, she does have considerable knowledge of geology; while Hamilton has pilot experience and is an expert in jet pack operation. Perhaps, in knowing her brother as she does, Susan may be able to discern some reason for their strange actions.

"Since we have only a few more days of sunlight remaining before this region of the Moon enters its periodic two-week night phase, I have scheduled the *Antares* to lift off at 12.00 hours tomorrow. Are there any questions?" Bergman asked, concluding his talk.

....

Precisely according to plan, the *Antares* blasted off from the lunar surface. Under the skilled piloting of Butler and Hamilton it was not long before it descended, on twin tongues of fire, in the immediate vicinity of where Frost and Baldwin had originally landed.

"We'll split up and commence a search for footprints or telltale impressions of the *Antares'* landing legs," said Butler, shortly after transmitting a report of their safe arrival to *Lunar Base*.

"If we each concentrate upon one quadrant, without moving beyond radio contact, it should allow us to pick up their trail with maximum efficiency," suggested Hamilton.

With no dissenting voice forthcoming, all four then proceeded to don space suits and jet packs. In minutes they had exited through the air lock and were trudging across the gray lunar landscape in their assigned search pattern.

It was to be Petrov who discovered the first tracks, pointing almost due north. Moments later, noting a second set of tracks that led southward, Susan began to follow the trail. Shortly thereafter, she came upon imprints of landing legs— much eroded by rocket exhaust gas—which had obviously been made by the *Antares* as it rested in the soft lunar soil.

After gathering about the earlier landing site of the *Antares*, the four searchers commenced following a clearly marked trail toward a steep escarpment that lay directly ahead. Reaching the base of the cliff, which extended for many kilometers in either direction, they noticed that a jumble of footprints led both to the east and to the west.

"I guess it would make sense to operate in pairs," said Butler, faced with the need for a decision. "Does anyone have a preference?"

Given a choice, Susan responded: "Mark and I will follow the tracks to the right, if you two would care to search in the opposite direction."

Accepting the proposal, the two groups parted company after first agreeing to rendezvous back at the starting point in exactly one hour. If at all possible, they would attempt to keep in periodic contact by radio.

Setting off toward the west, it was only a few minutes before Petrov uncovered evidence of their missing colleague's geological activity, in the form of chipped rocks and muddled footprints. "It sure looks like they stopped here for a while," said the Russian geologist, as he bent down to examine a portion of the cliff face from which soil had been excavated in order to acquire a rock specimen.

"Let's continue along the trail," suggested Butler, noting that the footsteps extended at least to the next rise on the undulating lunar surface.

Conceding a need for expediency, rather than indulging in any professional curiosity, Petrov soon rejoined his colleague and the two resumed their westward trek.

Meanwhile, Mark and Susan had wasted little time in reaching a position directly beneath the peculiar rock strata that had so intrigued Frost and Baldwin. "Looks like they jetted up to obtain a sample," opined Hamilton, examining a disturbed area which bore evidence of jet exhaust.

"I suppose we should go up and investigate," said Susan. "There's a ledge where one could stand in order to obtain samples."

"I'll go," Mark was quick to offer. "There's no point in both of us taking a risk when one would suffice."

"Be careful, Mark."

Activating his jet pack, Hamilton rose from the plain of Mare Imbrium and, with some dexterity, settled on the ledge beside the vein of peculiar rock strata. "They definitely landed here," he radioed back to Susan, noting several places where samples had been chipped from the cliff wall. There were also a number of imprints on the thin veneer of lunar dust which strongly implied human presence.

"Any clues as to why they decided to move the *Antares*?" asked Susan, not really expecting an affirmative reply.

"Nothing at all," answered Hamilton, likewise having no idea as to why they had made such a strange decision.

"I guess you might as well come down," said Susan. "Do you think you could break off a tiny sample of this unusual vein for later analysis?" she added, by way of an afterthought.

"No problem," Mark responded, removing a knife from a sheath below his right knee and prying loose a small chunk of rock, which he then proceeded to deposit in a convenient pocket.

However, instead of coming straight down, Hamilton made a rather fateful decision. "Why don't I continue up to the top of this mesa?" he asked Susan, over his radio link. "It seems a shame to have come so far without going the rest of the way. "Besides, I bet there's a terrific view from above."

"Just be careful, Mark," Susan repeated.

Launching himself from a projecting portion of the ledge, Hamilton soared upward to the summit of the high escarpment.

Effecting a safe landing, he began to explore his nearby surroundings. In a few short minutes he came across the footprints of his missing colleagues, which led toward a second but much smaller mesa some distance to the east. Moving to the edge of the cliff, so as to establish radio contact with Susan, he informed her of his discovery.

"I'm coming up," she said, reaching down to her waist for the jet pack control box.

But before Mark could respond, his companion had already achieved ignition and was rising to meet him. Arcing over the crest of the escarpment, she soon landed a short distance away with all the grace and finesse of a veteran gymnast.

"Well done!" proclaimed Mark, in praise of his star pupil. "You get better every time."

"I had a good teacher," she replied, walking over to where Mark was standing beside two sets of clearly discernible tracks.

"They seem to lead straight to yonder cliff. I have no idea what they expected to find, but they did come back the same way," said Hamilton, pointing to a returning set of tracks.

"I suspect their treasure map didn't live up to expectation, since there were no crown jewels in the *Antares* when it was found," deduced Susan.

“It sure looks like it was a wild goose chase," commented Hamilton. "But I suppose we are obligated to pursue their tracks to the bitter end of the road."

With the issue settled, the two searchers undertook to follow the trail of their lost companions. As expected, it led them straight to the 30-meter-high mesa which adorned the immediate eastern horizon. Somehow, they were not especially surprised to find that both sets of footprints came to an abrupt halt, amidst signs of rocket exhaust from jet packs.

"Here we go again," remarked Hamilton, as he looked up at what was an almost vertical wall of solid rock.

"I'm at a loss to understand what geological treasure one might hope to find on the top of this cliff," said Susan, preparing for yet another flight into the unknown.

"If I didn't know them both better I would be inclined to think that they were on a sightseeing expedition," commented Hamilton, as he lifted off with a burst from his jet thruster.

Following close behind, it was only a matter of seconds before Susan joined her companion on the top of this small but relatively flat mesa.

"That's weird!" exclaimed Mark, more than a little perplexed by his failure to find any trace of footprints. It was as if the two geologists had vanished into thin air.

"It can't be!" echoed Susan, equally dumbfounded by the absence of tracks. "They must have landed somewhere near here. We know that they just didn't fly off into oblivion, since they obviously returned in order to move the *Antares.*"

"Then where the devil did they go?"

"You know, Mark, this whole affair is fast beginning to resemble an episode of the old Twilight Zone series."

"I'm certainly tempted to agree with you on that assessment; but I have never been one to believe in magic. There must surely be a logical explanation."

"Let's spread out and search the entire mesa," suggested Susan. "They simply had to land somewhere on this small plateau."

Adopting a systematic search pattern, which would avoid confusing their own footprints with those of their missing colleagues, they were starting to become discouraged when Susan noticed a strange anomaly. "Mark! Come over here and tell me that I'm not imagining something," she shouted through her helmet radio.

"What is it?" he asked, coming swiftly toward her with long loping strides, so characteristic of astronauts cavorting about on the lunar surface.

"Look! What do you see from this particular sun angle when you gaze over there?" she said, pointing rather excitedly with a gloved finger.

Complying, Mark stared in the prescribed direction. "Seems to be a shallow depression or furrow, extending in a remarkably straight line to the east," he said, presently.

"You can only see it from this lighting angle," elaborated Susan. "When you move a short distance away the illusion vanishes."

"Perhaps it's not an illusion," said Hamilton, moving directly to where he judged the narrow furrow might be found.

"Stop where you are," advised Susan, as his path intersected the somewhat nebulous thin line.

Coming to a halt, Mark began to very carefully examine the ground about him. "It appears as if the lunar soil has been .... literally blown away!" he finally added.

"To cover footprints?" asked Susan, rejoining her companion. "It makes absolutely no sense."

"I certainly agree that it is a wild premise; but you must admit that the width of the furrow is just about right," said Hamilton. "What I can't explain is how (or why) the trick was accomplished."

"How can you be sure that anything was accomplished?"

"Take a close look at this rock, Susan. Do you see how it has been partially covered with dust; while this other rock, just a little further from the furrow, is completely uncovered?"

"So it is," conceded Susan. "Does this mean that we're obliged to follow the yellow brick road to some mythical Oz?"

"I'm open for a better suggestion."

"Feel free to lead the way, my courageous lion."

"Since it is obvious that the path leads eastward from the cliff edge, where they must have landed, I would suggest that we endeavor to find the Wicked Witch of the East," quipped Mark.

"Perhaps we'll end up encountering the Wizard instead," Susan retorted, as she trudged along in pursuit of her companion.

In a few minutes they arrived at the slight circular depression that had so fascinated Baldwin. There was something which appeared odd to Susan as she pondered the scene before them. Not only did the depression seem too circular, but even the texture of the underlying rock— if it could be called that— exhibited unusual features.

"What is it?" asked Hamilton, noting that she was prying rather vigorously at the substance with a knife.

"Take a look at this crack," she said, brushing away a thin covering of lunar dust. "It's quite deep and appears to follow the perimeter of the circular depression. Furthermore, it is definitely not normal rock!"

"What do you make of it?"

Before Susan could answer, their attention was diverted by a shadow that seemed to materialize from nowhere. Turning, they both stood frozen at the unexpected sight which they beheld. Standing a short distance away was a space-suited figure without a jet pack. Just as they were about to ask how either Butler or Petrov could have reached them without jet flight, a familiar voice came to them over their helmet radio: "Hello, Susan, it's your brother, John."

"Incredible!" exclaimed Hamilton.

Paralyzed with shock, Susan remained speechless.

"Please follow me," spoke the resurrected geologist, gesturing toward a nearby boulder, from which a sizable opening could be clearly discerned.

....

Meanwhile, having come to the end of the missing geologist's footprints, Butler and Petrov had commenced retracing their steps at the base of the escarpment. Eventually, reaching the starting point of their search, they stopped and looked in vain for Mark and Susan.

"Let's follow the trail eastward," suggested Butler, seeing no way in which they could miss their two companions as long as they stuck to the periphery of the cliff.

"Sounds like a good idea to me," agreed Petrov. "It could save us all some time."

In due course, they came upon the jumble of tracks beneath the peculiar rock vein which was situated quite high on the cliff face. Noting an absence of footprints, much beyond where they stood, it became obvious that any further searching would necessitate the use of jet packs.

"That unusual rock strata would definitely have appeal to Frost and Baldwin," said Petrov, staring upward at the formation. "In fact, no geologist could resist the urge to obtain a sample."

"There doesn't seem to be anybody up there now," stated Butler, after trying without success to establish radio contact with either Mark or Susan.

"Unless they're inside a cave or deep fissure of some sort," remarked Petrov, having spotted the nearby ledge which ran almost parallel to the vein in question.

"I guess one of us should go up and check it out," said Butler, mentally preparing himself for a flying belt caper.

"Let me go, Jerry. If they're not on the ledge I can at least avail myself of an opportunity to obtain a rock sample."

Concurring with the logic, Butler remained below to watch while his colleague soared up to the ledge to investigate. Finding only traces of earlier human exploration, he concluded that they must have continued up to the top of the high mesa. Relaying the information to Butler, he quickly obtained his sample and then proceeded to launch himself upward in pursuit of their two companions.

"Any sign of them?" asked Butler, observing that Petrov had crested the escarpment, which was estimated to rise about 400 meters above the floor of Mare Imbrium.

"Not a soul in sight," responded the Russian. "But I do see lots of footprints."

"I'll be right up," said Butler, wasting no time in activating the controls of his jet pack.

Effecting a safe landing, close to where his partner now stood, he began to study the muddle of tracks imprinted into the soft lunar soil. The trail clearly led to the east, where a second and much smaller mesa dominated the view.

"There's definitely two double sets of tracks going— but only one double set returning," perceived the geologist.

"Then they're somewhere down the road," said Butler. "Let's go and find them."

Arriving shortly at the base of the 30-meter-high cliff, it was at once apparent that yet another jet excursion would be required if they were to catch up with their colleagues.

"Since they didn't come down they must still be on top of the mesa," Butler deduced.

"Would somebody please tell me what's so fascinating about this particular plateau?" voiced Petrov.

"I can't imagine who could have started any gold rush rumor," remarked Butler, as he began to finger the controls of his jet pack.

Moments later the duo alighted on the western tip of the small mesa, only to find it devoid of visible humanoid life. Incredibly, their two companions had vanished from sight— in spite of the fact that there was very little that could conceal a space-suited figure!

"Where could they have gone?" asked Petrov, greatly puzzled at this latest unexpected development.

"They definitely seem to have been searching for something," said Butler, noticing a profusion of footprints which appeared to go back and forth in rather aimless fashion.

"Sure looks like they finally caught the scent of something," declared Petrov, after he eventually came across a double set of one-way tracks which led off to the east in a straight line.

"You're quite right," agreed Butler. "All of a sudden, for some reason, they ceased their zig zag pattern and took off in pursuit of whatever had caught their attention."

"There's only one way to find out what it was," said Petrov, his curiosity now fully aroused.

"Let's go," responded Butler, just as anxious to follow the new trail that had come to light.

Reaching the circular depression, which the low lighting angle of the Sun tended to emphasize, they stopped and surveyed their immediate surroundings.

"All the tracks seem to end in the vicinity of this shallow and remarkably circular depression," commented Petrov, noting a profusion of smudged imprints in the disturbed lunar soil.

"Here's several sets of footprints which lead away from this enigmatic depression," said Butler, pointing to tracks that seemed to go directly toward a sizable boulder, the only one close by.

"Better check it out," said Petrov, while thinking to himself that if you had seen one boulder you had seen them all.

"That's really strange," remarked Butler, as he approached the irregular shaped object, which measured about three meters in height and at least double that figure in length and breadth.

"What's strange?"

"The footprints come to an abrupt end and do not return!"

"Any sign of jet pack exhaust?" asked Petrov, as he hastened to rejoin his colleague.

"Negative!"

"People don't just vanish or dematerialize," stated Petrov, more perplexed than ever.

"I simply can't believe"....began Butler, who was still studying the footprints, when a portion of the rock face appeared to fold in upon itself— revealing a brightly illuminated interior!

As they both watched, in utter fascination, a space-suited figure emerged and walked toward them. "I'm John Baldwin," a voice came to them over their helmet radios. "Please follow me and all will be explained."

Totally mystified, the two searchers obliged and soon found themselves standing in what seemed to be an air lock chamber, although of a construction quite unlike anything that they had seen before.

"We've been expecting you," said Baldwin, touching a recessed area of the wall, which glowed a brilliant blue. In response, the door opening promptly closed behind them and air began to rush into the compartment.

"Exactly who is expecting us?" asked Petrov, still endeavoring to recover from the sudden shock of finding that Baldwin had somehow been miraculously resurrected from the dead.

"Is Frost with you? What about Mark and Susan? Who built this place?" Butler wanted to know, being just as astonished at the turn of events as his companion.

"I'm pleased to inform you that all of our colleagues are alive and well," announced Baldwin. "In fact, they're very much looking forward to meeting you and to tell you the great news."

"What great news?" asked Petrov, relieved to learn that their missing friends and associates were safe.

"The big news concerns positive proof that the human race is not alone in the universe," replied Baldwin.

"You mean to say that this structure is the product of an alien civilization, and that we are looking at technology from another star system?" voiced Butler, barely able to contain his excitement.

"Indeed it is," responded Baldwin. "Moreover, I am convinced that they are a morally advanced and benevolent race which could prove to be of invaluable assistance to Earth society."

"Where did they come from? How long have they been here? When can we meet them?" inquired Petrov.

"All questions will be answered in due time," said Baldwin, as the wall opened to disclose a ramp which sloped downward beneath the lunar surface.

Upon descending a long passageway they presently came to a circular chamber, from which branched a number of corridors. Turning to their left, the procession continued until they stood before a section of wall that glowed with a greenish hue. Placing his gloved hand on a recessed panel, Baldwin caused an opening to appear as if by magic. Ushering his companions inside, he activated sensors which served to seal the wall behind them and produce an entrance into what was at once perceived to be a well-furnished apartment complex.

"You may remove your space suits," Baldwin informed them, after they had stepped inside and the wall had resealed itself.

The two guests promptly complied, welcoming the opportunity to divest themselves of their bulky pressure suits and jet packs.

"So glad you could join us," said Frost, rising from a lounge-style chair to greet the new arrivals.

"What took you guys so long to find us?" remarked Hamilton, as he strode toward his companions.

"Welcome to Hotel Matusia," said Susan, joining the jovial reception committee.

"Why do you call this place Matusia?" Butler asked.

"Simply because it happens to be the name of the home world of its builders," she responded.

Chapter 5
AN EXPLANATION

As the joy and excitement of their reunion gradually subsided, all six lunar explorers began to contemplate the full implications of this momentous historical event. What, in fact, would be the impact upon Earth society as a result of this unexpected contact with an obviously superior space-faring humanoid race?

"You mean to tell me that you are able to converse freely with these alien beings?" asked Petrov. "Do they also speak Russian?"

"Actually, they have managed to acquire a reasonably good grasp of Earth's major languages," replied Baldwin. "In essence, they have been monitoring our planet for many centuries, carefully concealed within the confines of this underground base—a base which we chanced to discover quite by accident."

"And what are their intentions toward Earth?" inquired Butler. "Just when did they intend to make their presence known to us?"

"You may be assured that the Matusians are not evil monsters from outer space, with a desire to enslave mankind. On the contrary, I am convinced that they seek only to assist us with regard to our social and spiritual evolution," declared Frost.

"To put matters bluntly," said Baldwin, "they consider us to be greatly in need of direction and guidance."

"Amen, to that assessment!" commented Hamilton, recalling to mind the rather sordid course of Earth history with all its foolish wars, social injustices, and perpetual religious squabbles.

"As for the question of when they had planned to reveal their presence, I am told that they feel it could be extremely hazardous to their health to do so before the arrival of one of their great and powerful starships. Until such time they would be highly vulnerable to attack by any Earth faction in the possession of nuclear missiles," explained Frost.

"I believe their point is well taken," said Susan, entering into the conversation. "Offhand, I can think of several trigger-happy petty dictators who would prefer to shoot first if they thought the status quo might be threatened."

"Just when is this great starship expected, and what are its capabilities?" Butler hastened to ask.

"In about thirty of our years, I am so informed," responded Baldwin. "And yes, they do carry very formidable armaments by way of affording protection. Until then, neither Michael nor myself will be permitted to leave this base, since there is no possibility of explaining our survival without disclosing the alien's presence."

"What about your families back on Earth?" asked Susan, at once thinking of wives and children who had by now become resigned to their deaths somewhere on the barren lunar surface.

"I'm afraid that the security of this noble group of space-faring missionaries is of higher priority," responded Frost, with sadness of heart.

"Are we also to be held here until their ship arrives?" asked Petrov, more than a little concerned over the prospect of being separated from his wife and children for so many years.

"This option is still open, so we have been informed," replied Baldwin. "I do believe that the four of you will be allowed to return to the *Antares* if you sincerely promise not to reveal their presence."

"How could they be certain that we would keep our word?"

Butler questioned.

"They evidently possess some sort of device, comparable to our lie detector machine, only much more reliable," answered Frost. "In any event, it is an issue which they are presently discussing."

"Since they must have moved the *Antares*, in a desperate attempt to avoid a search of this particular region, would somebody be good enough to explain the details of their plan of deception?" asked Butler.

Baldwin volunteered to elucidate: "The thought that was foremost in the minds of the Matusians was to divert attention away from the immediate vicinity of their base. To do so they wore our boots, in conjunction with their own superior space suits and jet packs, and then proceeded to retrace our steps back to the *Antares*. After moving it to a different location they reactivated the transponder unit, which they had previously disconnected, and tampered with the radio. Deliberately leaving a trail to a nearby cliff, they seemingly jetted into oblivion— only to be picked up by one of their two spacecraft awaiting them in a clearing above. Their powerful jet exhaust then served to obliterate footprints and other telltale evidence."

"May it be assumed that they used some form of jet pack exhaust to remove footprints leading to the entrance of the alien base?" quizzed Hamilton, reasonably certain that he was on the right track.

"It would seem so," said Frost. "I guess what they hadn't counted on was Susan's keen eyesight and an unfortunate angle of illumination by the Sun."

"Never underestimate my sister," remarked Baldwin.

"What really surprises me is that they were able to operate the *Antares* without previous instruction," stated Butler. "I shouldn't have thought it possible."

"Never underestimate the Matusians either," advised Baldwin. "Their scientists are very knowledgeable and they are well-versed in the English language, both verbal and written."

"Still, they were taking a big chance," said Butler.

"Agreed," responded Frost. "But they were quite desperate. They simply could not risk any more searching so close to their base."

"Does this mean that the circular depression, near the boulder doorway, is another entrance to their underground complex?" asked Hamilton.

"Indeed it is," answered Baldwin. "It constitutes the covering for a hangar which houses two saucer-shaped spaceships."

"May it be further assumed that such craft could be a source of certain UFO sightings over the years?" asked Hamilton.

"I rather suspect so," Baldwin ventured to say. "Although I'm sure that the vast majority have either a perfectly natural and logical explanation, or are merely attempts by individuals to seek publicity."

"What do the Matusians look like?" asked Petrov, his curiosity aroused.

"They closely resemble ourselves, perhaps a little taller on average and with heads of glistening silver hair, which is evidently the norm. On the whole, I would have to describe them as being an especially handsome and highly principled race," Frost replied.

"How many of them are there presently on the Moon? Have they ever landed on Earth?" Susan wanted to know.

"I'm informed that this base has a stable population of some 120 souls, almost equally divided between male and female," answered Baldwin.

"There is one vitally important aspect of our contact with the Matusians, however, which must be mentioned," said Frost.

"What's that?" asked Butler.

"According to their scientists, it is extremely dangerous for biological life forms from one planet to intermix with another, since each has evolved with immunity to specific microbes and viruses. Unfortunately, there would be absolutely no resistance to those of another ecosystem. For this reason, it is necessary for our two races to be segregated and excluded from intimate physical association. In effect, we would likely end up by inadvertently killing each other," explained Baldwin.

"To answer the question as to whether or not they have ever set foot on Earth, I'm told that there has been a number of discrete visits, over the years, for the purpose of obtaining information. But in every instance it was necessary for them to remain enclosed within a protective isolation suit in order to avoid contamination," Frost informed the four recent arrivals.

"Tell me," began Petrov, "exactly how did you fellow geologists ever manage to stumble across the alien's underground base? It seems so well concealed that it must have been somewhat of a fluke."

"Blame it all on my eagle-eyed colleague," responded Baldwin. "If it hadn't been for his keen vision and curiosity we would not be in the situation that we now find ourselves."

"What happened?" asked Butler.

"It seems that he spotted a flash of sunlight reflecting off one of their surveillance cameras mounted on top of this 30-meter mesa. Jetting up to the plateau, it was only a matter of time before he stumbled upon the circular depression and began prying around its perimeter. At this point the Matusians felt that they had no choice but to subdue Michael with one of their stun weapons and take him inside as a long-term guest," explained Baldwin.

"Invariably, John came along in search of me and was similarly zapped after following my footprints into this same sensitive area,"said Frost, concluding the story of their abduction.

"I think our hosts should be made aware of our obligation to contact *Lunar Base* within the next few hours. If we fail to do so they're likely to start imagining all sorts of wild stories— not the least of which would probably include an encounter with little green men!" exclaimed Butler. "In fact, I wouldn't put it past Bergman to come after us personally in the *Hercules*."

"It is for precisely this reason that I believe you will soon be allowed to return," opined Baldwin. "They simply cannot risk matters getting even more out of hand with yet another confrontation."

Moving to a recess in the wall, Frost commenced pushing a series of buttons. In a few seconds he was rewarded by the appearance of a container filled with a pale orange-colored liquid. "Anybody care to sample what is possibly the best tasting of a variety of alien drinks?"he said. "I'm told that it is highly nutritious and fully compatible with the physiology of all advanced life forms."

"What does it taste like?" asked Petrov, willing to concede that he was beginning to acquire a thirst.

"I would say that it resembles a mixture of papaya and apricot juice," Frost answered, picking up the drink and offering it to his colleague.

"Which brings us to a very interesting question," said Butler. "What have you guys been using for food lately? I don't suppose that you have been offered a thick steak or roast turkey."

"Nothing quite so tasty, I'm afraid," responded Baldwin. "It seems that they manufacture their food by an elaborate chemical/biological process. While it is somewhat bland by our standards, it does seem to be satisfying and evidently contains all of the nutrients which we require."

"If you folks decide to stay overnight you could get to watch a choice of major league baseball games on what I would describe as a giant 3-D video screen. Or, perhaps, you might care to see a recent Earth movie or musical ballet," said Frost. "On the other hand, you could prefer an educational program dealing with Matusian culture."

"You might also want to freshen up with a shower before

dinner," said Baldwin, pointing to an adjoining room.

"No wonder you called this place the Hotel Matusia, Susan. These quarters are positively luxurious. They sure beat anything we have at *Lunar Base*," responded Butler.

Further conversation was interrupted by a flashing blue light on a nearby wall. "It's the Matusian's signal for a conference," said Frost.

"You're about to see our landlords," announced Baldwin, reaching for a button that would permit a two-way visual/audio conversation.

In an instant a section of wall became a large video screen, at the center of which stood three humanoid figures. So graphic was the picture, with its incredible depth perception, that they appeared to be standing right beside them.

"Greetings to all Earth citizens from your Matusian hosts. To those new arrivals who have not yet had an opportunity to converse with us, please be assured of our honorable intentions. My name is Kobar; while to my left is Ryona, my wife/mate. On my right is Jevad, one of our chief scientists and an astute philosopher. In your terms, I would probably be referred to as President of our small colony."

Introducing their new comrades, Frost anxiously awaited the alien's decision regarding their return to the *Antares*. "We have only a few hours before a scheduled contact with *Lunar Base*," he informed the Matusians.

"Thank you for your indulgence. We have given the matter much thought," spoke Kobar," and have concluded that it would be in the best interests of all if the four recent arrivals would return to their base. It is, however, most essential that every effort be made to conceal our presence for as long as possible."

"In order to give us some time, in which to learn more about each other, we have made preparations for you to communicate with *Lunar Base* from your present quarters," said Jevad.

"Hopefully, this will give us at least another Earth day before a final decision must be made," added Ryona.

"Will you agree to talk with your colleagues, over the radio we have constructed, and give them some excuse to delay your departure?" asked Kobar.

"But of course," responded Butler. "We would welcome this wonderful opportunity to learn more about your civilization."

"And I have a multitude of questions that come to mind with regard to cosmology and philosophy," stated Hamilton, highly excited at the prospect of leaping untold centuries into the future in terms of Earth knowledge.

"We shall be delighted to share our philosophy with you. As a matter of fact, it is the very purpose behind our interstellar travels to evolving worlds," said Kobar.

"It may come as a surprise to you, Professor Hamilton, but we have monitored several of your TV lectures. You will be pleased to learn that your crusade against all versions of Big Bang cosmology is well founded," remarked Jevad. "We look forward to a discussion on this subject before you are compelled to leave."

"But we do have much more to offer Earth society than philosophical insight, valuable as this may be. We are also prepared to give you a cure for cancer and the secret of longevity," said Ryona. "Would any of you care to guess our ages in terms of your years?"

"I should say somewhere between thirty to forty years," Butler finally volunteered an estimate.

"Then you would be in error by a considerable margin, as all three of us are over two centuries old!" exclaimed Ryona.

"Just how long do you people live?" asked Susan, astonished almost to the point of disbelief by how young looking the Matusians appeared.

"For some reason, which we do not fully understand, as we approach 300 years our health tends to deteriorate rapidly and the end is near. Until then our bodies retain the vigor of youth and our minds remain keen to the last," responded Jevad.

"And you think we could live just as long with the benefit of your technical assistance?" inquired Petrov.

"We have no reason to doubt it, since the physiology of our two races is remarkably similar. In addition to exploiting the genetic factor, a chief ingredient for humanoid longevity lies in adding special food supplements to one's diet," explained Jevad.

"You could sure make a fortune on Earth for the formula of this magic elixir," commented Susan.

"We have no interest in acquiring material wealth. It will be given freely to all with but one important provision," said Kobar.

"And what is that?" asked Butler.

"Since greater longevity would only serve to aggravate an already dangerous overpopulation problem on your planet, we would have to insist upon an effective plan of birth control. You simply cannot afford to increase the ratio of births to deaths without soon becoming overrun by people," cautioned Kobar.

"Which brings us to a related problem with Earth society that must be faced before you end up by destroying yourselves from within," said Jevad. "Your scientists have succeeded in prolonging the lives of many carriers of serious genetic defects— including those who would have died before the age of puberty— thereby allowing them to pass on these defects to their offspring. In effect, what is really needed is not so much a marriage license as a birth license. Mankind has now interfered with nature's way of preserving the integrity of the genetic pool, and by permitting unrestricted births it will not be long until almost everyone will be born with a serious inherited abnormality!"

"We fear that this manifest failure to adopt a sensible policy, with regard to the issue of birth control, will soon threaten the very fabric of your society if not corrected at once," advised Ryona.

"I certainly concur with your prognosis and advice," responded

Professor Hamilton. "This is a point which I have been trying to put across for some time."

"Unfortunately, we have an influential lunatic fringe, hiding behind a popular religious facade, who would preach against the very principle of birth control," said Susan.

"You may be assured that this is a subject which we intend to address upon the arrival of our great starship," stated Kobar.

"How big and how fast is your starship? In terms of our light-years, how distant is your home world?" asked Butler, momentarily suppressing a multitude of other questions which came to mind.

"To answer your last question first," said Kobar, "I would say that our planet resides in a solar system— not unlike your own—almost 30 light-years away. Although higher speeds are possible, the average cruising speed of our starship is about 20% that of light. To exceed this velocity is to risk serious damage from encounters with the micrometeorites of space. As for size, it is essentially saucer-shaped, measuring about 700 meters across by 70 meters high. It does, however, have a narrow cylindrical appendage— some 1,200 meters long by 40 meters in diameter— in the form of a powerful matter/antimatter type reactor, which provides the craft's thrust."

"Then your ship must have left Matusia about a century and a half ago in order to arrive here some 30 years hence," declared Butler, upon performing some fast mental arithmetic.

"That is indeed so," acknowledged Ryona. "We radioed for the starship immediately after your scientists exploded the first atomic bomb."

"Will your ship be able to defend itself from nuclear missiles, should certain Earth factions react in a hostile manner?" asked Hamilton, far from convinced that worst might not come to worst.

"Our starship carries a most impressive array of armaments, including laser-type weapons of incredible power which could easily annihilate a swarm of missiles," replied Jevad.

"But what we really fear is such an attack on our lunar colony. We lack any appreciable weaponry with which to defend ourselves, and would thus be highly vulnerable to a concerted missile launch," said Kobar. "It is for this very reason that we must remain concealed until assistance arrives."

"Your rapid advance in the development of nuclear warheads and missiles has caught us by surprise," admitted Jevad. "Of all the other races, of whom we have knowledge— either directly or indirectly— none comes close to matching the fervor of Earth leaders in their mad desire to construct weapons of mass destruction."

With such words of censure ringing in their ears, all six guest astronauts felt inclined to condemn Earth society in general. Holding a hasty conference among themselves, they were unanimous in agreeing to cooperate with their Matusian hosts in concealing their presence from the world.

Shortly thereafter one of the alien scientists, clad in a silver isolation suit, entered the apartment with a two-way communication radio which they had just constructed. Wasting no time, Butler proceeded to establish contact with *Lunar Base*, assuring them that all was well in spite of negative results to date. He had no difficulty in convincing Bergman that another day or two should be spent in exploring and gathering rock samples. This extra time would be put to good use in getting to know more about the Matusians. There was also the exciting prospect of obtaining insight into the true position of mankind in a universe which was now revealed to be blessed with an abundance of intelligent life forms.

After partaking of a meal consisting of an assortment of alien foodstuffs, one of which tasted something like chewy lima beans, a flashing blue light again signified a desire for a TV conference with their hosts. It was Kobar, with an invitation to take a guided tour of the colony. Six protective isolation suits, he informed them, would be delivered within the hour. It promised to be the opportunity of a lifetime for the Earth astronauts.

Accompanied by the same three principals, with whom they had recently held conversation, the six explorers passed through a series of corridors before emerging into a huge chamber, roughly the size of a very large auditorium. A profusion of strange and exotic vegetation could be seen adorning the banks of an oval pond filled with crystal-clear water. At the far end was a small but picturesque waterfall; while directly opposite an impressive fountain dominated the scene. Close by them were a number of bathers, including four shapely females wearing nothing more than their birthday suits — revealing that, in all important aspects, they were identical to the human form. The four males present likewise wore no covering whatsoever. It was quickly perceived that public nudity— at least in a swimming pool— was neither frowned upon nor unusual. More than one Earth visitor openly expressed regret of not being able to join in the frolic.

"This multipurpose park serves as our main recreation center," said Kobar.

"It's beautiful!" exclaimed Susan, echoing the precise sentiment of her companions.

"Over here we have a reasonable equivalent of what you call a tennis court," announced Ryona, pointing to a green carpeted area with a central net and a series of lines and circles imprinted upon the playing surface.

"Electronic sensors act to eliminate the need for line calls, and are considerably more accurate and totally unbiased," Jevad could not resist stressing, having once viewed a televised Wimbledon tennis match in which a player and referee had nearly come to blows.

Above them, at the center of the highly arched ceiling, hung an artificial miniature sun which illuminated the entire chamber. "Its intensity can be varied, so as to mimic conditions from sunrise to sunset," explained Kobar, noticing several of his guests looking upward at the solitary light. "Our cycle of night and day is very close to that of your planet, being almost 23 hours," he added by way of an afterthought.

The next section of the underground complex to be visited was a compartment housing the colony's primary fusion reactor. About the size of an average living room, it was capable of supplying the entire needs of the community. Two smaller units, in adjoining rooms, served as emergency back-up systems.

"How did you solve the formidable problems of controlled fusion?" asked Hamilton, painfully aware of the failure of Earth physicists to construct a functional reactor, in spite of numerous attempts and the expenditure of vast sums of money.

"That is a secret which we are prepared to share with Earth, once it is established that this knowledge will be used solely for peaceful purposes," said Kobar.

"I can readily see your point," agreed Susan. "It seems that mankind has utilized almost every major scientific breakthrough to devise still more powerful weapons of mass destruction."

"Your planet is currently at the stage where it could very easily destroy itself— or attempt to do so to any other civilization that it might encounter!" Ryona felt compelled to stress.

Not one of the six astronaut guests was prepared to dispute this pessimistic assessment of Earth society.

The tour soon led to a series of large rooms that contained numerous vats and highly sophisticated machinery, the function of which was to convert raw inorganic elements and minerals into nutritious edible organic compounds. Clearly, the Matusians had developed a technology far beyond the comprehension of 21st century mankind. The visitors could only marvel at the alien's ability to transmute basic material elements, mined from a barren lunar crust, into much needed food.

"Does this factory/laboratory supply all of your nutritional requirements?" asked Butler, greatly impressed with what he had seen.

"It is quite capable of supporting our normal complement of some 120 colonists. In fact, over the centuries we have been able to build up a surplus stock, sufficient to last us more than a dozen of your years," Jevad informed his audience.

Entering yet another section of the underground complex, they came to an exceptionally long compartment containing row after row of what resembled filing cabinets, along with an imposing array of electronic equipment of some kind. Beyond this immediate scene the visitors could view at least a dozen Matusians, each intent upon studying a particular video screen.

"This is where we monitor important Earth news, broadcast over a multitude of TV channels, in order to be versed in all of the latest developments," said Kobar.

"What did you ever do before we invented radio and television?" asked Butler. "Surely, your information must have been extremely limited in scope."

"Yes it was," admitted Kobar. "But then, at this less technically advanced stage of your evolution, it was not nearly so vital to obtain so much data. Incredibly, your race has managed to go from a rather primitive horse and buggy age to a dangerous nuclear age in the span of barely half a century!"

"We were greatly surprised when you made your initial space flight to the Moon, less than two decades after exploding the first hydrogen bomb. It was truly an amazing feat which required a considerable degree of motivation," Ryona stated.

"Unfortunately, the real motivation may be traced to the Cold War atmosphere which prevailed at the time. Threat of war always seems to inspire and bring out the inventiveness of mankind—quite regardless of whether the resulting product is beneficial or a serious menace to society," Hamilton philosophized.

"It is for this very reason that we feel morally obligated to intercede and assist your planet in forming one long overdue World Government," said Kobar, again stressing the need for urgent external intervention.

"At least the advent of your computer/satellite communications age has served the purpose of providing us with a wealth of information, allowing many gaps in our knowledge to be filled once we accessed your data files," remarked Jevad. "Prior to this time we were forced to resort to satellite probes and an occasional covert foray to Earth to copy (or purloin) records and books from selected archives."

"What I would really like to know," began Professor Hamilton, "is your relative status in the overall scale of higher life forms. In terms of Earth evolution, how many years would you say that your civilization has advanced beyond our present society?"

"It is almost 4,000 of our years— which is roughly two months shorter than yours— since we harvested the power of the atom," replied Ryona. "However, it should also be mentioned that we were likewise visited— at about the same time in our evolution— by a great starship from another solar system."

"Some three centuries later, under the guidance and sponsorship of this more advanced race, we were finally permitted to join a Galactic Federation of Planets— with a prime role being an obligation to assist emerging civilizations during the crucial years following the dawn of their own Atomic Age," Kobar elaborated.

"And now you are poised to reciprocate this assistance by helping us in our hour of need, so to speak. I find this attitude to be most commendable," said Baldwin.

"Hopefully, the time will come when Earth society has advanced to the stage where it is allowed to join our Federation in the great evolutionary saga of life," remarked Kobar.

"There is one thing that still puzzles me," said Susan. "Why have our radio telescopes failed to pick up signals between your starship and this lunar colony? I have to assume that you do communicate with each other."

Jevad undertook to explain: "We use a very narrow laser-type beam that cannot be detected by current Earth instrumentation, but which has spread sufficiently with distance that it can be received by our incoming ship. On the other hand, sending undetectable messages from the starship is not so simple. It was eventually decided to transmit a narrow beam of short gamma ray radiation—a wavelength which is infrequently monitored by your scientists. As it turns out, almost all conversation is outbound from the Moon, which greatly minimizes any chance of detection. So far we seem to have been lucky in this regard."

The final phase of their tour took the visitors to a huge hangar bay, in which resided two saucer-shaped spacecraft. Measuring about 20 meters across by some 4 meters high, they were told that the ships were powered by fusion reactors and could easily reach Earth in less than a day at optimum cruising speed. They were not, it was pointed out, designed for interstellar travel as they possessed neither the power nor the resources for such a long voyage.

"We have used these craft to explore the planet which you call Mars," said Kobar.

"And what did you find?" asked Susan.

"Our scientists found exactly what your own explorers have recently found— namely, that life had commenced there several billion years ago but was soon extinguished, for all practical purposes, when its atmosphere and water began to dissipate and the climate turned bitterly cold. It was just a little too small and too far from the Sun to nurture life forms beyond simple cellular organisms," explained Jevad.

"What would you say the odds are of a newly formed star giving birth to a planet capable of supporting advanced biological life?" Hamilton could not resist asking.

"If the star is between one-half and one and one-half times the mass of your Sun, the chances of producing at least one favorable planet are quite promising," replied Jevad. "Incidentally, we know of but two cases in which a solar system gave rise to a second suitable planet— and in each instance evolution had lagged behind on the less favorable world."

"Although astronomers of our late 20th century managed to discover large planets— comparable to the gas giants of our own Solar System—around several nearby stars, we were never able to detect bodies as small as the Earth, even though their existence could be reasonably inferred. But what I would like to know is whether a Jupiter-size body is essential for the formation of a biologically viable world," asked Susan. "We have theorized that this is so."

"It would appear to be a valid hypothesis," responded Jevad. "Of the close to thirty civilizations, of whom we have knowledge, their solar systems all contain at least one gas giant. Evidently, such a massive body is required in order to sweep up— by reason of its superior gravity — the myriad swarms of asteroid-size bodies that are formed early in the history of the system. Without such an object the incidence of catastrophic encounters would be so high as to preclude the emergence and survival of higher life forms."

"Never underestimate the many subtleties of nature," advised Ryona. "There is much that our respective worlds have yet to learn."

"Before you leave we must hold a serious philosophical discussion about life and the universe," suggested Kobar. "The science you call cosmology has always fascinated me since the days of my youth."

"I, for one, shall look forward to this unexpected opportunity. I'm quite certain that we can learn much from you," Professor Hamilton was most willing to concede.

Chapter 6
REVELATION

Some twelve hours after concluding their informative tour of the Matusian's lunar complex, Kobar fulfilled his promise to hold a philosophical discussion. Appearing with him on the large 3-D video screen was Jevad and two others whom the six astronaut explorers had yet to meet. Luvana, an esteemed historian/philosopher, was seen to be an attractive female with long silver/white hair. Mogab, a tall male with comparatively short hair of the same distinctive coloring, was revealed to be an astronomer/physicist of some renown.

"Since we are already versed in essential aspects of popular Earth views— relating to science, philosophy and religion— it is perhaps appropriate to commence with a description of our own cosmological interpretation of the universe," said Kobar.

It was Luvana who proceeded to give an account of how Matusian society had come to embrace the concept of universal reincarnation as the cornerstone of their philosophy— a viewpoint which, she was quick to emphasize, constituted a fundamental belief inherent in religions of all the advanced races with whom they had come into contact. The gist of her dialogue follows:

“As our civilization evolved to the point where it began to theorize that the soul could survive beyond death, it soon became evident that earlier primitive notions of multiple deities were hopelessly in error. Nor did the naive idea of a personalized God, with the power to admit or refuse entrance into a nebulous heaven, make much more sense as knowledge of our astronomical universe increased. Eventually, the principle of cosmic reincarnation surfaced as the only viable alternative to a highly chaotic and meaningless existence.

"Upon a purely philosophical basis, the many advantages inherent in the concept of reincarnation are extremely convincing if one would subscribe to the premise of a Just Creator. Any notion that we have but one all-determining life, in which to prove ourselves worthy of passing to some heavenly plane, is seen to be most illogical. For instance, what happens to the soul of one who dies in infancy? Should we rashly assume that it passes automatically to a higher existence, we are then faced with the rather disturbing thought that those who live longer are unlucky — in the sense that they are at risk of not making it, so to speak! Furthermore, it may be asked: What specific instant does a child cease being a child and become responsible for its actions? Clearly, any attempt to impose a time limit is quite absurd. A similar parallel exists with regard to adults. Since death shows no respect for either time or person, how can we fail to give all individuals an equal length of time and equal opportunity to evolve spiritually? To ignore this obvious deduction is to deny the very possibility of Cosmic Justice.

"This time impasse problem vanishes immediately one embraces the principle of reincarnation. By acknowledging the immortality of soul, or spirit, the mystery surrounding premature death (or any death, for that matter) is removed, since a subsequent rebirth will prevent the injustice which would otherwise ensue. If a spiritual entity deserves a particular level of existence once, it must surely deserve to be reborn into a similar physical body again— simply because nothing has transpired which would serve to change matters.

"Linked to the time aspect of reincarnation is the highly relevant phenomenon of biological evolution. In short, how are we to reconcile the idea of spiritual immortality with the implications of evolution? Assuming that our origin may be traced back to at least a microscopic beginning, then where can a line be drawn as to the specific stage in which one is suddenly blessed with the potential of rebirth? Exactly the same problem arises as must accompany any notion of a single all-determining existence. It takes very little reasoning to show that the answer to the first difficulty is also the solution to the problem posed by evolution.

"However, rather than attempt to infer a time limit where none may be inferred, or draw a line where none can be drawn, we are led to only one sensible conclusion. Invariably, it becomes a case of *all or nothing* with regard to the issue of a life after death. Either all forms of life are eligible for rebirth, or else it is a vain hope that does not exist at any level in the extensive hierarchy of life.

"Assuming that the universe is indeed characterized by a steady upward progression of spirit, through the various levels of biological life, it is to be noted that an extension of this premise to lowly matter is not without similar advantages in resolving the paradox of an imperfect physical universe and a Perfect Creator. An essential ingredient is the fundamental assumption of *free will*— a concept that not only agrees with our own experience, but which also relieves God of the responsibility of introducing imperfection into every facet of the material universe. It is undoubtedly a stroke of irony that the indestructibility of mere matter— as revealed by the conservation of mass-energy— may be adduced in support of the principle of spiritual immortality!

"Proceeding upon the assumption of spirit rising to great heights, from the depths of obscurity, we are immediately faced with a most intriguing observation. It is noted that, the further one goes down the scale of life, the higher the numbers encountered.

The difference in abundance is positively staggering. How could they all expect to evolve, individually, to more elevated levels? There can, of course, be just one logical conclusion. It must be deduced that— in strict conformity to some dynamic law— *many spirits (or souls) of a low order are combined, or fused, to produce fewer entities, but of a higher nature or status!* Only by recognizing the principle of *cosmic fusion* may we escape an otherwise hopeless situation.

"By way of analogy our mysterious universe may be likened unto a vast pyramid, with rows of steps extending from a broad base (which may be taken to represent many entities of low worth) to a peak or pinnacle at the top (which might be defined as a state of *Maximum Fusion: God)*. Since no valid excuse can be found to predict an end to this steady flow of spirit— up the Cosmic Pyramid — we are left with no alternative but to recognize the inherent right of all creation to rise to the height of Perfection, or Total Fusion. *Termination in God is invariably the Purpose and Motivation behind creation, and the Destiny of all spirit— ourselves included!"*

At this point in the discourse Mogab, the Matusian astronomer and physicist, began to speak:

"It was only after our philosophers had given us the concept of universal reincarnation that we were able to obtain a deeper insight into such phenomena as gravitation and radiation propagation. Once it was apparent that the principle of cosmic fusion extended to the very depths of subatomic matter, the true nature of gravitation now became clear. In essence, gravitation is an expression of the inborn desire of all creation to become fused into One Harmonious Whole. Acting to prevent this state of affairs are such properties as distance and motion which, together, introduce the phenomenon of time. (Were communion instantaneous there could be no time, motion, or distance and all would be Perfection, or God.) By assuming that gravitation is propagated at essentially the speed of light, the stage is set for a much better understanding of this mysterious cosmic force.

"Acknowledging the existence of vast swarms of minute quanta, at the lower extremities of a Great Cosmic Pyramid, it was a logical step to theorize that an exchange of these same infinitesimal quanta— at virtually light speed— could give rise to the force of gravitation. In short order, theory was devised which offered a highly promising explanation of how these tiny quanta might be absorbed and emitted, from a rapidly rotating mature material particle, so as to induce attraction. What soon became evident was that, while a preponderance of exchanged energy would indeed cause attraction among material bodies, a small proportion (comprising the larger quanta) must tend to impart repulsion. Further research permitted us to deduce a formula for this inferred factor of repulsion, once we realized that the ratio of these two opposing forces was linked to the very pattern of cosmic reincarnation— in the sense that a faster rate of spiritual evolution must imply a stronger repulsive factor. In contrast to gravitational attraction— in which a twofold increase of distance results in a fourfold reduction of strength— the repulsive aspect of this energy exchange takes the form of a twofold increase of strength with each fourfold increase of distance. The key calibrating ingredient lay in identifying the starting point as the diameter of a proton nucleus, in conjunction with the supposition that initial repulsion is equal to the square root of attraction.

"Upon such a basis a number of celestial mysteries were soon found to have a ready solution. Missing mass problems, in which galactic extremities and the random motions of galaxies within a bound cluster would seem to imply the presence of unseen mass, can all be explained as a consequence of this repulsive aspect of gravitation. Likewise, minor perturbations in the orbits of certain planets, binary stars, galactic spiral structure, and an expanding universe may also be seen to have a common explanation. (This repulsive force becomes equal to that of attraction at a distance of close to 17 million light-years.) Of particular importance to the science of cosmology, this factor of gravitational repulsion removes any need to postulate an explosive origin of the universe in order to account for the observed recession of the galaxies.

"Yet another consequence of inferring a great preponderance of recently created infinitesimal matter forms, inhabiting the vast expanse of space, is the effect it must have upon radiation seeking to propagate the enormous distances between the galaxies. Since no physical interaction can take place in zero time, there will be a delay factor imposed upon radiation— a factor which will manifest itself in terms of enhanced redshifts, or wavelength shift toward the red end of the spectrum. In turn, this would act to preclude a simple extrapolation of distance with the time of propagation. Considering that radiation must propagate at the speed of light relative to the motion of the prevailing gravitational field— regardless of strength— it follows that extreme redshifts will be indicative of very long transit times. Upon contemplating the high redshifts that are observed in the more distant galaxies and quasars, it may well be deduced that this radiation has been in transit for many tens of billions of years beyond the point where such objects would be deemed to be receding at the velocity of light— namely, a universe radius of about 18 billion light-years."

It was Kobar who could not resist commenting upon the beliefs held by many Earth scientists. He spoke as follows:

"When we first learned of the high regard accorded to a Big Bang explosive origin of the universe, by so many of your otherwise astute astronomers and physicists, we were greatly surprised. Not one of all the advanced civilizations, of whom we have knowledge, had ever given the Big Bang concept much credence. We could hardly believe some of the erroneous interpretations made by your scientists. Not only have they ignored the possibility that extreme redshifts could be caused by interaction with swarms of infinitesimal quanta, in the depths of space, but even the so-called relativistic formula— used to reduce redshifts to below light speed — is convoluted logic. In point of fact, it serves the purpose of reinstating the *law of addition of speeds*— a firmly established and valid law of nature from which all radiation was supposedly (and rather magically) exempted! Incredibly, another widely accepted formula, depicting the rapidly mounting difficulty of accelerating a body as light speed is approached, was thought to be due to an increase of mass — ostensibly, becoming infinite at the velocity of light, an obvious impossibility. In actuality, this perfectly legitimate equation really describes the declining efficiency of gravitation (or applied force) as the velocity of light is approached. (Light speed is seen to represent the escape velocity of quanta from association with a mature material particle.)

"Upon acceptance of the correct view of radiation propagation, all objections to a Steady-state (continuous creation) cosmology are now promptly removed. For example, the numbers of faint extragalactic radio sources, which appeared to increase with distance at a greater rate than could be accounted for by a simple increase of space/volume, will be seen to be the result of detecting radiation from considerably more than one 18 billion light-year age/radius universe. Rather than being due to observing more sources in a smaller volume of space, such radio telescopes were observing far more *time* than distance, which permitted detection of multiple generations of celestial creation. Moreover, even the microwave background, which so many of Earth's scientists still proclaim to be proof of a Big Bang cosmology, was later shown by others to be merely a reflection of the average temperature of matter in the cold isolation of deep space.

"To an unbiased mind, there is conclusive proof of Big Bang fallacy merely by examining galaxy redshifts within the confines of our own Local Supercluster. It so happens that the average redshift, per million light-years (MLY) of separation, is of the order of some 22 km/s. But since all members of our supercluster are greatly constrained by gravitational attraction, this would require the true rate of cosmic expansion to be considerably higher— at the very least, double such a figure. Therein lies an insoluble problem for supporters of any form of Big Bang cosmology, since a velocity this high would give an age/radius of the universe of less than 7 billion light-years! Considering that many stars of our Milky Way's globular clusters are at least 15 billion years old, this would be seen to pose a fatal contradiction.

"The problem for Big Bang proponents becomes rapidly worse when we assess galactic redshifts in terms of distance traversed since the time of their birth. Should we adopt a figure of 15 billion years, as being consistent with the ages of our oldest stars and the present observed expansion rate of the universe, then it may be calculated that a system now 20 MLY distant (with an average recession velocity of some 330 km/s over the past 15 billion years) will have receded about 16.5 MLY since formation. A galaxy currently situated 40 MLY distant will have moved away by not less than 33 MLY; while another at 100 MLY will be adduced to have traveled over 82 MLY in this same interval. If we go back to the time of their birth we are confronted with the absurdity of having condensed our entire Local Supercluster — consisting of thousands of galaxies — into a tiny volume of space barely 30 to 40 MLY in diameter! Such enormous density would clearly possess a gravitational field so strong that no system could ever manage to escape to greater distances. Upon the basis of a solitary Big Bang explosion there is just no way in which they could have receded to their present positions — revealing that there is a very substantial *time delay* factor imposed upon such radiation by reason of interaction with the inferred distance/repulsion (D/R) quanta and the ubiquitous interstellar medium.

"Further confirmation as to the validity of the D/R factor is to be found in a study of galactic redshifts immediately behind and in front of the great Virgo Cluster, which has an average redshift of some 18.2 km/s per MLY. By coincidence, this dense cluster lies almost in a direct line between us and the cosmic center (which will be discussed shortly), and is concentrated at a distance of 50 to 60 MLY from our Milky Way. At a distance from us of 30 to 50 MLY, the average redshift is 27.9 km/s per MLY of separation. At the other side of the Virgo Cluster, between 60 to 80 MLY distant, the average redshift is only 15.3 km/s. If this large discrepancy is due solely to gravitational attraction from the massive cluster, then why is the group closest to us some 9.7 km/s higher; while the opposing group is only 2.9 km/s lower than this centrally located cluster? Since both groups do not vary by the same amount, there is clearly a more subtle factor involved — one which must surely be due to interaction with the repulsive quanta so theorized to permeate extragalactic space.

"Enlarging upon the premise of continuous creation, one may deduce that matter is introduced into the universe at a level far below that of the most elementary known particle. Drawn toward a central meeting point between neighboring superclusters, by the repulsive force of the larger gravitational quanta, it is to be inferred that an exceedingly massive black hole will eventually be produced— thereby facilitating the production of vast swarms of electrons and positrons. Spiraling deeper into the vicinity of this swirling concentration of mass, multitudes of protons only are created due to favorable rotation of the central black hole. As contraction of the cloud continues, so the velocity of rotation must also increase. Ultimately, as the speed of light is approached, intense outward pressure becomes sufficient to literally blast the bulk of these newly created matter forms into the depths of space in a mammoth Small Bang explosion — thus accounting for the primordial helium which was erroneously deemed to have come from a Big Bang explosion. With the protons soon capturing free electrons, great numbers of hydrogen atoms are produced and become the main source of fuel for the stars. The supermassive black hole core, surrounded by a considerable amount of hydrogen/helium gases, now becomes the quasar nucleus of what will eventually evolve into a giant galaxy."

Further dialogue was provided by Jevad, who continued the story by making the positively startling prediction that the very universe is enclosed by an impenetrable physical boundary! His contribution to the discourse follows:

"Of itself, the actual premise of continuous creation involves a violation of the firmly established law known as the conservation of energy— whereby the total mass-energy content of the universe is considered to be a fixed commodity. In order to avoid the spectacle of a steady increase in the size of our physical universe, and yet satisfy the dictates of perpetual creation, it is quite obvious that stability may only be maintained at the expense of postulating a literal disintegration of an equivalence of existing matter. Just as there is birth and death in the realm of biological life, so must our physical universe be subject to the same limitation if we are to infer a cosmos that is infinite in time.

"Valuable insight into the nature of this proposed annihilation factor is inherent in a proper understanding of how radiation is propagated, within an expanding universe, upon acceptance of the law of addition of speeds. At the point where galaxies are receding at the velocity of light— relative to the center of the universe — any inflowing radiation will be moving at the same speed as the outward flowing quanta of an expanding universe. In effect, this radiation will become trapped to form an encircling shell of energy of truly incredible strength, since a universe that is infinite in time must allow radiation to build upon radiation for an eternity. Such an invisible shell may well be described in terms of an encircling black hole, which acts to absorb and annihilate any star or planet that strikes this fateful barrier at the velocity of light! Hence, it may be deduced that many celestial objects exist only in the form of ghostly images — the actual sources themselves having long since undergone disintegration in response to a fundamental cosmic law requiring the conservation of mass-energy."

Mogab, the Matusian astronomer, now undertook to expound what promised to be a most intriguing cosmological model of the universe. His dialogue follows:

"Confronted with the prospect of one day finding ourselves at the brink of encountering this impenetrable energy barrier, it became essential to determine our proximity to the nearest boundary of what was presumed to be a closed universe. Fortunately, there was a way to do so by utilizing quasars— by far the most luminous objects in nature— as celestial beacons, in conjunction with one important feature inherent in our cosmology of an expanding universe.

"By reason of the outward flowing of repulsive gravitational quanta, there must be a pronounced bending of quasar images, as radiation from all distant objects— not in a direct line of sight with the cosmic center and nearby edge— interacts with this outbound stream and is caused to follow curved trajectories. In every instance this *cosmic arcing*, or deflection of images, will be toward the center of the universe. Thus, if theory is correct, there should be a most noticeable clumping of quasars in one direction of the heavens, with a corresponding shortage focused chiefly at right angles. There should, however, be another very dense concentration in exactly the opposite direction of the sky, since radiation from many generations of quasars is still fighting a strong headwind, so to speak, and will be in a state of near entrapment in the direction of the closest cosmic edge. Observation reveals that this is indeed the case, with amost pronounced difference in numbers implying that our Milky Way galaxy is situated relatively close to this portentous energy barrier.

"What permits a distinction between the cosmic center and the nearby edge is the fact that quasar luminosity is a strong function of age, in the sense that the brighter the object the more youthful it must be. Since many quasars will be extinguished prematurely upon reaching the boundary of the universe, it may be adduced that the immediate cosmic edge will be characterized by a preponderance of younger and brighter quasar images of higher than average redshift. Yet another distinguishing feature will be a relative shortage of high luminosity quasars of low redshift— simply because there will be less room for their formation between ourselves and the edge before we both reach this fateful barrier. In contrast, the central regions of the universe will exhibit a mixture of high and low redshift quasars with lower than average luminosity at higher redshifts. This theorized dichotomy is well confirmed by observation, and clearly indicates that the closest cosmic edge lies in the vicinity of the constellation of Sculptor, in the Southern Hemisphere. Accordingly, the cosmic center would be seen to reside in the region of Coma Berenices, in the Northern Hemisphere.

"Further proof of this inferred principle of radiation arcing is evident upon a study of the many quasar images to be found near the coordinates of massive galaxies. To the astonishment of astronomers, lacking insight into the effect of repulsive quanta upon radiation, far more quasars appeared to be located in close proximity to giant galaxies than could be ascribed to chance alone. What was also noted was that, for a certain distance range beyond these centers of mass, there was an equally disproportionate shortage of quasar images — impressive evidence that such images had been displaced toward the galaxies in question. The explanation, of course, is to be found in what might be termed the *galactic arcing* of radiation— whereby the larger repulsive quanta, emitted from the galaxies, acts to bend radiation so as to make it appear much closer to the intervening concentration of mass.

"By good fortune, the very manner in which repulsive quanta interacts with radiation — in the vicinity of the nearby cosmic edge— affords a means of determining our proximity to this impenetrable boundary. In this particular direction of the sky a relatively small line of sight separation, between sources, is capable of producing quite different redshifts, as radiation must find it increasingly difficult to propagate toward the central portions of the universe. If one is able to deduce the true linear separation of two closely bound galaxies (whose images originated in the direction of Sculptor), it becomes possible to calculate their distance from the nearby edge — as a function of radiation transit time — from their respective redshifts. Analysis of a number of suitable galaxy pairs, with highly discordant redshifts, tends to imply that our Milky Way presently resides within a few million light-years of the cosmic boundary.

"One other promising method of determining our proximity to the cosmic edge involves monitoring the redshifts of nearby galaxies— centered upon the constellation of Sculptor — as there is reason to suspect that they will undergo a gradual reduction with the passage of time. Whereas it had previously been mentioned that gravitation is propagated at essentially light speed, it is probably more accurate to state that such energies— including the larger repulsive quanta— are ejected from a source at a slightly higher velocity. (The viable premise that gravitation can flow from a black hole, while radiation cannot, is a strong indication that this must be so.) In this event, a difference of only a fraction of one percent can be shown to have a significant impact upon radiation that has been in transit for many millions of years. Since the last D/R quanta (emitted from a long extinguished galaxy) will be seen to have passed us before the arrival of its last radiation, it follows that our Milky Way will have less repulsive quanta to eject toward such incoming radiation— energy which would otherwise serve to retard it by way of enhanced redshift. As a direct consequence of this abrupt cutoff of the means with which to slow inbound radiation, a situation must prevail whereby the non-velocity redshift component of many local galaxies is reduced by reason of extinction at the cosmic periphery!

"This enigma of declining nearby galactic redshifts, which was actually reported by certain Earth astronomers toward the latter years of the 20th century, is capable of providing a new and potentially more accurate method of deducing our position with respect to a rather fateful cosmic edge. Further monitoring, combined with research into the velocity differential between radiation and D/R quanta, should one day give us a somewhat better assessment of our present location. Meanwhile, preliminary evidence would seem to indicate an interval of between a few thousand and a few million years remaining to us before this impending cataclysm overtakes our region of the Milky Way — with indications that it could actually be much closer to the lower figure!"

It was Luvana, the Matusian historian/philosopher, who ventured to describe how they had developed what could only be termed a highly intriguing concept of universal reincarnation. Her next contribution to the interview follows:

"Both theoretical and observational evidence tends to lend strong confirmation to the concept of a bound and finite physical universe. It must, however, be stressed that the existence of an enclosed system does not preclude the possibility of *other* universes! It could well be that our own universe is as one relatively minute cell in another structure far greater than we might dare to imagine. Nevertheless, it is perhaps prudent to reserve comment to that which is conducive to investigation. In so doing, it can be shown that a most unique series of mathematical relationships link the realm of the ultra-small with that of the ultra-large — a feature which would seem to indicate that, for all practical purposes, our own universe constitutes a bound system sufficient unto itself!

"By way of our illustrating the close interrelationship of such cosmic extremes, we might refer to five rather curious numerical associations involving the immense sum of 10^{40} (one followed by 40 zeros). These similarities may be described as follows:

(1) At very close proximity, the electrical charge of a pair of positive/negative particles exceeds the strength of their mutual gravitational influence by close to 10^{40}.

(2) The density ratio of highly degenerate neutron stars, in relation to the average density of matter throughout the expanse of our enclosed universe, is of the order of 10^{40}.

(3) Stretched out in a straight line, it would take about 10^{40} proton nuclei to reach the distance at which the galaxies are receding at the speed of light.

(4) The repulsive aspect of gravitation, at a distance equal to the diameter of a proton nucleus, is seen to be some 10^{20} times weaker than attraction — in essence, repulsion is revealed to be the square root of attraction.

(5) The square root of the number of protons, within our enclosed universe (10^{80}), is none other than 10^{40}.

"In each instance these relationships may be considered to be an expression of fusion versus non-fusion. Essentially, the phenomenon of gravitation may be defined as an inborn desire for fusion — of intrinsic worth expressed over the depths of space. It is, in fact, a reflection of a particle's ability to achieve attraction or communion with the physical universe as a whole. In contrast, the electrical force of a particle is a manifestation of this same worth compressed to a volume of space equal to that of its immediate self— the halo of energy enveloping the material body in question. Since there is good reason to suspect that the value of congealed energy/spirit fused within a proton or electron does not exceed that of the surrounding halo by an exorbitant figure, it follows that exposure to another charged particle will produce a magnified reaction that is largely in proportion to the value of spirit fused within. Hence, it may be inferred that roughly 10^{40} of the smallest units of creation (which we might designate as an "A") likely constitutes the level of the proton. In a sense, the electrical force of a particle may be viewed as an indication of achieved fusion; whereas gravitation may be considered to be a sign of potential fusion associated with Destiny.

"A philosophical basis for the inferred D/R factor would thus seem implicit in theory. It is surely more than a coincidence that, at the point where the force of repulsion first becomes manifest, it does so as the square root of the number of these most elementary units of creation that are believed to characterize such a mature particle as a proton. Moreover, it is essential that a twofold increase in the strength of this repulsion induce a fourfold increase of distance in order to achieve a balance between the rate of new creation and that of cosmic evolution. In effect, *it is actually the rate of spiritual advancement which determines the expansion rate of the universe!*

"With a total of 10^{80} protons comprising our physical universe, and 10^{40} fused "A"s per proton, it will be inferred that Perfection— or any one level within the Great Cosmic Pyramid— is equivalent to some 10^{120} "A"s. Expressed in terms of spiritual evolution, this Ultimate State at the top of the Pyramid would involve approximately 400 occasions of doubling, or cosmic steps. Accordingly, an entity of the status of a proton would be seen to reside 1/3rd of the way toward the top, having already climbed some 133 steps (equal to 10^{40}) from its origin as an infinitesimal "A". Upon this premise, slightly less than one percent of all the mass-energy in the universe is likely to be incorporated into basic material particles. This ratio of minute quanta to actual matter is in excellent agreement with the dictates of the Steady-state creation model, which imposes strict limitations as to the relationship between average total density and the rate of cosmic expansion.

"A most exciting prospect which now emerges is that of determining the universal *time constant* of spiritual fusion. For it must be an integral feature of theory that all levels of spirit, within the Great Cosmic Pyramid, will manage to double their worth in some common interval of time. A solution to this problem will afford useful insight as to the average time that an individual must live in order to achieve one doubling of status. It should also give us some idea as to when one might expect a future rebirth.

"Assessment of this time aspect of reincarnation involves the rate of annihilation at the edge of the universe, since all spirit from disrupted life forms will be compelled to seek rebirth on appropriate planets elsewhere. In terms of the planet with which a spirit was last associated, considerable time could elapse between incarnations, as displaced spirit must share available body-forms on other worlds. (Time, of course, simply does not exist to spirit until it is reborn into another biological form.)

"In theory, it could well be that those who succeed in increasing their intrinsic worth, in excess of the average, will be rewarded by a longer postponement in their next rebirth— thereby enhancing the likelihood of securing an existence in a more favorable environment. Conversely, one who has made relatively little or no progress may expect to be reborn in a fraction of this time— quite possibly, in less desirable circumstances should a regression be involved. Thus it is conceivable that nature could permit us some latitude with regard to determining the specific moment of rebirth within an evolutionary era on a planet.

"Invariably, the rate of expansion of the universe must constitute a key factor in determining the time constant of cosmic evolution. Why does the universe double in size every 12 billion years or so? Why not some other figure? Obviously, the greater the rate of any expansion the sooner a world will experience annihilation at the edge of the universe. Since disintegration must be balanced through creation, it follows that the introduction and evolution of new "A" is closely related to recession of the galaxies. The issue, therefore, becomes one of determining how "A" is introduced with respect to each cycle of cosmic doubling. The one logical possibility to emerge must surely embrace the premise that *one entire level of new "A" is created in the span of 12 billion years, and is able to evolve to a state of Perfection in this same interval!*

"Should such be the case, it must follow that the time required by spirit, to double its worth, may be determined by dividing the overall cosmic cycle by the number of steps separating "A" from Perfection. Subsequently, a period of roughly 30 million years, per occasion of doubling, may be derived upon dividing 12 billion years by the sum of 400. However, since only 1/400th of an entire level of new "A" will be created in a period of 30 million years, it means that just one spiritual entity in 400 may actually have a conscious (or physical) manifestation at any given instant. But if 30 million years is the allotted time, for one entire level of spirit to double in status, this restriction will introduce an additional factor of 400 into the time permitted for a physical incarnation. Dividing our 30 million year period by this further factor of 400, we are left with about 75,000 years as the average elapsed time between doublings.

"Yet another factor is imposed by annihilation at the cosmic edge, as it takes time for new stars and planets to form and biological entities to evolve— a factor that is related to status. Calculation of the average age of matter, within the framework of Steady-state cosmology, reveals that only about one part in twenty will be as old as the overall period of cosmic doubling.

"The final factor, in deducing our reincarnation cycle, involves knowledge of humanity's position in the Great Cosmic Pyramid. (While a relatively minor factor, the more advanced the life form the less time that will be available for a physical manifestation.) With a hydrogen nucleus established at step 133, this problem may be resolved by determining the ratio of hydrogen to mankind throughout the expanse of the universe. In this regard, it may be estimated that there are roughly 10^{53} protons (equal to 177 doublings) for every human. Adding this sum to the 133 doublings, so deemed to characterize a proton, we are led to believe that man presently resides at about the 310th step out of a maximum of 400. (An error of one million in computing the ratio of man to proton will only make a difference of about 6%, and a million million by just 12%.)

"Applying this information to reincarnation of the human soul, we may derive an interval of approximately 4,800 years (or almost 70 lifetimes of 70 years) as the average time that must be served as a conscious manifestation in order to double our intrinsic worth. In terms of Earth evolution, however, two highly relevant questions come to mind. During what past age did we last live? Moreover, in what future era are we likely to be reborn?

"Considering the need to accommodate spirit displaced from other worlds, in conjunction with the overall cycle of doubling which is of the order of 30 million years, reincarnation could take the form of a projection well into the future and very likely into another planetary environment. Thus, if man requires 4,800 years as a conscious entity to achieve one doubling of status, over a period of 30 million years, it will be tantamount to an elapsed time of almost 6,200 years for each year of a past life. With an average life expectancy of 70 years this would imply a rebirth some four or five hundred thousand years into the future. However, if only 1/400th of an entire level of new "A" is created per 30 million year cycle, in terms of Earth evolution the *apparent* elapsed time will be less that the *actual* time by an identical factor. What most likely transpires is that man is actually reborn some hundreds of thousands of years from now; but in relation to past environment it will be equivalent to an evolutionary era only a thousand years or so into the future.

"In contemplating the future of mankind, as a biological species, it may be theorized that successive doublings will require some 75,000 years in terms of Earth time. The eventual passage of man, beyond his present frail and transitory human form, could very well lead us to infer a solution in such astronomical curiosities as *neutron stars and celestial black holes!* Best described as immense concentrations of mass-energy, contracted into super atomic particles, the ratio of mankind to this highly fused state of matter should permit computation of the number of steps or doublings needed to achieve this inferred evolution. With such being the case, it may indeed be said that human destiny is to be found in the stars!

"There are convincing arguments for linking humanity's future to a phenomenon that, at first glance, might be considered quite bizarre. Not only does this unique state of matter possess all the attributes of total fusion— thereby constituting a spiritual entity of a certain leve — but there is excellent agreement of numbers which would relate theory with observation. It is surely more than a coincidence that an estimate, of all stellar black holes/neutron stars likely to exist in the universe, should equal the probable number of Earth-type planets that are allowed to fulfill their evolutionary roles. It can also be shown that the quantity of "A" fused within a typical stellar black hole (some 10^{58} protons x 10^{40} "A"s, or about 10^{98} fused "A"s), when multiplied by the number of such objects in the entire universe, is very likely of the same order as the total spiritual worth (or "A" content) of one complete population of Earth-man multiplied by the quantity of all other worlds of a similar evolutionary level! Since it is most inconceivable that man could ever expect to conclude his evolution toward Perfection, without there being some transient stage, we may well deduce that such highly compacted celestial objects do indeed constitute the required medium.

"In predicting the future of mankind, in his evolution and passage through subsequent occasions of doubling, it is to be inferred that some 17 doublings— each of about 75,000 years— will be needed to evolve beyond the human form. Upon this basis, little more than a million years will suffice to complete man's evolutionary saga on the planet Earth. (Accordingly, any difficulty in contacting intelligent life on other planets may be due, in part, to spirit evolving beyond the biological state. In effect, large numbers of highly advanced civilizations will be seen to have already come and gone in the relatively short time span allocated for human supremacy.)

"One can only speculate as to the details involved in subsequent evolution. Presumably, further progress is facilitated by means of stellar black hole entities establishing reciprocal communion with similar entities— interactions of a non-physical nature and not restricted to the velocity of light. Finally, upon attaining the ability to express instantaneous or Total Communion, time will cease to exist for such advanced entities and a literal fusion into God will ensue. Somehow, as a consequence of Black Hole Minds concluding this momentous transition from the physical world of imperfection and time, the energy so released is manifested as a new generation of "A" within the confines of our celestial universe."

The concluding speech in the Matusian's lecture was made by Kobar, as he endeavored to convey some idea as to the current status of their cosmological views. He summarized as follows:

"Without a doubt, a truly amazing picture has emerged which allows us to glimpse a glorious destiny that must surely exceed one's wildest dreams. Our respective races now stand at the threshold of a bold new field of scientific and philosophical inquiry. At long last, after eons of primitive groping for the meaning of existence, we have before us considerably more than mere conjecture as to what lies beyond the human form.

"But while a physical universe of finite size is thus theorized, by reason of an annihilation factor equal to that of creation, a paradox nevertheless seems to arise when we contemplate a connection with the spiritual aspect of cosmic evolution. If spirit forever rises from an infinitesimal quantum (or "A") to a state of Perfection or

God, then may it not be deduced that— with the passage of time—God is becoming increasingly more Omnipotent? Conversely, might it also be argued that God was less of an Entity in the distant past? The issue of a finite physical universe is therefore seen to differ from the issue of spiritual evolution in one crucial respect. In essence, our physical environment may be likened to the role of a catalyst— a medium which remains unchanged in the long run, while yet facilitating an endless progression of spirit up the Great Cosmic Pyramid.

"Conceivably, a solution to this Eternity paradox may be found in an important attribute of Perfection— namely, a state in which *time* has literally ceased to exist. Without the phenomenon of time such properties as distance, dimensions, or size become meaningless terms. Likewise, the concept of quantity — being related to size in the physical world — is similarly shrouded in nebulosity should there be no time. Devoid of both time and size, the apparent problem of an ever-increasing and evolving Creator tends to fade into oblivion. Looked at through the eyes of mortal man there does indeed appear to be a contradiction. At the level of Perfection this seeming paradox may very well have no substance."

"Exactly how would you define the general term of *soul* or *spirit?*" asked Hamilton, posing a problem which had long been the subject of debate among Earth philosophers. "May it be looked upon as a segment of Perfection, or whatever God consists of?"

"Essentially, yes. We have chosen to describe this universal spark of life as a degree of *Cosmic Love*," replied Luvana. "In bare essence, a spiritual entity is so believed to consist solely of a specific *degree of unselfishness* — with such attributes as memory and biological consciousness being a product of imperfection and time. Upon this basis, the ultimate level of God or Perfection may well be depicted as a state of *Total Unselfishness*."

"It is for the purpose of evolving above our inherently selfish nature— toward a state of *Universal Love* — that we owe our mundane existence," summarized Kobar.

More than one guest astronaut stood in deep thought, before the blank video screen, long after their hosts had concluded their most informative interview. There was no question but what Earth society was on the verge of a momentous upheaval — once the presence of the Matusians became known.

Chapter 7
RETURN TO EARTH

Within the span of the next ten hours an important decision was made regarding the Matusian's four most recent guests. Upon passing a much superior version of Earth's lie detector test, the way was now open for their return to *Lunar Base*. Unfortunately, there was still no hope of allowing Frost and Baldwin to leave, as it would be quite impossible to explain their presence without revealing the fact that they had made contact with an alien civilization.

"I wonder what they would have done if one of us had flunked their test," remarked Petrov to his companions, as the group anxiously awaited a signal for another video interview with their hosts.

"I'm sure that they would have persuaded the rest of us to invent some sort of wild story— probably based upon a runaway jet pack — in order to account for the absence of one of our colleagues," Hamilton theorized.

"Actually, there would really be little option but to do so, when you come to think about it. However, I must admit that it would be pushing the jet pack hypothesis to the limit," commented Susan.

"I can just imagine how the manufacturer's stock would begin to tumble at the thought of another alleged failure," said Butler.

"What a tangled web of deception we are sometimes compelled

to weave!" philosophized Baldwin.

"Why, in heaven's name, did I have to be so damned inquisitive when I inadvertently glimpsed one of their surveillance cameras?" lamented Frost, feeling a measure of responsibility for their present predicament. Further conversation was cut short by the familiar flashing blue light, which signified the Matusian's desire to converse with their astronaut visitors.

"We have good news to report," announced Kobar, who appeared on the screen alongside his wife, Ryona, and another Matusian whom their Earth guests had yet to meet.

"This is Bordak, captain of one of our two spacecraft," said Ryona, introducing a tall male seated to her left. Wearing a colorful purple and white costume, which tended to blend well with his long silver hair, he compared favorably with any captain starring in Earth's 20th century Star Trek series.

"As you must know, we deeply regret the necessity of detaining two of your colleagues until the arrival of our starship," began Kobar. "But there may be a way to circumvent the problem which threatens to separate husbands from wives and children for what promises to be a lengthy thirty years."

"What we propose to offer is an opportunity to unite such families here on the Moon, if this can be done discretely and with little risk of exposure," said Ryona. "If the wives of Frost and Baldwin consent to the plan, captain Bordak has agreed to land his ship in a remote area where there would be minimal danger of discovery."

"In the event that one of the wives should decline this offer, we feel that a simple denial of our existence— by the four returning astronauts —will suffice to counteract what would almost certainly be interpreted as hallucination on the part of an emotionally disturbed widow," said Kobar, unable to think of a better way to state the matter.

"I don't think there will be any hesitation by Janet in accepting your very kind offer," remarked Baldwin, exceedingly jubilant at the prospect of being with his wife and two-year-old daughter, Jane.

"Nor do I anticipate the slightest doubt with regard to my wife, Carol," said Frost, likewise overjoyed at the possibility of being united with his wife and four-year-old son, Thomas.

"Then it remains merely to arrange a rendezvous time and site," concluded Bordak. "Do you have any suggestions as to where a night landing might be made without attracting too much attention?"

"I can think of one secluded clearing, in the middle of a pine forest, that is about a hundred miles from Earth's major space base at Cape Canaveral," Hamilton finally ventured to say, interrupting the silence of his comrades.

"By any chance, would it happen to be that same spot, in the Ocala National Forest, where we picnicked during a hiking trip shortly before leaving for *Space Station Orion*?" asked Susan.

"Why not? It's a small circular clearing, about 40 meters across, level and surrounded on all sides by tall pine trees. It also has an infrequently used gravel road passing to within 100 meters of the site," responded Mark.

Moving toward a nearby console, Bordak commenced pushing a series of buttons. In a few seconds a detailed map of Florida appeared on screen. Simple adjustment of a dial served to greatly enlarge the region of Ocala National Forest. "Can you point out the approximate location of this clearing?" he asked.

Upon approaching the map, which had been so magnified as to fill the entire video screen, Hamilton complied by placing his finger on a section to the northwest of Juniper Springs. "This region should be quite deserted after midnight," he said.

"If you place a cluster of three blue lights at the center of the clearing, in the configuration of a triangle, we will detect it and consider it to be a sign that all is well to land. Just be certain to stand under cover of the trees and away from our exhaust blast as we come in," said Bordak.

"Now that we have determined the place, we still have to establish the time," Kobar reminded them.

"There is also the question of who is best suited to speak to the wives," added Ryona.

"I do think Susan is an obvious choice to contact her brother's wife, Janet," suggested Kobar. "In fact, she is probably the most logical person to approach Carol as well."

"How soon could you return to Earth without arousing suspicion?" Bordak asked Susan.

"My tour of duty has barely started. Unless someone can pull some strings I'm afraid they expect me to serve the full four-month term," Susan answered.

"Perhaps a ring, instead of a string, might expedite matters— if you accept my proposal of marriage," said Hamilton, looking directly into Susan's eyes.

"Come to think of it, Mark, you did say that you wanted to propose to a prospective mate amidst lunar surroundings. I hereby accept, in front of witnesses from two worlds," responded Susan, putting both arms around her man and giving him a passionate kiss.

"I do know of two qualified astronaut/astronomers who might be willing— if not anxious— to replace us on short notice," commented Hamilton, after acknowledging congratulations from colleagues and Matusians alike. "The fact that I'm on rather good terms with the chairman of Earth's space program may also prove helpful."

"Do you really think they would go for it, if we requested an early return so as to get married on Earth?" asked Susan.

"One can only try."

"There is perhaps an inducement which we can provide," interjected Kobar. "We can present you with the secret of obtaining controlled fusion energy— a gift which we were planning to give your society upon the arrival of our great starship. It will almost certainly cause leading Earth physicists to demand your immediate recall in order to acquire first-hand information."

"I have some insight into nuclear physics, of course, as it is a requirement of every professional astronomer. But will it be enough to understand a process which has hitherto defied our best minds?" questioned Hamilton, beset with grave doubts as to his ability to pull off the charade.

"It may seem somewhat ironic, but the breakthrough in technology is closely related to a formula which you actually pioneered yourself a few years ago, in a paper dealing with the manner in which a quasar is able to liberate so much energy," Jevad informed the astronomer, having just made an appearance on the screen.

"You know about that paper?" Hamilton asked, caught completely by surprise at the alien's knowledge of his work. It was considerably more astonishing to be told that he had unknowingly come close to solving a long-standing problem in nuclear physics.

"Jevad is confident that he can fill in any missing gaps that may tend to prevent you from grasping the principles involved, and to do so with only a few hours of tutoring," said Kobar, smiling at the puzzled look on Hamilton's face.

"We will provide you with all the relevant data needed on a tiny disk that will fit your most popular computers. In addition, the disk will contain a more detailed account of our previous discussion with regard to cosmology and philosophy— including our views of cosmic reincarnation," said Jevad.

"Since this information is something which we want Earth society to have, in any event, we can see no harm in revealing it sooner instead of later," explained Kobar.

"You may, of course, be assured that I will do my very best to propagate your superior knowledge," responded Professor Hamilton. "But I can't help thinking that I would actually be guilty of an act of plagiarism, so to speak."

"At the time of announcing our presence we will make it clear to the world that we induced you to publish in your own name, as a matter of expediency and at our specific request," said Kobar, aware of the threat to the scientist's professional integrity which was bound to surface some thirty years hence.

Agreeing to the proposal, it now became a question of deciding upon a suitable time for the Matusian spacecraft to land on Earth. Lacking a convenient means of communication, the rendezvous would have to be prearranged and, if at all possible, augmented with a code which could be used to abort the mission if something were to go wrong.

"How about 3 A.M., in the dark of night, exactly three weeks after you set foot on Earth?" asked Bordak. "Would that give you enough time? We would know when you arrived simply by monitoring your news channels."

"Sounds acceptable to me," said Hamilton. "Incidentally, I do believe that I can offer a means of aborting the landing, if it should be necessary, although it might leave a gap by as much as several hours in our ability to cancel."

"Please elaborate," spoke Kobar.

"I have a colleague by the name of Phil Bonham, currently on *Space Station Orion*, with whom I occasionally converse from my office at the University of West Palm Beach. Since he is not scheduled to return to Earth for another three months, and you evidently monitor all radio messages to the station, we could use this conversation (or lack of such) as a form of code. If I should make a call to him it would signify that a landing is inadvisable. No news would mean that all is well and to proceed according to plan," responded Hamilton.

Accepting the idea in principle, it was not long before a more sophisticated scheme was devised, utilizing key words, which would permit the choice of alternate times and locations in which to carry out the intended rendezvous.

"There is perhaps one little favor which the two of you might do for us, if you have time during this three-week interval," said Kobar, referring to Mark and Susan.

"And what might that be?" asked Susan, overjoyed at the favorable turn of recent events, and more than willing to please the Matusians in whatever way she could.

"In view of this unique opportunity, our historians have made a brief list of certain data which they would like to obtain for their records. If you could assist them it would be most appreciated," stated Kobar.

"You have only to ask. If it is within our ability to supply this information we shall feel privileged to oblige," responded Susan.

"We thank you for your cooperation, and look forward to hosting the wives and children of your two fellow astronauts," said Kobar, concluding the interview.

Within the hour, clad in a protective isolation suit and carrying a small computer with a keyboard similar to that of an I.B.M. machine, Jevad was admitted to the quarters of the Earth visitors. Presenting a tiny disk to Professor Hamilton, he inserted a duplicate into the computer and commenced his lesson. In short order, a large wall screen displayed the schematics of a controlled fusion reactor. Quite incapable of being converted to an explosive device, it was able to generate prodigious amounts of cheap energy, with complete safety and absolutely no pollution. "You will find that this disk is fully compatible with your computers, and printouts can be readily made of all the data contained therein," he informed his attentive pupil.

Totally fascinated by Jevad's lecture, and tempted at times to kick himself for failure to realize how close he had actually come to understanding certain facets of nuclear physics— yet to be grasped by the world's foremost authorities— Hamilton was oblivious to the fact that some three hours had elapsed by the time Jevad had finished his tutoring. Incredible! In such a short interval man's knowledge in the realm of physics had been advanced by what might have otherwise taken centuries. He could not resist wondering how many more near miracles— in numerous fields of science and technology— might soon be made available to Earth society by reason of the alien's presence. It tended to boggle the mind to think that a great wealth of knowledge was to be given freely to scientists of all nations, and that he was about to become a central figure in dispensing such information.

Three days after leaving *Lunar Base* the four returning astronauts had donned their space suits and jet packs, bade farewell to their alien hosts, and exited from the boulder air lock. Retracing their steps to the edge of the first cliff, they wasted no time in jetting down to the larger mesa some 30 meters below. Multiple sets of tracks led to the brink of the 400-meter cliff— a distinctly visible pathway that the Matusians planned to do their best to eradicate once their guests had departed.

"I suppose we should gather a few choice rocks for the sake of putting on a front," said Petrov, his mind far removed from the science of lunar geology as he stooped to chip off a sample from a nearby rock.

"Our own tiny craft sure doesn't compare with their saucer ships," remarked Butler, gazing down at the small orange dot of the *Antares* which lay to the south.

"I only hope we all live long enough to see the great starship when it arrives some thirty years from now," commented Susan, as she prepared to descend to the plain below.

In little more than an hour they reached the *Antares*, from whence they promptly notified *Lunar Base* of their intention to lift off for the return flight. Unfortunately, they were still so enraptured by the magnitude of their discovery that they overlooked one detail. In short, they neglected to dispose of a two-day supply of food, water and oxygen, so as to account for what would have been consumed during their stay at the Matusian colony. It was to be only one of a chain of seemingly innocent anomalies and circumstances that, when taken together, were destined to adversely affect Earth history.

....

Arriving safely and without incident at *Lunar Base*, the four adventurers were greeted by a welcoming committee at the air lock. One hour later they were ushered into Bergman's office for a taped debriefing session. Giving no hint as to their momentous discovery, they merely told of following the footsteps of Frost and Baldwin along the base of the escarpment. They went on to describe the ascent of the two missing geologists up to the rock ledge with the peculiar strata, and of their subsequent visit to the top of the first mesa. Of their sojourn to the second 30-meter plateau there was, of course, no mention.

"Then you still haven't the slightest idea as to why they should suddenly decide to move the *Antares* to another location more than 40 kilometers away?" asked Bergman, clearly disappointed that this latest expedition had failed to solve the mystery.

"We're completely baffled by their action," lied Petrov. "We did find evidence that they had taken rock samples from several locations at the original landing area, but no reason to explain why they chose to up and leave for this other site."

It was Bergman's next question which served to alarm the four converts to the Matusian cause. "If they obtained samples, then why were none found in the *Antares* when it was recovered at the second landing site?" he asked, in bewilderment.

Obviously, the question was one which could not be answered satisfactorily without recourse to the truth. Nevertheless, Petrov elected to voice a rather lame response. "I suppose they either discarded them or simply forgot and left the samples in their suit pockets," he finally uttered.

"Just what I needed to convince my superiors that the personnel of *Lunar Base* are all sane scientists that know what they are doing!" lamented Bergman. "It isn't bad enough that we can't explain why they moved the *Antares*, but now we find ourselves dealing with the case of the missing samples. Truly, we have before us an enigma within a mystery."

"Perhaps it would be wise to refrain from mentioning this latest anomaly in your report to Earth authorities," suggested Hamilton, hoping to pacify Bergman. "What they don't know won't hurt them, and I'm sure that none of us present will be anxious to broach the subject to anyone."

"I'm afraid that it only gets worse," said Bergman, recalling something which had struck him as odd at the time he heard of Frost and Baldwin jetting to the top of the 400-meter mesa, after first stopping at the peculiar rock ledge.

"How come?" asked Butler.

"When the *Antares* was found, it was noted that none of the spare jet pack tanks had been used. How could they have accomplished all of these flights on just one tank of propellant and one tank of oxidizer? Unless I'm badly mistaken, they would not have had sufficient fuel to make a safe descent from the second site mesa. Why would they be so foolish as to risk their lives by not switching to fresh tanks?" responded Bergman.

At this point, all four astronaut/scientists could sense that their plan of subterfuge was in jeopardy, and that they might well have to chance revealing the alien's presence to their immediate superior.

"There's yet another anomaly which I would like cleared up," continued Bergman, deciding to lay all his cards on the table. "In checking over the *Antares*, Yashin has just informed me that hardly any food or water was consumed; in fact, even the consumption of cabin oxygen is more conducive to the requirements of less than one day — not the three days that you were gone. What the devil did you guys eat, drink and breathe for at least two missing days?"

On the verge of being forced to confess to the truth, further conversation was interrupted by the loud and insistent ringing of Bergman's telephone. It was Dr. Lin Chang, with news of a serious accident to Kovakov, who had lost a great deal of blood when a power cutting tool had slipped and severely gashed a leg. In desperate need of a transfusion, it seemed that Petrov was the only member of the colony who was a proper match for his Russian comrade's rare blood type.

"We'll resume this discussion later," said Bergman, informing them of the mishap and turning off the audio tape recorder. "I think we had all better get over to sick bay as soon as possible."

Moving swiftly down a narrow corridor, they almost collided with Adam Wentworth, the American journalist. Describing what had happened to Kovakov, in just a few words, they quickly rushed past him with thoughts riveted solely upon their stricken colleague. Momentarily pondering whether to follow them, Wentworth soon decided upon a course of action which was to have immense repercussions.

Instead of heading for sick bay, he proceeded directly down the corridor to Bergman's unlocked and deserted quarters, desirous of obtaining first-hand information on the debriefing session which had been so dramatically cut short. Quickly rewinding the tape, he began to copy the playback with a tiny recorder of his own. Still uncertain of the nature of his "scoop," he turned the machine off at the precise point of interruption and quietly exited the compartment unobserved.

It was to be some three hours later, with the emergency over and Kovakov out of danger and under the expert care of both Dr. Chang and Dr. Mitchell, that the meeting with Bergman was reconvened in his quarters. This time, by insistence of the confessors, there would be no taping of conversation until he had heard the details of what would be told in strict confidence. Needless to say, it was a story which left the commander of *Lunar Base* on the verge of being speechless.

"And that's about it," announced Hamilton, upon concluding their explanation for the strange disappearance of Frost and Baldwin.

"The defense rests," said Butler, feeling that the actions of the small group had been morally justified.

"I trust that you can see the necessity of withholding word of our discovery until the arrival of their great starship," voiced Susan.

"It would clearly be a disaster of the highest magnitude if this noble race was to be attacked by some foolish faction on Earth," added Petrov, still a little tired from his donation of blood to Kovakov.

"Incredible as your story may seem, I do believe what you say and I'll support your cover-up attempt to the best of my ability — but with one provision," Bergman finally replied.

"What's that?" asked Susan.

"If the plans given to Professor Hamilton for a fusion reactor prove to be bona fide, I will consider it to be conclusive evidence of the Matusian's good faith," Bergman answered.

"Then I shall have to get busy and work on my presentation of this momentous scientific breakthrough," said Hamilton. "I think I can talk certain of my associates into covering for me, so as to free more time."

"Meanwhile, I'll erase the initial taped debriefing and we can prepare a new one without mention of any anomalies. But we may have to take Yashin into our confidence if I can't convince him to forget about the *Antares*' consumables," Bergman told them.

"Let's just hope that nothing else intervenes to complicate matters," opined Hamilton, as he fingered the tiny disk that would require many hours of deep study before its contents could be made ready for publication and distribution.

....

Some ten days later, with Susan's valued assistance, Professor

Hamilton managed to complete a scientific paper outlining plans and listing specifications for a controlled fusion reactor. Seeking the opinions of the two highly respected physicists currently at *Lunar Base* (American Brian Erskine and India's Sanjay Singh), he was rather amused by the astonished looks on their faces as they studied the text of his thesis.

"You could sure make a fortune with this totally new approach to the problem. I can see no reason at all why it wouldn't work," said Professor Erskine, his mind continuing to reel from a multitude of startling revelations.

"I concur with my fellow physicist's opinion," commented Professor Singh, likewise impressed to the point of utter amazement at what he had read. "It is certainly most generous of you to offer it— without asking for royalties of any kind— to the entire world."

"There are some things which should belong to the public, instead of being controlled by a handful of wealthy individuals," responded Hamilton, doing his best to live with the masquerade which had been thrust upon him.

"How do you propose to make this information available to the various nations of Earth?" asked Singh.

"Assuming that you guys are unable to find fault with the paper, Bergman has agreed to an electronic transfer of data to my Miami publisher. In turn, a consortium of publishers have consented to print and distribute free copies to major news sources, science journals, and also to a broad spectrum of physics research laboratories. By so doing, no person or group will be allowed to obtain a patent on the principles involved," explained Hamilton.

"You must be on exceptionally good terms with your publisher for them to do this without compensation. Every company that I know of worships the profit motive above all else," stated Erskine.

"Actually, I did promised to supply them with an even more appealing treatise dealing with cosmology and philosophy— one which, I feel, could easily become a bestseller," Hamilton informed his colleague.

"When do you expect to finish this new work? Furthermore, how is it that you seem to be so inspired to produce such masterful works on the Moon, instead of back home on good old terra firma?" Singh could not resist asking.

"With the help of Susan, my co-author, we hope to complete the manuscript within a month. Fortunately, the vast bulk of this work was prepared beforehand, you might say," replied Hamilton. "As for inspiration, I suppose it could be said that the Moon does harbor unsuspected powers capable of enhancing man's perception. Sometimes you just have to get away from the distractions of earthly life in order to think clearly. Incidentally, if I were you I shouldn't give credence to the Big Bang model of creation, as it is on the verge of blowing up."

"You may be assured, Mark, that we do plan to give Bergman our unanimous approval of your ingenious concept for a controlled fusion reactor— one that will invariably satisfy the world's great hunger for a safe, cheap, non-polluting and inexhaustible energy supply," said Erskine.

....

The next few weeks saw everything go according to plan. Professor Hamilton was already being hailed as a genius and a celebrity, with numerous offers to lecture at prestigious universities. Accordingly, it had been a simple matter for Bergman to use this as an excuse to arrange for his return on the first lunar shuttle. With Mark and Susan having expressed plans for an early wedding on Earth, it had likewise been easy to include her as a passenger aboard the *Moonbeam*, now awaiting departure to *Space Station Orion*. As fate would have it, among those returning was Adam Wentworth, the American journalist. In his pocket was the tape so surreptitiously obtained of Bergman's initial debriefing session— a record which had since been erased and replaced by a much less incriminating second version.

Carrying with them the newly completed manuscript, which they entitled *Science and Philosophy*, its dual authors presently entered the *Moonbeam* through the docking tube that connected it to the silver land shuttle. In high spirits, they looked forward to a life together which promised to be both eventful and prosperous. It was with some regret that they found themselves leaving friends and colleagues behind at *Lunar Base*; but the thought of giving Frost and Baldwin's wives the good news concerning their husbands was more than adequate compensation. They anticipated a pleasurable and rather emotional meeting with Janet and Carol, who had been resigned to their fate for considerably more than a month.

Amidst tongues of orange flame the Moonbeam lifted from the lunar surface, slowly arcing over to a direction which would point it to where the crescent Earth would be some three days hence. Minutes later, floating in a weightless state over to a cabin window, Mark and Susan watched the Moon as it gradually receded into the distance. Three days later, through the same porthole, the pair gazed upon the sight of *Space Station Orion* as it grew steadily larger before their eyes.

Spending one full day in the synthetic gravity of the station's rotating wheel, the duo entered the air lock of the *Rigel*, one of four Earth shuttle craft which regularly serviced the international space station. It was not long after departure until friction with the upper atmosphere brought a semblance of gravity, which soon began to feel increasingly oppressive. Flame spewing from the craft's heat shield totally obscured whatever view might have been possible, were one able to overcome the strong "G" force now pushing them deep into their reclining seats. Finally, just when it was starting to become tiresome, the pressure eased and the *Rigel* commenced a glide path that would bring it close to the designated runway now awaiting them at Florida's Cape Canaveral. A few short bursts with maneuvering jets— an option lacking on earlier shuttle models— brought them directly over their target. In a matter of minutes the craft had rolled to a stop and was being towed to a terminal, where a welcoming committee stood ready to greet them.

As they stepped down a ramp to the red carpet, which led to a nearby building, their legs did not feel quite so sturdy as when they had left almost two months ago. (It would, as they well knew, take a few days for their bodies to recover from the effects of prolonged reduced gravity.) Among the VIPs present were such dignitaries as U.S. President Adolph Harker and Florida's Governor Charles Dagle, along with a flock of top physicists from several nations. Ignoring the lot, both Mark and Susan cast their eyes upon a solitary figure standing in the background. It was Janet, Susan's sister-in-law, who was the focus of their attention. Looking alone and forlorn, they could hardly wait to see the expression on her face when she was informed that her husband was alive and well.

While Hamilton was promptly cornered and subjected to a seemingly endless number of introductions, Susan rushed over to Janet Baldwin and embraced her, not daring to disclose the good news at this point in time. Compelled to endure interviews by a host of television personalities, it was several hours before the two somewhat weary celebrities were allowed to escape their clutches and leave with Janet for her three-bedroom Vero Beach bungalow. They decided to defer word of John's enforced stay at the Matusian base until after they had arrived. It would not do to have a highly emotional driver at the wheel of their vehicle in the heavy early evening traffic.

At last, following a genuine steak dinner with fresh vegetables, and with Janet's two-year-old daughter fast asleep, they undertook to reveal the great secret regarding her husband. Intending to deny the entire story, should it be necessary in order to protect the Matusians from discovery, they were relieved by the instant and affirmative response. As anticipated, Janet was not only willing but most anxious to take her infant daughter and join her husband on the Moon— even if it meant living in partial seclusion for the next thirty years.

With Frost's wife still remaining to be contacted, they were momentarily dismayed to learn that Carol had returned to her native Australia the previous week. While constituting a minor setback, it was far from a problem. In fact, the very thought of spending a honeymoon on the other side of the globe, away from reporters and physicists alike, seemed to possess definite appeal.

Having decided upon a small wedding some three days hence, they would make plans to fly to the city of Brisbane the following morning to meet with Carol. Again, should word leak out of an alien presence on the Moon, they were prepared to brand it a hoax. In the unlikely event that Carol would decline the Matusian's offer, and ever make mention that her husband was still alive, it could always be ascribed to a nervous breakdown. There seemed little danger that anyone would take such a story seriously.

The next afternoon the two authors attended a meeting in Miami with Hamilton's publisher. Signing contracts, and turning over the revolutionary new manuscript, they were promised swift publication. With all the flattering publicity, which had accrued as a result of the fusion reactor, it was bound to become a huge financial success. The thought foremost in their minds, however, was simply to convey essentials of the superior cosmology and philosophy of the Matusians. Once more, there was a feeling of guilt over what might well be construed to be an act of plagiarism. On the other hand, there was consolation in knowing that it was not their fault that sudden wealth was about to be thrust upon them. One just had to learn to live with infrequent occasions of serendipity.

Chapter 8
COVERT ACTIVITY

With no church affiliation, Mark and Susan were married a few days later in a small civil ceremony and with only minimal news media coverage. Surrounded by a wall of luxurious semi-tropical vegetation, Janet's home made an ideal setting for the wedding. She would miss the daily swim in her sparkling pool, along with frequent walks on a nearby beach. But having just leased it to the newlyweds, Janet knew it would be in good hands for what was expected to be almost half a lifetime. The very thought of shortly being reunited with her husband made her feel like a young bride-to-be.

The following morning, after a refreshing dip in the pool, Mark and Susan departed for the airport. It was their intention to combine a brief honeymoon with their mission to contact Carol. Unable to dodge every news reporter, who appeared to have nothing better to do, they were asked point blank by one television personality whether they planned to meet with Frost's widow while in Australia. With a short connecting flight already booked from Sydney to Carol's home town of Brisbane, there was nothing to be gained by giving a negative reply. Free to acknowledge that they had spoken to Carol by telephone a few days earlier, they merely said that they hoped to express condolences in person. There was, of course, no hint as yet of any connection between

Frost's wife and an alien presence on the Moon.

With money no longer a major consideration, the couple had elected to fly by supersonic jet nonstop from Miami to Honolulu. After a one-hour layover they would fly directly to Sydney, Australia. Boarding a small commuter jet, they were scheduled to arrive in Brisbane a scant twelve hours from the time that they had left Florida. In terms of technology, the world had clearly made amazing advances during the span of the past two centuries. They could not help wishing that Earth society had made the same progress with regard to many long-standing economic problems. Nor had there been any appreciable change in such realms as religion and philosophy, where archaic views still dictated the actions of mankind. It was the fervent hope of the newlyweds that their recent fortuitous contact with the Matusians would soon serve to remedy matters.

Catching a few hours of sleep at their hotel, they telephoned Carol and were promptly invited to have dinner with her at the Frost residence on the outskirts of the city. Accepting, they took a taxi to the address that they had been given. It was a beautiful villa, replete with colorful vegetation, and featuring a picturesque garden with a kidney-shaped swimming pool. As was the case with Janet, it would be a sacrifice of sorts to give it all up for what promised to be a lengthy confinement— in very restricted quarters— hidden below the barren lunar surface. It was, they now came to realize, somewhat less than a foregone conclusion that Carol would be willing to take her young son and commit themselves to thirty long years of seclusion.

As the two girls embraced in friendly reunion, Mark could sense that the past couple of months had acted to rob Carol of much of her youthful exuberance. Thomas, having recently celebrated his fourth birthday, also seemed to have aged and matured in this same interval. Needless to say, they would have to wait until he had gone to sleep before they dared to disclose the good news that Michael, her husband, was still alive and well—although destined to spend the next thirty years on another world a quarter of a million miles away.

Just when they had begun to suspect that Thomas was one of those children who are allowed to stay up until all hours of the night, Carol finally took him to his room and put him to bed. Spending some time reminiscing their days together in Florida, it at last seemed safe to conclude that Thomas had fallen asleep, and that the time was now ripe to reveal their great secret.

"Carol, we have some very exciting news to tell you about Michael; but you must promise not to tell a soul. If you do, then we shall be compelled to deny every word of the story that we are about to tell you," Susan told her.

"What do you mean?" asked Carol, somewhat bewildered. "Does it concern the manner in which Michael died?"

"Your husband is not dead; nor is Susan's brother, John. They are both alive and well and anxious for you to join them on the Moon," said Mark.

"I .... I don't understand," replied Carol, her confused mind tending to reel at the words she had just heard.

"I think that you had better hear the story from the beginning," voiced Susan. "You will then see why we are unable to risk disclosing the momentous discovery which has been made on the Moon."

During the span of the next hour her two guests proceeded to give an account of the bizarre series of events which had transpired during the past couple of months, eventually concluding with the plan to transport Thomas and herself to the Moon, if she so desired. By the expression on Carol's face they could tell that she could hardly wait to leave.

"Of course we will go," she said, through the tears of joy that ran down her cheeks. "It's the most wonderful news that I have ever received! Thomas will be so happy to go. He simply adores his father— even to the point of crying for hours when he was told that he could not go with him to *Lunar Base* when Michael left on his last mission."

"So you think Thomas won't mind leaving this beautiful home for a thirty-year stay inside an alien colony?" asked Susan.

"He would be willing to move anywhere to be with his father," Carol replied, continuing to wipe away the tears which marred her pretty face.

"Including the Moon?" reiterated Susan.

"Especially the Moon."

"It is vitally important to understand that, under absolutely no circumstance, must Thomas learn that his father is still alive until you are both about to board the Matusian spaceship," said Susan. "As you very likely know, a small child is not one to trust with a secret, and disclosure could easily jeopardize our entire mission."

"You may be assured that he will not be told about his father before the proper time," responded Carol, ecstatic over the thought of being united with her husband, whom she loved deeply.

Unfortunately, and quite unbeknown to the three adults now conversing in Michael's study, young Thomas had awakened and crept downstairs from his second floor bedroom. Intent on sneaking to the refrigerator for a chocolate bar, which was strictly forbidden, he was in the process of returning from his successful foraging expedition when he happened to hear his father's name mentioned through a door which had been left slightly ajar. Moving closer, he was able to learn that his mother intended to take him to the Moon to be with his father. On the verge of shouting for joy, he quickly changed his mind when he heard that he was not supposed to know anything about the trip. With a half-eaten candy bar in his hand, he suddenly had thoughts concerning his fate should he be caught. Afraid of discovery, he quietly slipped back to his room undetected and buried the bar's incriminating paper wrapper amongst other refuse in a convenient wastebasket. With the telltale evidence hidden, he soon went to sleep amidst dreams of cavorting about the Moon with his father.

Arising early the next morning, no less excited than his mother, he was understandably reluctant to make mention of what he had chanced to overhear the previous evening. His unauthorized visit to the refrigerator was bound to get him into deep trouble. Nevertheless, the immense secret which he possessed kept surfacing in his mind, and it was all he could do to suppress the urge to blurt it aloud to the world. Exhibiting remarkable restraint for one so young, he said nothing to the one person in whom he should have confided.

By misfortune, an opportunity arose later that same afternoon when a news reporter and his companion photographer called at the home to interview Carol. It seemed that they had found out about the visit of Mark and Susan and sensed that a story might be forthcoming. What they really wanted to know was just how close their friendship had been with Michael, and if they had conveyed details of his death that had not leaked out to the general public. Unwilling to give them a reason to suspect that there was anything to hide, she invited them in and very discretely answered their questions. While the photographer was busy talking to Carol, and having her pose for several pictures by the pool, the reporter managed to draw Thomas aside and began to speak to him.

"Hello, Thomas, my name is Henry Hogan," he said. "I'm a reporter from the *Brisbane Sentinel*. By any chance, do you know what your two visitors of last night had to say?"

A little shy, Thomas made no effort to speak, merely dangling his feet in the shallow end of the pool.

"Can you swim?" Hogan asked, hoping to get the child to talk.

"My father taught me last year," he finally replied.

“I suppose you miss your daddy very much. I'm so sorry about what happened," said Hogan, encouraged that he had at least gotten some response. He was quite unprepared for what followed.

Triggered by thoughts of his father, and unable to contain his secret any longer, Thomas abruptly blurted out: "My father is still alive, and I'm going to the Moon with my mother to live with him."

Startled, to the point of disbelief, Hogan decided to humor the boy. "Do you mean to say that you intend to go to *Lunar Base* as an astronaut when you grow up?" he asked.

"No! We're going to be picked up by a big spaceship and taken to a city on the Moon. Susan's brother is there, too," Thomas added.

Still trying to figure out where the child could have incurred such a wild notion, Hogan's interrogation was soon cut short by the approach of Carol and the photographer. Disappointed to have missed the Hamiltons, his companion wanted a picture of Frost's widow with Thomas to wrap up the session. It had turned out to be an interview which, on the surface, seemed quite unproductive in that it conveyed nothing new with regard to the tragic Frost/Baldwin lunar saga. This impression, however, was to be far from the truth.

Later that same evening, in a downtown Brisbane pub, Hogan ran into an old acquaintance by the name of Jason Stanley. Now the editor of a somewhat notorious tabloid magazine, the two proceeded to get into conversation over a couple of beers. Before long Hogan found himself mentioning the weird remarks of Carol's young son. At once fascinated, and forever on the lookout for a sensational story — no matter how bizarre — Stanley pressed his friend for more details.

"Do you intend to publish this story?" Stanley finally got around to asking.

"If I did I would probably find myself looking for another job," responded Hogan. "My editor would likely laugh at me before tossing me out of his office. Kids that age are prone to invent fantasies, especially when they lose someone to whom they are deeply attached."

"My magazine doesn't have such qualms."

"You mean that you want to publish it?"

"Why not? It could make a terrific story and would be a cinch to sell a lot of copies."

"Just don't mention my name if you do publish, even though it did happen the way I told you."

"I rather doubt if anybody could prove or disprove the words of a four-year-old," said Stanley.

"I can prove that Thomas did say what I have repeated to you," responded Hogan, pulling a small tape recorder from his pocket.

Listening to a playback of the conversation, Stanley's mind was made up. He would feature it in the next issue of his bi-monthly magazine, which was due to hit the newsstands in another six days.

Spending only four days in Brisbane, Mark and Susan flew back to Florida, confident that all was well and assured that Carol and Thomas would follow a few days later. Leasing the home to a trusted sister, Carol hoped to excuse her prolonged absence by telling friends and relatives that her urge to travel was simply due to a need to get away from a house that held too many memories of her beloved husband. Flying a zig zag course, so as to mask her final destination, Carol planned to make overnight stops in Tahiti, Hawaii, Los Angeles and Atlanta. They would meet with Mark and Susan at Vero Beach, Florida, several days prior to the scheduled rendezvous with the Matusian spaceship.

The very same day that Carol and Thomas left Australia, as fate would have it, Stanley's tabloid featured a most sensational headline: "Alien Spaceship to take Frost Family to Moon." The story then went on to give an account of Thomas' statement that both of the missing lunar geologists were alive and living in an alien underground city on the Moon. As to how Thomas acquired this seemingly wild notion, it was speculated that— if the story was to be believed— it must have been through an overheard conversation between his mother and the two visiting celebrities. Was it, the article pointed out, just a mere coincidence that Carol had spoken to Mark and Susan Hamilton the evening before? Although a tabloid with a somewhat sleazy reputation, the story was nevertheless remarkably accurate in describing events as they really happened.

....

Picked up almost immediately by certain headline-seeking tabloids, in several countries, it was only a few days until a similar version of Stanley's article appeared in one of America's most popular tabloid magazines. Thus it transpired that the wife of Martin Wiley (a high ranking CIA official) came to purchase a copy of the story at a local newsstand. Showing it to her husband later that evening, the fat was now in the fire. Reaching for the phone, he hastily summoned a number of key associates to an early morning meeting in his Pentagon office. Looked upon by most readers as yet another spurious attempt to attract the attention of a gullible public, to Wiley it was the vital missing link to a rather enigmatic tape that had reached his desk the previous day. In his mind, there was something very peculiar going on at *Lunar Base*, and he was determined to expose it at all cost.

It was almost 8.15 A.M. when presidential aide Robert Perkins entered Wiley's office. Seated to the left of Wiley was General Earl Turnbull, a U.S. Air Force officer currently serving NASA in an advisory capacity. On his right sat Colonel Edward Tyson, of the U.S. Marines, a long-time friend of the CIA official.

"Sorry to be late for the meeting," apologized Perkins, dropping his heavy 260 lb., 6'-2" frame into a vacant chair. "Now what's all this crazy talk about an alien presence on the Moon?"

"It would appear to be more than speculation. I think you will agree with me once you listen to this tape which has just come to my attention," said Wiley, as he began a playback of Bergman's original debriefing session.

"How did you come to acquire this tape?" asked Turnbull, more shocked than puzzled after hearing this distinctly different version of the second *Antares* expedition to the Teneriffe Mountains.

"It was brought to me by Adam Wentworth, the journalist. To hear him tell it he was looking for a news scoop and simply took advantage of an opportunity to copy a recording of Bergman's initial interview with the returning astronauts," Wiley answered.

"I don't believe this is the same information that was supplied to the press," declared Perkins.

"I know for a fact that it isn't," said Wiley. "I had Franklin Turcott, Chairman of the International Space Agency, fax me a copy of the report from their headquarters at Cape Canaveral."

"Are you sure that the voices on the tape are authentic?" Turnbull wanted to know. "It could be a subtle attempt to stir up trouble and jeopardize our plans to explore space. Unless I've been misinformed, that journalist is a Bible thumper with totally archaic views of the universe."

"I wondered the same thing, which was why I had our lab boys run a voice comparison test yesterday. They tell me that everything checks out affirmative," Wiley responded.

"Then what do you make of this subterfuge? Why would Bergman want to submit a revised second version?" asked Perkins.

"Probably because the answers that he was getting were not making much sense," opined Tyson, entering into the conversation.

"But why were they not making any sense?" voiced Wilely. "To me, that is the real question."

"And what thoughts do you have on the matter?" Perkins asked, not at all clear where the discussion was leading them.

"Until last night I was admittedly quite confused myself, before my wife handed me a magazine story which I would normally dismiss as an irresponsible fabrication," said Wiley, presenting each member of his audience with a copy of Stanley's article.

Some minutes later, after digesting the story, Turnbull got up and began pacing the floor. Finally, he stopped and asked Wiley point blank: "Do you really believe that the kid was telling the truth, and not imagining the whole thing?"

"Yes, I do. It explains everything, right down to the very last anomaly. Is it just a coincidence that the Hamiltons chose the city of Brisbane, of all places and at the other side of the globe, for a honeymoon of a few days— unless there was some ulterior purpose in mind?" responded Wiley.

"Is Frost's wife still in Australia? Furthermore, what about Baldwin's wife? If the one is supposedly going to the Moon, to be reunited with a lost husband, then it's logical to think that the other received the same invitation," deduced Perkins.

"I can have an operative in Brisbane on the job in a matter of hours," replied Wiley. "As for Janet Baldwin, I could put a tail on her by early afternoon."

"It might also be a good idea to include the Hamiltons, since they seem to be involved with whatever is going on," suggested Turnbull.

"Just be careful if you should decide to use phone taps or bugs on Hamilton and his wife. They have become world celebrities, in the eyes of many, and it would be unwise to risk censure with no solid evidence against them," advised Perkins.

"I'll get on it right away," said Wiley. "If there's a conspiracy to withhold information of an alien presence on the Moon I intend to find out."

"Keep me informed of developments. Meanwhile, I'll see to it that President Harker is apprised of the situation, which I want classified as top secret," announced Perkins, lifting his considerable bulk out of a chair that was far from comfortable.

Later that very same day Wiley received what he promptly interpreted as confirmation of his alien hypothesis. The CIA agent in Brisbane had called to inform him that Carol Frost and her young son had already left on what was alleged to be an extended vacation. Her immediate destination, he learned, was Tahiti. Instructing his man to follow them to the far corners of the world, if need be, he fully expected the paths of the two "widows" to cross somewhere in the very near future. Smiling to himself, he picked up the phone to call Perkins and Turnbull. He would also contact his friend Ed Tyson, and arrange for the two of them to fly to Cape Canaveral the following day, where they could be closer to the scene of the drama which he felt was about to unfold.

....

At about the time that Wiley and his associate were en route to Florida, Janet returned home from shopping at a nearby mall. In her hand she held a copy of a tabloid magazine with headlines boldly echoing Stanley's disturbing article. Showing it to Susan, as she lounged by the pool with two-year-old Jane, she sat down beside them and awaited her reaction.

"My God!" exclaimed Susan, as she finished reading the story.

"How could this have happened?" Janet wondered aloud, alarmed by the thought that the alien rendezvous might have to be scrubbed.

"Mark! Come and read this," shouted Susan to her husband, who was swimming laps in the pool.

"What is it?" he replied, climbing out of the water and reaching for a towel that was draped over a nearby chair.

"I can only surmise that young Thomas must have awakened and come downstairs, where he evidently overheard some part of our conversation with Carol," said Susan, handing Mark the article.

"Will this change everything?" asked Janet, after Mark had read the entire story and turned to face the girls.

"I think it might be advisable to contact Phil Bonham, on *Space Station Orion*, and code a message postponing the pickup for a while. If we wait long enough the story will die a natural death," answered Mark, upon giving the matter some thought. (He was, of course, quite unaware of the incriminating tape which had come into Wiley's hands.)

"When Carol phones us we'll just have to convince her that she should continue to play the role of a tourist traveling about the country, as if she had no intention of coming to Florida," said Susan. "As long as she keeps in periodic touch with us we can inform her as to a new rendezvous time."

"What if they decide to tap our phone?" asked Janet.

"Do you think Carol has seen the article yet?" Susan inquired of her husband.

"Probably negative on both counts," responded Mark. "It's rather unlikely that anyone would take such drastic action, with only a four-year-old's wild tale as incentive. As for Carol, I'm sure she will call the moment that she is aware of the story."

In this latter assessment Mark was to prove somewhat of a prophet, as Carol phoned later that afternoon from Los Angeles. Highly excited and apologetic, she had just spotted the bold headlines of Stanley's article as she passed a local newsstand. Purchasing a copy, she was appalled by the accuracy of the disclosure. Upon confronting Thomas, she finally coaxed a confession out of him. He had, as Mark and Susan already deduced, overheard a portion of their conversation with his mother. Understandably, she was concerned that the planned rendezvous might be canceled. Faced with the possibility of being watched— or even have their phone tapped in the near future— Mark decided to have Carol check into a specified Daytona Beach motel under an assumed name, which he proceeded to give her. He would contact her, at this location, if there was any change of plans. Otherwise, he would pick them up on the prescribed evening and drive them to the Ocala National Forest landing site. It was most vital, he emphasized, that they not be traced to the motel — or even to the state of Florida— if it could possibly be avoided. Wishing her well, Mark ended the conversation, trusting that Janet's phone call had not yet been monitored by any government agency.

Later that evening, endeavoring to contact Phil Bonham, on *Space Station Orion*, Mark was thankful that he had been so cautious in his talk with Carol. Quite unexpectedly, his friend had returned to Earth the previous day, in response to a serious illness in the family. In effect, any ability to cancel or change their planned rendezvous was thus negated.

Two days after Carol's phone call Mark had good reason to become more than a little apprehensive. Returning from giving a lecture at the University of West Palm Beach, he was conscious of a car that seemed to be following him ever since he left the university. When he took the Vero Beach exit from the freeway the vehicle also exited. Winding his way through several side streets, as a test of suspicion, he noted that the car continued to track him. Stopping briefly at a small shopping plaza, he hoped that this act might allay any fears of the driver that his shadowing attempt had been exposed, since his erratic course could be interpreted as merely a search for a specific store in an unfamiliar section of the city. Without a doubt, he was now firmly convinced that they were under surveillance.

The very next day Mark proposed a scheme to find out just how suspicious a certain faction had become, and to ascertain how far this party was prepared to go in order to obtain information. He had Janet phone a friend and arrange a social call that evening. Taking Mark and Susan with her, along with two-year-old Jane, they would leave the house vacant for a few hours after dark. The intention was to tempt his stalkers into committing an act which would betray them. Making sure that the windows were securely locked, Mark carefully wedged toothpicks between the door and door frame of all the home's outside doors. If opened, a rather minuscule piece of wood would drop unobserved to the ground in the dim light. Were they to return and find evidence of entry, it would be a clear indication that the residence had been searched and/or bugged— along with a warning that their phone was probably tapped.

Returning from the visit, it was noted that the front door had not been disturbed. However, it was soon apparent that their worst fears had been realized. Upon examining a rear door, Mark discovered a toothpick lying on the floor. A silent search of the home disclosed a tiny electronic bug planted underneath a sofa. Turning up the volume on a television set in the den, while Janet put her daughter to bed, Mark and Susan began a whispered conversation.

"I think we should leave the bug where it is, otherwise they might suspect that we're on to them," Mark whispered into Susan's ear.

"Where there's one there's bound to be more— probably, one in every room," Susan whispered back to her husband.

"I agree," came the low-voiced reply.

Further searching served only to confirm their assessment of the situation. Before long they discovered two more devices. One was located inside a room thermostat near a dining area; while the other was behind a dresser cabinet close to their bed.

"Is there no respect for privacy in one's own bedroom?" asked an indignant Susan, over the loud music coming from a radio which they had turned on.

"Shall we give them a big thrill tonight?" suggested Mark, in a subdued tone of voice.

"Do you want me to moan and groan, or should we merely rock up and down on the bed?" she whispered, giving her husband a sharp dig in the backside with an elbow.

"Your choice."

"How about both?"

"Why not? We're still newlyweds."

Awakening the next morning to the blaring of music from an

alarm clock/tape player, Mark leaned over and gave his nude and curvaceous wife a passionate kiss. "You really put on a performance last night," he whispered. "But don't you think you were overacting just a little— especially the part where you let out that series of incredibly loud ear-piercing screams."

"Who was acting?"

Responding to Susan's statement, Mark decided that another kiss was in order.

Unable to converse freely inside Janet's home, for fear of their conversation being overheard, Mark had suggested a picnic lunch at the local beach. Not willing to risk the possibility that Janet's vehicle might be bugged, they restricted talk during the short drive to the ocean. More than once, Mark felt certain that a car was following them. It was not the same color as the one that had been used to monitor Mark's journey from West Palm Beach, which seemed to indicate that whoever was behind it all was blessed with considerable resources— probably, the CIA, Mark thought to himself as Janet drove the car into a parking lot close to the surf.

Settling down on a couple of large beach blankets, the three adult sunbathers at last felt free to talk without whisper or loud music to conceal speech. It was highly disconcerting to be subjected to such covert observation, with only a four-year-old's strange story as a basis for motivation. Or, was there some other reason which had hitherto escaped them?

"It just doesn't make any sense. Why are they going to so much trouble on so little evidence?" asked Janet, quite bewildered by all the clandestine action of late.

"I wish I knew," confessed Mark. "There must surely be more to it than what meets the eye."

"You don't suppose that Bergman has betrayed our confidence, do you?" asked Susan.

"I rather doubt it. He strikes me as a man of his word— besides, he could have turned us in long before we left the Moon.

However, I do believe that there must have been a leak from some source at *Lunar Base* — but how, or by whom, I have no idea," confessed Mark, gazing up at the clear blue sky.

"In any event, we had better give serious thought as to how we propose to leave undetected for our forest rendezvous," said Janet, abruptly bringing Mark back to the planet Earth.

"There is also the tricky matter of arranging a plausible story to cover the disappearance of Janet and her young daughter, should there be inquiries down the road," Mark hastened to point out.

"We could pretend that she took Jane to visit relatives out of state. Her car could later be found abandoned in some isolated area, with their absence being attributed to misadventure. While it might drive the police nuts and send them on a wild goose chase, it would at least afford an explanation of sorts," suggested Susan.

"For what it's worth, in thirty years the record could at last be set straight when all is revealed," stated Mark.

"I'll agree to that, unless anybody can come up with a better scheme," said Janet, looking out over the sparkling blue waters of the Atlantic Ocean. She could not help recalling how often she had been to this very spot with her husband. Currently, the love of her life was a quarter of a million miles from this beautiful beach, but she would much prefer to be with him— even if it was beneath the airless surface of the Moon.

Deep in contemplation for some time, Mark eventually spoke: "I think I've worked out a plan which should work, if I can enlist the help of certain students of mine."

"Please elaborate," said Susan, echoing Janet's exact thought.

Sifting a quantity of golden sand between his fingers as he talked, Mark began to expound a scheme to elude their unwelcome stalkers. "What do you think of it?" he finally asked.

"Sounds good to me," answered Susan.

"You have my vote," agreed Janet.

"Then I guess I'll have to get busy and make a couple of phone calls .... from a pay phone, of course," he was quick to add.

....

The morning before the night of the scheduled alien rendezvous, Janet loaded several suitcases into the trunk of her car. Taking Jane with her, she drove off amidst a chorus of well-wishes. As expected, another vehicle promptly pulled out from a side street and began to follow at a discrete distance. Taking the northbound freeway, she exited near Cape Canaveral and headed west toward Orlando. Bypassing the city to the south, Janet soon entered the sprawling Walt Disney amusement complex and parked. Four hours later, after mingling with every crowd she could find and positive that they were no longer being shadowed, Janet and her daughter met with one of Mark's students at a prearranged location. Slipping the fellow a generous sum of money, she accompanied him out of the complex and into a van parked some distance away from her car, which was almost certainly being watched. By mid afternoon she was relieved to join Carol and Thomas at the prescribed Daytona Beach motel.

Shortly after Janet's departure Mark summoned a taxi. Taking Susan with him, and briefcase in hand, they were driven to a Vero Beach commuter rail station. Catching the first southbound Bullet Train, they got off at West Palm Beach and promptly took a cab to the university campus, noting that they were being followed by two men wearing suits that were a little too warm for the mild weather that prevailed. Watching them exit a second cab, from the concealment of a doorway, they moved swiftly along several winding corridors and then took an elevator up to the top level of an adjoining parking garage. Confident that they had shaken their quarry, Mark soon found the van that he had been looking for. Greeting his trusted student, he handed him an envelope of money and entered the vehicle with Susan. With the accomplice driving, and his two passengers safely hidden within, the van left the multi-level parking lot and headed northward. A few miles away from the university the driver stopped and bade Mark and Susan good-by. Undetected, Mark was now free to complete a leisurely trip to Daytona Beach. Pausing for lunch, they arrived minutes after Janet and Jane had been delivered by Mark's other student.

Spending an enjoyable afternoon on the beach, the girls went on a shopping spree to replace the wardrobe which Janet had left behind. The question soon arose of supplying growing children with clothing and shoes of increasingly larger sizes as they matured. It was almost more than Mark could do to convince both Carol and Janet that the Matusians had a technology which was surely capable of producing such items. Finally agreeing to travel with minimal baggage, they had a late dinner and returned to the motel for a few hours of sleep prior to their 3 A.M. rendezvous with the alien spaceship.

Loading all their luggage aboard the van, along with a briefcase full of computer disks containing much of the Matusian's requested data, they left the motel about an hour after midnight. Driving west on a main road, which traversed the heart of Ocala National Forest, it was not long until he turned north after passing Juniper Springs. Proceeding down a narrow and deserted stretch of road for several miles, Mark eventually came to an even more desolate intersecting gravel trail, which he followed for some distance. Reaching their destination, he pulled off the poor excuse for a road and parked beside an exceptionally large live oak tree that served as a handy reference point. Taking flashlights and the three prescribed blue identification lights, Mark and Susan entered the pine forest. After stumbling around in the dark for a time, it was with much relief that they came upon the small clearing.

"It sure would have been a great deal easier to find in daylight," remarked Susan, as the two prepared to lay out their signal lights.

"At least it's a clear evening, so the Matusians should have no trouble locating the site," said Mark, turning on the first beacon.

"So far, the gods seem to be favoring us. I just hope that they don't turn fickle," Susan commented, clicking on the second lamp.

"We have thirty minutes to spare," announced Mark, looking at his watch. "Why don't you stay here while I go back for the others?"

"I'll point my flashlight to guide you through the trees, as our landing lights are directed upward and are not easily perceived from the ground," responded Susan.

Taking his bearings from the stars overhead, Mark returned to the van. With his briefcase under an arm, and a large suitcase in each hand, he again entered the woods. Both Janet and Carol followed with flashlights in one hand and a child in the other. More than a little grateful for Susan's guiding light, it was not long before they all arrived without incident at the clearing.

"Now the waiting game commences," said Mark, placing the bags at the edge of the trees and looking up at the night sky.

Two sleepy children clung by their mother's side, not quite aware of what was about to transpire. They knew only that they would soon be united with their fathers in some far away place called the Moon. To Thomas, it was a dream come true, as he was prepared to move anywhere in the universe to be with him.

Gazing upward into the heavens, which seemed to be filled with a million stars, they noticed one that suddenly appeared much brighter than the others. It was also moving directly toward them, growing visibly larger and brighter with every passing second.

"Right on schedule," said Mark, once again consulting his watch.

Taking cover under the trees, they stood in fascination as the alien spacecraft, with surprisingly little noise, slowly settled in the middle of the clearing. Abruptly, a door slid open to reveal an illuminated interior. Seconds later a ramp was lowered to the ground.

Luggage in hand, Mark and Susan raced toward the ship, with the others close behind. Greeted by a figure enclosed in an isolation suit, the four passengers were quickly ushered aboard. Three minutes later the saucer-shaped craft rose vertically into the night sky with its cargo of four humans, most of the requested data, and a limited amount of personal luggage. In moments it was gone.

Gathering up the three blue lights, and quickly extinguishing a smoldering patch of grass scorched by engine exhaust, Mark and Susan returned to the van. In an hour they would be back at their Daytona Beach motel. Come morning, they would return the vehicle to Mark's friend at the university.

"It sure looks like we pulled it off unobserved," remarked Susan, as they turned onto the main highway with not one headlight to be seen in any direction.

"So it would seem," said Mark.

Chapter 9
CONFRONTATION

Watching an early morning television news broadcast, from the comfort of his Titusville hotel suite, Wiley immediately became suspicious upon learning of an overnight UFO sighting in the sky above the Ocala National Forest. Having already received word of Janet Baldwin's mysterious disappearance at the Walt Disney complex, along with failure of his operatives to shadow either the Hamiltons or the Frost "widow," he was certain that there had to be a connection. If he was not mistaken, both the Frost and Baldwin families were at this moment aboard an alien spacecraft en route to the Moon. Reaching for the phone, Wiley proceeded to make a number of calls. Should his hunch be correct, he might soon have all the evidence that he needed.

By mid morning a fleet of Air Force helicopters was diligently scouring the region of the UFO sighting. At just about the same time that Mark and Susan were returning the van, one of the search craft radioed to say that they had found something of interest. Within minutes Wiley and Tyson were on the scene and bending over to examine the telltale marks of three oval depressions on the ground, in the middle of which lay a circular patch of scorched earth.

"It was the burned patch which first drew our attention to the spot," said the helicopter pilot. "As requested, we tested the area for radioactivity, but the results were negative."

"There's no question in my mind but what the alien craft landed here last night," Wiley remarked to Tyson, who was busy video taping the evidence. "It must have been fairly large, judging from the size and depth of the impressions."

"I agree," said Tyson. "What's our next step?"

Wiley's response was to address the pilot. "Take us directly to NASA headquarters at the cape," he ordered.

By early afternoon Wiley had managed to convince his superiors that an alien spaceship was, at this instant, very likely approaching the Moon with the families of both Frost and Baldwin. Of the present whereabouts of the Hamiltons, he had just received word that they had only now returned to the Vero Beach home of Janet Baldwin. During the course of a conversation with Perkins, at the White House, he was given assurance that President Harker would immediately order *Lunar Base's* orbiting telescope to be trained on the suspected mesa at the southern edge of the Teneriffe Mountains.

"Do you think Bergman will interfere with your attempt to record the UFO landing?" asked Tyson, seated alone with Wiley in a borrowed NASA office.

"I'm sure that he will try to do so if he can," Wiley answered. "He's obviously committed himself to concealing an alien presence."

"Then how do you propose to stop him, if he should choose to intervene?"

"Perkins said that Harker plans to send a coded message to Ron Harland, a recent arrival and a CIA agent masquerading for us as a communications specialist, giving him orders to monitor the target area," replied Wiley.

"How could Harland do that? He's not an astronomer."

"He is to enlist the discrete services of James T. Bradley,

an American astronomer, who will presumably honor a direct request from President Harker."

"What if Bergman tells him to do otherwise?"

"In that event, Harland will restrain him by whatever means is necessary," Wiley answered.

"Is Harland armed?" asked Tyson, knowing full well that it would be in violation of an international agreement which expressly forbid weapons of any kind at *Lunar Base*.

"Affirmative."

"I just hope that he doesn't have to use it and end up creating a global incident," said Tyson.

"So do I," responded Wiley.

"How long do you think it will take for the alien ship to reach the Moon?"

"Good question. Offhand, I should say it will be substantially less than the two or three day capability of the *Moonbeam*, or its newly commissioned *Lunik* sister ship," Wiley answered.

"Any chance that it has already landed?"

"It's possible, of course, but not likely. They have no idea that we're on to them and would not wish to waste fuel needlessly."

As events turned out, by 3 P.M. Florida time— exactly twelve hours after the forest rendezvous— the returning spaceship was detected by the orbiting lunar telescope as it touched down at the Matusian base. It was yet another in a series of misfortunes for the alien's cause, as there was an even chance that the telescope would be at the far side of the Moon at the moment the ship landed. Bad luck seemed to be the order of the day.

With all the proof that he needed, upon receiving telemetry of the alien craft, Wiley decided to act. By 6 P.M. he had arranged for the FBI to pick up the Hamiltons and escort them to his office at the Cape Canaveral NASA complex. Joining Wiley and Tyson for the interrogation were General Turnbull and presidential aide Robert Perkins, who had just flown in from Washington.

Playing the Wentworth tape to the pair, along with video images of the forest landing site and the UFO arriving at the Teneriffe mesa, he eventually asked: "Would either of you two please oblige by offering us an explanation?"

Confronted with overwhelming evidence of their participation in an alien presence cover-up, both Mark and Susan felt they had little choice but to tell the truth. Somehow, there was small consolation in knowing that exposure of the Matusians could not be blamed on them.

"No wonder you guys got suspicious," said Hamilton, referring to the incriminating Bergman interview tape. "How, in heaven's name, did Wentworth ever manage to obtain a copy of this conversation?"

"I guess you might say that he was an opportunist who just happened to be in the right place at the right time," answered Wiley.

Giving a detailed account of their amazing lunar adventures, the accused astronauts made a strong plea for discretion in revealing the alien presence to a world characterized by a number of unscrupulous governments— many of which possessed nuclear missile capability.

"They are definitely no threat to Earth society. In fact, they have already demonstrated their desire to assist our planet by giving us the secret of a controlled fusion reactor," said Hamilton, freely acknowledging the Matusian's role in what was clearly a momentous scientific breakthrough.

"Then you admit that they gave you this technology as a gesture of good will?" asked Perkins.

"Yes, of course! It was the only way they could convey this precious gift without disclosing their presence. Upon the arrival of their starship, some thirty years from now, they promise to give Earth many more scientific treasures. Meanwhile, our world will be allowed to reap the benefits of a cheap, safe, and virtually unlimited energy source," replied Hamilton.

"They must have really taken a liking to you to have supplied such valuable information," remarked Perkins, wondering to himself if this trust could not be put to some use.

"I suppose you might say that it was a case where someone had to be selected. Like Wentworth, I just happened to be in the right place at the right time," Hamilton responded.

"As citizens of the United States of America, would the two of you be willing to come to Washington and tell your story to President Harker?" asked Perkins.

"As citizens of the universe we would be most anxious to speak to Harker, if only to receive his assurance of honoring the Matusian's wish to remain concealed and unknown to any hostile power on Earth," said Hamilton.

"I fully concur with Mark," agreed Susan. Having never voted for the man, she had always regarded Harker to be a poor choice for this important office.

"I believe an early appointment can be arranged," said Perkins, reaching for a telephone and placing a call to the capitol.

....

At exactly 10 A.M. the following morning Mark and Susan were escorted into the White House for a meeting with President Harker. Accompanying them were the four interrogators from the previous evening.

"I trust that you had a pleasant flight," said Harker, greeting the astronauts with what might be interpreted as a combination grin and smile. "Please be seated. It seems that you newlyweds led a lot of people on a merry chase for a while. If you should ever consider a career in the CIA, I have a feeling that our friend Wiley could use your services."

"I'm afraid that our interests are presently much less mundane," responded Hamilton. "Our immediate concern involves the safety of the Matusians, as there is fear that at least one hostile faction on

Earth will seek to destroy them once they have learned the purpose of their mission."

"And why would anyone wish them harm if, as you say, they are a highly advanced and benevolent race?" asked Harker, shifting his 60-year-old, 226 lbs., 6'-0" frame in a leather chair that sat behind a luxurious teakwood desk.

"Simply because their philosophical views are so much superior, to those held by Earth leaders, that there is bound to be resistance to change," answered Susan.

"This would seem to be a rather profound indictment of world religions and society in general," said Harker, lighting up a cigar and exhaling a great puff of smoke.

"There is a great deal more to the issue than merely antagonizing proponents of popular religious beliefs. I rather suspect that their desire to rectify a host of social and economic injustices will incense many political leaders," informed Hamilton, seeking desperately to avoid inhaling the obnoxious cloud of smoke which drifted silently toward him.

"We think it would be in the best interests of Earth society if the Matusian's presence were to remain a secret until the time is ripe for disclosure," opined Susan.

"Tell you what," began Harker, "I'm prepared to make a deal with you. If you agree to lead a small delegation to meet with the aliens, I'll personally guarantee not to reveal their presence to the world—at least for the present. We would like a chance to talk with them and hear what they have to say first-hand."

"I guess we don't have much choice," responded Hamilton, still trying to elude the fumes which had begun to annoy him.

"When might we expect to leave?" asked Susan.

"How about in a week or so?" suggested Turnbull. "We should be able to schedule the *Moonbeam* for a clandestine flight about then."

"Fine with us," said Susan, beginning to wish that Harker would either choke on his foul cigar or succumb to lung cancer—whichever might occur first.

"Agreed. I'll have Wiley, our professional bloodhound, keep in touch with you at your Vero Beach residence," Harker announced.

"Is it permissible to remove your electronic bugs— especially from the bedroom?" asked Susan.

"So you did notice them? I suppose we should have guessed as much when we heard nothing incriminating," remarked Wiley.

"Before you cloak-and-dagger characters talk any more shop, I shall be obliged if our lunar adventurers would be so kind as to describe the interior of the Matusian underground complex," said Harker. "I've always had a fascination for futuristic alien cities."

....

Some six days later, at Cape Canaveral, Harker's contingent of three boarded the waiting space shuttle *Polaris*. Disembarking shortly thereafter, at *Space Station Orion*, were U.S. Vice President Joseph Donovan, Senator Fred Nixon and General Earl Turnbull. Accompanied by Mark and Susan, the five were greeted by Peter Hawkins, commander of the orbiting satellite.

"To what do we owe the unexpected pleasure of your visit?" asked Hawkins, as he proceeded to honor his guests with a grand tour of Earth's international space station.

"I would appreciate it, Peter, if you would keep our mission confidential for the present," answered Vice President Donovan. "At the moment, I am only free to say that we are leaving tomorrow on the *Moonbeam* in order to follow up certain clues relating to the Frost/Baldwin affair."

As a former U.S. Air Force general, used to years of obedience to authority, Hawkins declined to press the issue further. "I hope you are successful in your venture, whatever it may be," he said, as he continued to escort them around the station.

Some four days after the delegation left Earth, the *Moonbeam* entered into lunar orbit. Piloted by Frank Wallace and copilot Ken

Johnston, the craft then went on to make a safe landing at the southern edge of the Teneriffe Mountains— on the same upper mesa which housed the underground Matusian colony.

....

Quite by chance, while doing a routine test of equipment and without any knowledge of the *Moonbeam's* flight, Paul Cooper picked up the craft on *Lunar Base's* radar screen. Puzzled, when there was no response to his repeated attempts at radio communication, he continued to track it as it began to orbit the Moon. He watched in amazement as it descended into the region of the Teneriffe Mountain— at just about the same location as Frost and Baldwin had set down some months ago. Wasting no time, he summoned Bergman and apprised him of the unidentified spacecraft.

Aware that the Matusian spaceship should have returned more than a week ago, from its scheduled Florida rendezvous, Bergman was at once apprehensive at this unexpected sighting. He decided to contact Frank Wallace, at *Space Station Orion*, with intention of confirming the status and whereabouts of the *Moonbeam*. Ostensibly, the ship was undergoing a minor overhaul at the station. Informed that Wallace had departed on the *Moonbeam* with five passengers, three days earlier, Bergman was really concerned. Upon learning the identities of the passengers, hopes of concealing the alien presence seemed to be completely dashed. With the newly operational *Lunik* due to dock at *Orion* in a matter of hours, on a return flight from the Moon, there was no other known Earth spacecraft that could have shown up on Cooper's radar screen. It had to be the *Moonbeam* — with the Hamiltons leading a strictly American delegation to the Matusian underground complex! Having already stuck out his neck, in support of alien concealment, it was now little short of obvious that his position as head of *Lunar Base* was in jeopardy.

"Should we get the astronomy department to scan this region

with the orbiting telescope?" asked Cooper, interpreting his superior's next move.

"Yes, by all means. Get Bradley and Bial working on it right away," answered Bergman, fully expecting to be axed in the near future.

Minutes later, after viewing a computer-enhanced image on a video screen, there could be no question but what they were looking at the *Moonbeam* perched atop a small mesa— exactly where the Matusian base was reported to be situated!

"Why would the *Moonbeam* choose to ignore our attempts to achieve radio contact?" asked Cooper, at a loss to understand developments. "Furthermore, what seems to be the big attraction at this particular location?"

Realizing the futility of trying to conceal evidence of the alien presence, Bergman decided to bring the entire matter out into the open. Calling all personnel to a meeting in the Operations Center of the base, he began to tell them about the discovery of the Matusian lunar outpost. With no reason to offer only a partial explanation of the many clandestine events which had recently transpired, he told an astonished audience everything he knew. Bergman concluded his speech by informing them about the *Moonbeam* having just landed at the alien base with what was clearly an American only delegation.

"Don't you think it is grossly unfair, if not highly unethical, to restrict such an important contact to representatives of one nation?" asked Petrov, the senior Russian member of the International Team at *Lunar Base*.

"Indeed I do!" exclaimed a somewhat disgruntled Bergman. "This is precisely why I am now in favor of letting the whole world know about the Matusians."

At this point James Bradley, the astronomer who had been induced to record the return of the alien spaceship to its lunar base, felt a need to speak. Rebelling against ingrained ties of vain nationalism, he likewise supported the public's right to be informed about the momentous encounter with another spacefaring race. Accordingly, he promptly confessed his role in President Harker's covert monitoring of the Matusian spacecraft.

As a consequence of Bradley's confession, Bergman began to suspect that Mark and Susan had been persuaded (or coerced) into leading the American delegation to the present encounter. Having as yet no knowledge of Wentworth's highly incriminating tape or of Stanley's article he was, of course, still in the dark as to why there had been the slightest suspicion.

Nevertheless, the very presence of the *Moonbeam*, with its list of VIP passengers, plainly bespoke of the necessity for a drastic change of plans. Casting aside all pretense of allegiance to any particular flag, Bergman showed both maturity and courage in renouncing what he considered to be a serious violation of the spirit of international cooperation. Within the span of the next ten hours he intended to draft and broadcast a speech to Earth, describing in detail all that he could about the alien encounter on the Moon. For better or for worse, knowledge of the Matusian presence would no longer be a secret possessed by a select few.

....

Meanwhile, following an uneventful landing of the *Moonbeam*, about a hundred meters distant from the boulder entrance to the alien lunar outpost, Professor Mark Hamilton had exited alone from the craft's air lock. Clad in a protective space suit, minus jet pack, he made his way directly to the concealed door. While still in the process of searching for the unobtrusive button, which would afford entry, a section of rock suddenly slid away to reveal another similarly suited figure standing in the illuminated interior.

"What are you doing here, Mark?" asked John Baldwin, over their suit radios, having recognized Hamilton's face through the clear plexiglass visor of his helmet.

"It's a long story, John. But at the moment I must speak to

Kobar on a matter of some urgency," replied Mark, recognizing Baldwin more by voice than by visual observation.

Cycling through the alien air lock, it was not long before Mark was deep in conversation with several of the Matusian leaders. Upon describing in some detail the unexpected and unfortunate series of events which had brought him back to the alien base, Hamilton went on to express the sincere regrets of his colleagues that their presence had been compromised. There was, he informed them, still hope that the small American delegation, now aboard the *Moonbeam*, could persuade President Harker to withhold news of their discovery.

Displaying no visible emotion, Kobar extended an invitation to the three VIPs to enter the Matusian underground city. They would be most willing to talk to them if, by so doing, they might be convinced of their peaceful intentions and desire to assist an Earth society that was badly in need of assistance and guidance.

"Please feel free to escort your delegation into the quarters that we have prepared for Earth guests," said Kobar, over the giant 3-D video screen which covered much of one wall. "You may be assured that we will do our best to make their stay a pleasant one."

Thanking the Matusians for their hospitality, Mark replaced his helmet and soon made his way back to the *Moonbeam*. En route, he could not help thinking how ironic it was that the present situation had arisen chiefly because of their sense of compassion. Had they never offered to unite two loving families, their presence on the Moon would likely have remained a secret for the next thirty years. Such, he reflected, was just one more consequence of living in an imperfect universe.

Less than forty minutes later, leaving both pilots behind in the *Moonbeam*, Mark and Susan exited the craft with their three VIP delegates in tow.

"This large circular depression where the Matusians launch and retrieve their two saucer-shaped spaceships," said Hamilton, pointing to the external covering of the base's giant elevator shaft.

"And this is the artificial boulder which contains the air lock entrance to the underground city," Susan informed the visitors, at least one of whom found it hard to believe that they were about to cast eyes upon alien technology— technology from another star system, in fact.

Activating the concealed door button, Hamilton guided the procession through the air lock and downward into the series of passageways that led to their assigned apartment complex. Entering, they were promptly greeted by Michael Frost and John Baldwin, the two missing astronauts who had once been presumed dead. Behind them stood their wives and children. Mark hastened to introduce the three guests.

"Welcome to the luxurious quarters which our kind hosts have so generously provided," said Janet, prior to introducing herself and two-year-old daughter, Jane.

"I'm Carol Frost, and this is Thomas, my four-year-old son," the taller woman responded.

"So you're Thomas, the young man who is destined to go down in history?" remarked Vice President Donovan, extending a gloved hand that was declined as the boy chose to cling to his mother.

"Please remove the rest of your space suits and make yourselves more comfortable," said Susan, in the process of doing so herself.

"May we bring you something to eat or drink?" asked Janet. "I'm afraid the food is a little different from what we are accustomed; but after you get used to it it's really quite good."

Before long a flashing blue light signified the Matusian's desire for a video conference. Responding to the request, Mark wasted no time in establishing a 3-D communications link. He derived a measure of amusement from observing the expressions on the faces of Harker's delegates when the sharp holographic images of Kobar and several others appeared as if by magic on the wall screen. It was just as if they were sitting right next to them.

"We hope that you had a pleasant journey from Earth. It had been our desire to remain hidden until the arrival of our great starship, some thirty of your years from now. But it seems that fate has prescribed otherwise," said Kobar, introducing himself, his wife Ryona, and the female historian/philosopher known as Luvana. Also present was another tall male by the name of Tygus, who was described as being the Matusian equivalent of a psychologist.

"I am Vice President Joseph Donovan of the United States, and this is U.S. Senator Fred Nixon and General Earl Turnbull of the U.S. Air Force," responded Donovan, pointing out his two associates.

"As you have already been told, we came from another star system, almost 30 light-years distant, many centuries ago. Our sole purpose is to assist emerging civilizations to safely traverse what is surely the most critical stage of humanoid evolution— namely, the dawn of the Atomic Age, with an inherent temptation for unethical exploitation of nuclear energy. Unfortunately, it is a sad fact that not every society is able to pass through this phase without developing weapons that threaten to destroy their world. It is our sworn duty and moral obligation to intercede and, wherever possible, to prevent this from happening," said Luvana.

"You are certainly engaged in a very noble and highly challenging profession," commented Donovan. "But just how do you propose to accomplish such a difficult task? If our planet is typical, you would be up against many governments with leaders unwilling to listen to reason. Our own United Nations organization has failed miserably in all attempts to achieve global disarmament."

"Indeed, we are presently confronted with what is tantamount to many virtual dictatorships, with leaders who would not hesitate to unleash their deadly arsenals of atomic and biological/chemical weaponry if provoked," confessed Senator Nixon.

"Your rather volatile situation has already been duly noted, which is why we have sent for our powerful starship. If ever there was a planet that required assistance, in order to avoid a holocaust, it is surely Earth," remarked Tygus, the Matusian psychologist.

"Exactly how do you propose to disarm and unite the many belligerent factions currently in office?" asked Turnbull.

"Our starship possesses the means with which to accomplish this task with minimal casualties and damage to property," Kobar was quick to answer. "For defense, it carries an impressive array of laser-type cannons and fusion bomb torpedoes of incredible power—quite sufficient to destroy any number of nuclear-tipped missiles that might be launched against it."

"Surely you would not use this great destructive force against an uncooperative government?" voiced Senator Nixon, beginning to wonder what manner of crisis Earth might be faced with in the foreseeable future.

"Of course not!" exclaimed Ryona, resenting even the slightest insinuation that any Matusian would deliberately inflict harm. "We consider ourselves to be a morally advanced race that positively abhors violence."

"As we understand the situation, the problem lies with a blind willingness of individuals to follow leaders, without respect for conscience," said Tygus.

"What our starship will likely do, should it become absolutely necessary, is to remove obnoxious and dangerous leaders by a far more humane means. Among its capabilities are batteries of powerful stun beam projectors and gas launchers, which can temporarily paralyze the population of entire cities, thus facilitating the prompt removal from office of those deemed to be a threat to world peace," explained Kobar.

"Well, I do suppose that is one unique and admittedly efficient way of getting rid of unwanted opposition," conceded Turnbull.

"But how would you go about uniting a divided world, with so many different religions and economic creeds?" asked Donovan.

"By the simple expedient of providing a superior philosophy of life," replied Tygus. "We have been studying the course of your global history for some centuries. Regrettably, it has been a case of one foolish conflict after another— with false religions and social injustices at the root of the problem."

"What might be the nature of this more advanced philosophical outlook?" the senator wanted to know.

Using as few words as possible, Luvana undertook to describe Matusian philosophy. Dwelling at some length upon the twin issues of evolution and reincarnation, she then proceeded to weave them into a coherent picture embracing a physical cosmos comprised of entities ranging from infinitesimal quanta to giant galaxies of stars with supermassive black hole cores. It was an indifferent revelation to Turnbull and Nixon; while to Donovan, a staunch Roman Catholic, it posed a most heretical and unacceptable contradiction to his ingrained beliefs.

"Do you have no room in your philosophy for Jesus Christ?" asked Donovan, visibly shaken by the Matusian lecture on a topic to which he had a decidedly closed mind.

"I'm afraid this is a rather naive viewpoint which is not shared by any other civilization with whom we have come into contact," said Kobar. "In fact, when you stop to ponder the vast number of other star systems and civilizations in our wondrous universe, the very notion of a deity visiting the planet Earth—while ignoring all others— must be considered somewhat childish."

At a loss for an answer, Donovan could only hope for a change of subject, as it was not every day that one's philosophy would be so negated by plain logic and scientific evidence. "What about social and economic injustices? What changes do you propose?" he asked, by way of diversion.

"Like yourselves, we also evolved the concept of democracy, after having had our fill of bad kings and despots," began Luvana. "In contrast to the outcome on your world, however, we soon realized that this principle had little chance of working unless it was accompanied by reasonable equality of wealth. As long as it costs enormous sums of money in order to be elected, and the wealthy control both the means and ability to utilize the very persuasive news media, the public is unlikely to be blessed with good government. In effect, the residents of most nations on Earth are deluded into thinking that they live in a democratic society— when it would be far more truthful to describe it in terms of *rule by the wealthy*!"

"Yet another difference between our respective worlds, with regard to the democratic principle, is to be found in one's right to vote. While you base this privilege upon the sole criterion of age, we found it desirable to initiate a program of rather stiff tests, so designed as to weed out the incompetent and those lacking in moral principles. We could see no merit in allowing the vote of the village idiot to carry as much weight as that of one of high intellect and capability," said Ryona.

"And this improved the caliber of elected officials?" questioned Senator Nixon, having never considered such a restriction himself.

"Indeed it did. Nevertheless, the issue of a more equitable distribution of wealth is of prime importance— without which the democratic process becomes more of an illusion than a reality," stated Tygus.

It was Luvana who chose to comment on the two opposing economic systems presently characterizing Earth society:

"We found that the best results were obtained from a mixture of what you would define as capitalism and communism. While the profit motive may give incentive to a business owner, and pride of ownership should be encouraged, problems arise when too much power and wealth end up in the possession of too few individuals. Quite simply, there is just so much wealth to be distributed, and when one receives a greater than average share another must go without. In essence, millionaires are only produced at the expense of pushing others into poverty.

"Of all the major businesses which should be placed under public control, finance is by far the most important. With no reason to charge interest for the use of money, a government would be free to loan funds to its citizens for merely administrative costs—thereby greatly reducing the expense of housing and other worthwhile projects. As long as the loan is repaid, and the amount of money in circulation is made to coincide— through appropriate taxation—with available consumer's goods, there will be no inflation and economic stability is assured.

"In addressing the question of unemployment, a constant threat among capitalist nations, the problem is easily resolved by merely lowering the age of retirement in order to produce the required jobs. Conversely, should there be a shortage of labor, then the obvious solution would be to raise the age at which one receives a pension.

"As to the vital issue of a redistribution of wealth, it is clear that some arbitrary figure must be derived which would act to reward initiative without becoming excessive. At Earth's present level of development, it is perhaps prudent to limit individual wealth to no more than ten times the average yearly income. Thereafter, one's personal income should probably be restricted to an amount not to exceed about four times that of a typical worker. Upon the basis of such guidelines, it should be possible to achieve a much more harmonious balance between one's intrinsic worth to society and one's financial reward."

At this juncture of the interview it was Kobar who undertook to dwell upon certain fundamental human rights:

"Of all the crimes perpetrated against humanity by a government, a most despicable practice is one of drafting its citizens into military service and forcing them to obey the commands of another. This is nothing less than outright slavery of body and soul, and a violation of the sacred right of an individual to follow conscience! Without a doubt, it constitutes a criminal act which must be outlawed upon a global basis, and any government guilty of such conduct should be removed by whatever means is necessary. Were nations unable to force men into armies, it would be very difficult to wage much of a war. It would, in fact, be tantamount to compelling aggressive leaders to fight their own battles alone and unsupported.

"Contrary to popular opinion, it is an injustice against a child to withhold information and attempt indoctrination of any specific religious dogma. An inherent right of every child is to receive an education free from prejudice, so that it is enabled to construct a philosophy of life that could truly be considered one's own. Children are natural born imitators and trusting of parental guidance, and it is unethical for parents— who may have little sense of reality— to thrust their biased views upon them as though there was no possible alternative.

"A further blatant disregard for human rights concerns such issues as birth control and genetic defects. Although still opposed by a number of short-sighted religious factions, the practice of birth control is most essential to the rights of the unborn. To bring an unwanted infant into the world, by parents who are unwilling or unable to care for it, is a crime against the child. (Ironically, an act of abortion is by no means an automatic injustice against the unborn, since the soul of one so terminated does not perish but must be reborn into another fetus of the same evolutionary status.) Also linked to the principle of birth control is the propagation of genetic defects. Due to the advance of medical science, many individuals are living longer and passing defects on to their offspring— parents who would have otherwise died before the age of puberty. With the current rate of degradation of Earth's genetic pool, it will not be very many generations until most infants are born with a serious inherited defect. The time has clearly come for the world to initiate a system of genetic testing and birth licensing."

"When your powerful starship arrives, will there be an attempt to impose these views upon us?" asked Vice President Donovan, his mind still reeling with thoughts of religious conflict.

"The aforementioned recommendations have already been prepared and will be relayed to our ship during the next scheduled transmission, some two weeks from now. We have every reason to believe that they will be followed to the letter," replied Ryona.

"Needless to say, initial priority is the establishment of a World Government, which will act to outlaw all nuclear weaponry and the use of chemical/biological agents. Subsequent priorities will involve the abolition of armies, and the formation of an International Police Force capable of ensuring global peace," said Kobar.

"We shall also press for a common language," announced Ryona. "For a planet so advanced in technology, it is no credit to Earth society to find its citizens still babbling in multiple tongues."

"Regrettably, there are many on Earth whose philosophical outlook has continued to remain in the Dark Ages," remarked Hamilton.

Chapter 10
NEFARIOUS REACTION

Following an extensive tour of the Matusian's tiny city, President Harker's delegation retired to guest quarters for a meal of alien cuisine and a much needed rest. It had been a long and eventful day, which had left the VIPs startled— if not outright shocked— by the revolutionary changes planned for Earth society. Visibly impressed by the advanced technology of this space-voyaging race, they were most in awe of the two saucer-shaped spaceships which were currently berthed in the underground hangar. Privileged to have been allowed aboard one of the craft, they had been fascinated by the interior of the ship and of its amazing capabilities. Although unable to cruise between the stars, it did constitute an excellent vehicle with which to explore the Solar System. Time and food, they were told, were its limitations when it came to overcoming the vast distances involved in interstellar travel.

"What do you think this stuff is made from?" asked Senator Nixon, chewing vigorously on something which resembled cubes of hardened yellow squash. "As you say, it really isn't so bad once you get used to it."

"All of their food is a mixture of certain native lichen and a variety of synthetic organic compounds. It contains every amino acid protein and nutrient needed to sustain the human body," explained Professor Hamilton.

"Can they eat our food?" inquired Turnbull.

"We gave them some of our food packs to analyze," said Susan. "With four exceptions, they informed us that they could indeed digest everything that they tested— once they had treated it to remove all traces of harmful bacteria and virus entities."

"And what were the exceptions?" Donovan wanted to know.

"Evidently, they just can't stomach anything containing garlic, onions, mustard or vinegar, which we use as condiments," replied Frost. "They say that these substances react to their system as a form of poison."

"I'm not really surprised," said Hamilton. "I've always had an aversion to that kind of junk myself. We seem to have a great deal more in common than just science and philosophy."

After finishing their meal, which more than one VIP visitor viewed as a culinary adventure, it was unanimously decided to call it a day and get some needed sleep. Perhaps, more refreshed, the Matusian's ambitious plans might appear more palatable and less disruptive of the status quo. What was not anticipated was the impact of Bergman's broadcast to Earth, which occurred while they slept. It was to have implications far beyond what might have been foreseen.

Not content with a simple account of how Frost and Baldwin had stumbled upon the alien colony, and of the subsequent escapades which had ensued in an attempt to conceal their presence, the commander of *Lunar Base* had elaborated at some length upon the Matusian's desire to rectify a host of global injustices. In particular, he stressed their avowed intention to redistribute wealth in a more equitable manner. He also told of the powerful starship which was en route to Earth—with the capability to enforce these changes should the need arise.

The very next morning, within one hour of opening, the New York stock market abruptly crashed with record losses. Before authorities managed to intercede and stop all trading, most commodities had plunged to less than one-half of their previous value! It was truly a financial disaster for those who lived and controlled huge corporate empires by the power of stock certificates.

Nor was panic restricted to the economic scene. Leaders of the world's most popular religious movements were in a state of absolute shock. News of the alien outpost was posing questions which could not be answered upon the basis of naive church dogma. Adding to their problems was the release of Mark and Susan Hamilton's new book, which expounded much of the Matusian's advanced scientific and philosophical views. Unless something could be done to negate this great wave of information, it was fast becoming apparent that such leaders might not have any flocks to lead in the very near future!

Reacting to Bergman's surprise disclosure, the Matusians soon began to weigh their limited options. Now that there was no point in trying to conceal either presence or motive, they decided to tell their side of the story to the entire world. Accordingly, they informed President Harker's delegation that they proposed to beam a televised broadcast — in all major languages— to Earth some twelve days hence. On this momentous occasion they would outline their ideas for economic and social reform, trusting in the cooperation and support of mankind for changes which would surely benefit all of humanity.

By way of facilitating acceptance of their many reforms, the Matusians planned to announce several more priceless gifts which they were prepared to offer the world. In addition to their previously welcomed contributions of controlled fusion and scientific/philosophical insight, they would supply a cure for cancer and the means with which to virtually triple the human life span. On the whole, it promised to be an opportunity beyond expectation— especially when one considered that the abolition of poverty, the spectacle of war, and the demise of false philosophies would be the only price asked.

Horrified at the swift turn of events, Harker's delegation cut short their visit and returned to Earth via *Space Station Orion*. At the request of the Matusians, the Hamiltons elected to stay at the alien outpost, where they were expected to play a key role in the forthcoming global TV spectacular. Along with their other guests, the inclusion of Mark— with his recent surge to fame— would surely make it easier for the world to accept the advice of alien beings from another planet. The fact that they were of a higher evolutionary level would not make it a simple task, as living with a bruised ego was never really one of mankind's greatest virtues.

....

Exactly six days after President Harker's delegation had first arrived on the Moon, a secret meeting was convened in the White House. Seated around a large oval table were a total of sixteen of the world's richest and most influential men. In addition to a number extremely wealthy billionaire industrialists, financiers, communications tycoons and oil barons, there were top representatives of the Christian and Islamic faiths. (Although the pope himself could not attend, due to ill health, Cardinal Manzella was given full authority to act in his place.) There was one purpose on the minds of this hastily assembled group, and that was to find some way to neutralize the serious threat now posed by the Matusian presence on the Moon. Unless promptly and effectively checked, it promised to overthrow the very economic and religious structure of the entire planet!

"You say that their powerful starship is not due to arrive for some thirty years?" questioned Ahmed Kassem, owner of an inordinate percentage of Middle East oil wells.

"That's what they tell us," responded Vice President Donovan. "At our age, we shall not live long enough to greet them."

"Or be around to face the wrath of an irate commander of a

huge and powerful space battleship, if we should act to wipe out their lunar colony," General Turnbull felt inclined to mention.

"Then the real issue becomes one of deciding whether to take matters into our own hands, for the sake of buying a lifetime of status quo, or to submit now and incur premature loss of all that we cherish," opined President Harker.

"In a word, yes," said Senator Nixon, himself a multimillionaire who had much to lose if the masses were to follow the Matusian's advice and redistribute wealth.

"Exactly how would you propose to negate this infidel alien influence which threatens us?" inquired Muhammed Bakr, an Islamic fundamentalist leader who was not noted for his tolerance of other viewpoints.

"We are led to believe that their base has little or no defense capability," answered Turnbull. "Even a small atomic bomb should be able to do the job, as long as it is placed strategically."

"Is there no other way? Could the base not be captured without destroying it?" asked industrialist J.P. Moriarty, thinking of the advanced technology which he would have liked to exploit.

"Negative! I'm afraid it's a case of all or nothing," Turnbull informed the American billionaire.

"In the name of our Lord Jesus Christ, and for the sake of having to defend the faith, I am prepared to absolve those partaking in such a venture," remarked Cardinal Manzella.

"Unfortunately, the problem does not lie solely with the alien outpost. We would still have to consider the staff at *Lunar Base*, as there is every reason to suspect that they will support the Matusian's cause," said Senator Nixon.

"Bergman has certainly sided with them," stated Donovan.

"In other words, we cannot destroy the aliens without being forced to eliminate the many incriminating witnesses at our own base," advised Turnbull.

"The general is quite right," agreed Harker. "It must be made to look as though the Matusians attacked first and we were compelled to retaliate. Needless to say, the plot would fail should there be any survivors left to dispute our story."

"It is better that a few should perish for the sake of many," said Bakr. "If you require volunteers for a suicide mission, I do believe that I can be of assistance."

In view of the religious leader's suspected connection with more than a few terrorist bomb attacks, several members of Harker's group suppressed an urge to make a sarcastic reply. Instead, it was Robert B. Hurst, owner of a vast newspaper and television empire, who chose to comment: "We may well be in need of your services," he said.

"Why not simply launch a salvo of nuclear missiles toward the alien base— preferably, from a submarine?" asked Jason A. Goldberg, a leading financier.

"It must be made to appear as though the Matusians initiated any hostilities. Unless we knock out our own *Lunar Base* we would have no excuse to attack them," explained Harker.

"Then you would propose a missile strike against both bases?" remarked Moriarty, looking toward Turnbull for confirmation of his deduction.

"Quite impossible," responded the general. "Such a launch would be detected by other nations and it would become obvious that Earth had instigated the attack— with the U.S. being the most logical suspect."

"Just how would you go about it?" asked Ahmed Kassem, the world's foremost oil baron.

"A far more subtle plan is to deposit a small atomic bomb close to the alien underground base. Detonated by a timing device, it should easily destroy the Matusian outpost. A second bomb, exploded a short time later at *Lunar Base*, could eliminate all embarrassing witnesses," suggested Turnbull.

"Wouldn't it be evident that we started the war if we destroyed the alien complex first?" Hurst was quick to point out.

"Not if we made our initial landing at *Lunar Base* and seized possession of communications. We could always claim that the aliens had attacked and captured the station before our military expedition arrived. Our force then retaliated and blew up the Matusian base in order to prevent them from sending reinforcements. During the course of a fight to recapture our own installation the aliens destroyed it and escaped in one of their saucer spaceships," explained Turnbull.

"I see what you mean," began Goldberg. "We must first start any covert strike by going after our base's communications center, lest news of an attack be radioed to Earth."

"But how could we launch an expedition to the Moon without the rest of the world becoming suspicious? And what about *Space Station Orion*? Wouldn't somebody be bound to blow the whistle on us?" asked Senator Nixon.

"It is not inconceivable that *Orion* might have to be sacrificed," Turnbull conceded, rather reluctantly.

"My God! Where does it all end?" Cardinal Manzella wanted to know, fast becoming worried by the way the plot was beginning to escalate.

"I do believe that our best plan would be to sabotage *Orion's* communications and hijack either the *Moonbeam* or the *Lunik* with a small band of armed mercenaries. There are presently so many terrorist groups now active in the world that it would be difficult to place blame— especially if a dozen factions later claimed it to be their work," said Turnbull.

"How might we explain the presence of these mercenaries on *Orion*? Wouldn't they have had to arrive on one of our shuttle craft from Cape Canaveral?" asked Harker, starting to have second thoughts as to the feasibility of what was rapidly developing into a scheme rife with complications.

"Moreover, who could we possibly get to pilot the spacecraft, assuming that everything else goes according to plan?" inquired Donovan.

"There are still several details to be worked out," admitted General Turnbull, fidgeting in his seat. "We will probably be compelled to resort to threat at gunpoint. Yet another alternative is to kidnap loved ones as an inducement to follow our orders."

Flinching visibly, Earth's two religious delegates nevertheless remained silent. To their closed minds, it was vital that the faith be preserved— no matter what nefarious criminal acts it might entail. Before the meeting was over the course of Earth history would be decided by a handful of men— men who had chosen to place wealth and misguided reverence ahead of such virtues as unselfishness and common sense.

....

A scant four days before the Matusian's scheduled broadcast to the world, the *Polaris* shuttle lifted off from Cape Canaveral. Secretly smuggled aboard and concealed in its spacious cargo bay were two small low-yield atomic bombs equipped with timing devices. Also aboard were six armed fanatics, led by Colonel Tyson, who were masquerading as technicians and scientists. Docking at *Space Station Orion*, it was not long before two of the impostors had succeeded in neutralizing all radio and TV communication, to the extent that repairs would require numerous replacement parts from Earth. It was deemed most improbable that operation could be restored in less than a week.

Lacking weapons of any kind, there was nothing that the personnel on *Orion* could do to prevent a transfer of the two atomic bombs from the shuttle into the *Moonbeam*, which was currently docked at the opposite end of the station's hub. Already fueled and ready for departure, it was a simple matter for the six invaders to compel astronaut Frank Wallace— at gunpoint— to pilot the ship. Unaware of the deadly cargo, or of the hijacker's intentions, he permitted himself to be taken aboard the lunar shuttle. Told that his wife and young son, back home in Atlanta, would come to great harm if he did not cooperate, the *Moonbeam* left Earth orbit en route to the Moon with the shanghaied pilot very reluctantly at the controls.

Removing certain vital electronic components, so as to prevent Wallace from conveying news of the hijack, his captors gave no hint that they were planning to destroy *Lunar Base*— with all of its inhabitants! Had they done so, he would have deliberately fired the craft's engines and sent the *Moonbeam* on a one-way trip to outer space. As it was, he skillfully guided the ship to a safe landing at *Lunar Base* some three days later, completely oblivious to the chain of momentous events that would shortly transpire.

Entering the station, the invasion force promptly brandished their weapons and ushered the surprised populace into one easily guarded wing of the underground complex. As a precaution, and being unsure of his reaction to their cause, they relieved the equally astonished CIA agent of his automatic pistol. In short order, Ron Harland found himself herded in with the rest of the prisoners. Seizing control of the base's communications, they undertook to distribute their two nuclear devices. Loading one aboard the *Antares*, they planted the second bomb inside a small storage compartment, welding the door shut and hiding the torch among canisters of rocket fuel in the hangar bay. It was capable of being armed from afar by a remote control device which resided inside a jacket pocket of Colonel Tyson. They were now free to tackle their main objective.

Again compelling Wallace to act as pilot, Tyson and two of his associates in crime entered the *Antares*. With him were Louis Flynn and Mario Piazza, trusted recruits of General Turnbull. Both were mercenaries proficient in acts of violence, as well as being religious extremists who were prepared to risk all to preserve their distorted views. While exceedingly poor in philosophical and moral outlook, their recently opened Swiss bank accounts each held the sum of three million dollars— payable to their wives and children should they fail to return. Remaining at *Lunar Base* to guard the prisoners were three Islamic fanatics: Abdul Mezar, Akim Hussem and Hammid Kabul. Supplied by their revered leader, Muhammad Bakr, they had been quite willing to offer their services for little more than the glory of having their names go down in history as martyrs defending the faith.

With Tyson acting as copilot, by reason of a crash course that had been arranged in a NASA flight simulator, Wallace taxied the craft out of the hangar. Three hours after arriving at *Lunar Base* the schemers lifted off in the *Antares*. Their destination was the base of the 30-meter cliff containing the Matusian underground complex. Minutes later, on tongues of orange flame, the small craft settled gently onto the lunar surface at the prescribed site.

"Why can't you tell me what this is all about?" asked Wallace, for yet another time, as he shut down the engines.

"You don't want to know!" barked Tyson, getting out of his seat and preparing to put on his helmet.

"Why don't I want to know?" insisted Wallace, still unaware of the bomb which had been hidden from his view.

"Just sit over here and be quiet," ordered Piazza, motioning to an empty seat beside him.

Accessing the ship's storage compartment, Flynn and Tyson began to move the nuclear device toward the air lock, allowing Wallace to catch a glimpse of the cylindrical object.

"Good heavens! You actually plan to blow up the alien base!" he exclaimed, finally realizing what they were attempting to do.

"Their destiny is out of your hands," said Piazza, pointing his gun directly at Wallace's chest.

Watching in sheer frustration as the deadly bomb was being slowly maneuvered into the air lock, Wallace eventually saw his chance as the guard's attention was momentarily diverted by a sharp clang, when a corner of the cylinder clipped the door.

Leaping for the gun, he managed to knock it from Piazza's hand and it clattered across the floor of the cabin. Unable to reach it, as his somewhat huskier opponent had a good grip on him, he lunged toward the control panel, pulling the man with him. His intention was to hit the button that would fire the craft's main engines. If it became necessary, he was prepared to crash the *Antares* rather than let them carry out their diabolical plot. Unfortunately, his fingers fell inches short of the mark and the two tumbled to the floor together.

"Grab the gun!" shouted Tyson through his helmet radio link to Flynn, as he rushed to assist Piazza.

While the three wrestled on the floor, Flynn retrieved the weapon. Stepping closer, he fired point blank at the helpless astronaut. The bullet struck Wallace in the back of his head, killing him instantly where he lay with his hands about Piazza's throat.

"You didn't have to do that!" shouted Tyson. "Now we have no experienced pilot to get us home."

"He couldn't be trusted any more. In fact, he was trying to blast off and would probably have destroyed the *Antares* rather than let us fulfill our mission," argued Flynn.

"I suppose you're right. He did seem determined to commit suicide by his excited reaction to the bomb," Tyson conceded, upon giving the matter some thought.

"Do you think you can fly this thing by yourself?" Flynn asked the newly promoted copilot to pilot, assisting Piazza to his feet.

"There doesn't appear to be much choice. The return trip to *Lunar Base* should be quite interesting," responded Tyson, not at all pleased by the unexpected turn of events.

"I guess we had better get on with the task at hand," said Flynn, motioning to the sinister looking silver canister residing in the air lock of the *Antares*.

Exiting the craft, the two conspirators proceeded to dump Wallace's lifeless body on the ground and commenced dragging the bomb across the lunar surface to the bottom of the 30-meter cliff face. Opening a covering panel with a special socket wrench, they peered inside at the timing mechanism.

"What should we set it for?" asked Flynn. "Do you think ten minutes will give us enough time to get away?"

"Sounds just about right," replied Tyson. "If we make it much longer they might be able to whisk the bomb away in one of their spaceships before it goes off."

"Too little time isn't all that great either," remarked Flynn. "Are you sure the rocket engines will start without delay?"

"If they don't we'll be in big trouble," Tyson responded, as he punched a series of buttons to activate the nuclear device.

"What's the cancellation code?"

"Six .... six .... six," announced Tyson, entering the numbers which would have to be inserted in order to cancel the timer.

"Can I bolt the cover on now?"

"Be my guest."

"There, that should do it," said Flynn, tightening the last bolt and pocketing the wrench.

"Then let's get the hell out of here!" voiced Tyson, making a run for the *Antares* which stood some thirty meters away.

Reaching the craft, they quickly cycled through the air lock and prepared to lift off. In moments the ship rose vertically atop a stream of flaming exhaust gases and climbed high above the alien mesa, eventually arcing over to a southwest trajectory which was intended to return it to *Lunar Base*.

"Will we get to see the explosion?" asked Piazza, gazing out a side window of the *Antares* in the direction of the Matusian plateau.

"Affirmative," replied Tyson, his eyes transfixed on several dials in front of him. "But whatever you do, don't look directly at it; the bright light could blind you for life."

"What about other harder forms of radiation?" Flynn asked, as he suddenly wondered if their superiors had told them everything they should know about atomic blasts.

"There's no air, so we don't have to worry about any shock wave," Tyson announced to his associates.

"You didn't answer my question," Flynn persisted.

"You don't want to know," responded Tyson.

"The last time you uttered that phrase it didn't bode so well for the one you were addressing," Flynn recalled.

"Guilty, as charged. Anyhow, we'll be too far away to have any worries about radioactive fallout," Tyson replied.

"I repeat. You still haven't answered my question relating to radiation. This craft has very little in the way of protective shielding," complained Flynn.

"I suppose it's possible that we may incur a modest degree of radiation exposure," Tyson finally acknowledged.

"How modest?" inquired Piazza, expressing more than a casual interest in the conversation between his two associates.

"If you're worried you could have a doctor at *Lunar Base* check you out when we arrive," said Tyson, as the craft neared the apex of its trajectory.

"I wouldn't count on them to give an honest evaluation— not after the way we treated them," responded Flynn.

"Don't all physicians have to take some sort of oath?" asked Piazza, moving as far away from the window as he could.

"They may choose to forget, in our case," said Flynn.

"Not much longer to wait before the alien base is terminated," announced Tyson, glancing at his watch.

Commencing a countdown, as the last seconds drew near, it was not long before a brilliant flash flooded the cabin with the light of multiple suns.

"Holy Christ!" exclaimed Piazza, as he at last gained sufficient courage to look out the window after the burst of radiation had subsided. "There's a huge mushroom cloud of dust that's rising quite rapidly."

"I sure wouldn't want to be near one of those things when it exploded," declared Flynn. "And just think, this is the smallest one that we have in our arsenal!"

It was a statement which caused his fellow crew members to pause for reflection. Could the Matusians really have succeeded in their plan to abolish atomic weaponry on Earth? Was it possible that, in defending the status quo, they had made a terrible mistake when they annihilated the alien outpost? Whatever their thoughts, it was clearly too late to change the course of history by wishing that they had aborted the mission. What was done was done, and they would have to live with the consequences for the rest of their lives.

Descending, in the general vicinity of *Lunar Base*, it was by no means certain that longevity was guaranteed. Landing, it soon became apparent, was not nearly as easy as taking off. Wasting a great deal of fuel in trying to maneuver the craft closer to the base, Tyson commenced his final approach. Successfully dodging several small craters, he was not quite so lucky when it came to avoiding other hazards. With a jarring thud, one of the *Antares*' landing legs buckled when it struck a protruding boulder, causing the ship to list at an obscene angle.

"Well, at least we're still alive," commented Piazza, releasing his seat belt and promptly colliding with a wall that now more closely resembled a floor.

"How far do you suppose we are from the base?" asked Flynn, being a little more cautious in sliding out of his seat.

"Probably only a kilometer or two," answered Tyson. "Another good question might be to ask in which direction."

"You mean you don't know?" Piazza wondered aloud.

"Let's all put on our helmets and find out," said Tyson, also inclined to exercise caution in extracting himself from what was in truth a reclining seat.

Exiting the damaged *Antares*, the three climbed a nearby hill to get their bearings. To the northwest they could glimpse the top of the *Moonbeam*, as it rested a short distance from the hangar entrance to *Lunar Base*. Within an hour of the crash landing they managed to traverse the intervening ground and rejoin their fellow conspirators inside the station.

....

Observing the *Antares* as it approached the 30-meter-high plateau, which housed their underground base, the Matusians had immediately displayed the view on the TV screen of their Earth guests. Informed that all attempts to establish radio contact had failed, suspicion ran high among both races. The moment that the surveillance cameras had disclosed the cylindrical object, mere suspicion turned to outright alarm. Nor did the spectacle of a body being dumped from the ship do anything to dispel this notion.

"Quick! Get into your space suit and jet pack, John," Hamilton shouted to his companion, already dashing toward a storage locker containing their astronaut equipment. There was not the slightest doubt in his mind but what the metallic object was an atomic bomb!

With record speed the two climbed into their suits and rushed toward the boulder air lock. They exited just in time to see the *Antares* lift off, eventually vanishing to the southwest.

"I don't know how much time we have left before it explodes," said Mark, making his way as fast as he could toward the point where the cameras had shown the cylinder to be located.

"What are we going to do if we can't disarm it?" asked Baldwin, matching Hamilton stride for stride.

"Let's face up to that problem when we come to it," said the astronomer, already beginning to formulate a course of action should worst come to worst.

Upon reaching the edge of the cliff they soon spotted the ominous silver canister. It was about 40 meters to their right and some 30 meters below them. Utilizing their jet packs, they promptly descended to the floor of the much larger mesa and approached the object.

"Damn! It's not going to be possible for us to disarm the bomb," shouted Baldwin, over their radio link. "There's no way that we can access the timing mechanism."

"If only we knew when it was set to explode we could at least assess our options," lamented Hamilton. "As it is, I fear that we can't wait for our Matusian friends to do something."

"Even if we should be successful in removing the covering panel there is still no guarantee that it could be defused in time," stated Baldwin, looking around for the direction of the nearest edge of the 400-meter-high plateau.

"I'm afraid that we're fresh out of alternatives," said Hamilton, with the same thought in mind. He was also searching desperately for the best place to push the deadly cylinder over the precipice.

"The southern face appears to be the closest, even though it must be a good 300 meters distant. Let's get this thing moving before it's too late," suggested Baldwin, clasping a convenient hand hold and commencing to pull.

Together, they slowly dragged the bomb toward the edge of the steep cliff, thankful for the reduced lunar gravity which allowed them to move a 600 lb. object as though it weighed no more than 100 lbs. Upon reaching their destination they were relieved to find a spot, only a short distance away, which was free of projections that might strike the falling canister. Rather than risk a chance that the shock would detonate the explosive trigger mechanism, they decided to move it an extra ten meters.

"How long do you think it will take for the bomb to impact the ground below?" asked Baldwin, as they prepared to shove it over the brink.

"Offhand, I should estimate a little over 20 seconds, in view of the weak gravity," Hamilton responded, as they gave the device one final push.

"Then let's get out of here!" cried Baldwin, turning to run.

"Fire up your jet pack, John! It's not only faster but we must clear the 30-meter cliff in order to gain cover from the radioactive fallout," exclaimed Hamilton, proceeding to do so himself.

Rising at full throttle, the two shot up and away from the center of the impending explosion. Clearing the summit of the smaller mesa, they arced over to horizontal flight, eventually touching down some 40 meters from the boulder entrance. Sprinting for the air lock, they were suddenly thrown off balance as the ground beneath their feet shook as though from a powerful earthquake. Behind them a blinding flash of light and a swiftly rising cloud of vaporized lunar rock and soil told of the violent release of nuclear energy. Momentarily dazed, they managed to pick themselves up and stagger toward safety. Casting a hasty look behind, they could see that a large portion of the massive plateau had abruptly vanished.

"I do hope the door mechanism is functional," panted Baldwin. "That was some blast!"

"If it doesn't open we're in big trouble when the fallout starts to settle," said Hamilton, glancing upward at the deadly cloud which loomed above them.

Just as they were about to find out by activating the hidden button, a section of the rock entrance slid away and multiple gloved hands reached out to pull them inside.

"That was certainly a close call. Why didn't you guys invite me to your picnic?" Frost greeted them, through the radio link built into their helmets.

"We didn't have time to send an invitation. It was one of those things that come up without notice, and you just have to be in the right place at the right time," Baldwin responded.

"We're disappointed that you missed the live performance," said Hamilton. "It really was quite spectacular— especially the part with the mushroom cloud."

Cycling through the air lock, the two heroes were promptly rushed to a decontamination center. After flushing away a modest amount of radioactivity from their suits, they were soon pronounced fit and allowed to return to their quarters, where they received passionate hugs and kisses from their wives.

Thirty minutes later Kobar initiated a TV holographic broadcast to his Earth guests. "On behalf of my fellow Matusians, I thank you both profusely for your courageous action which has saved our small city," he began. "Had it not been for your quick response we should all be dead."

"On behalf of Earth society, we are thoroughly ashamed of this wanton act of savagery," apologized Hamilton. "May we inquire as to the extent of damage and casualties?"

"Fortunately, only the lower levels incurred more than superficial damage. Unfortunately, two of our citizens were killed and about a dozen injured by collapsed walls and ceilings," responded Kobar.

"We're so sorry this had to happen because of us," said Frost—a sentiment promptly echoed by Baldwin.

"It was just a fluke series of coincidences and misfortunes," said Kobar. "Do any of you have a suspicion as to who might be behind this nefarious attack?"

"It seems clear to me that President Harker's delegation must somehow be involved," replied Hamilton. "No other faction would have had the resources to instigate such swift and violent reaction."

"I suppose that the rather strange look on their faces, when they learned of the stock market crash, should have been an indication of what to expect," added Susan.

Chapter 11
LUNAR BASE

When the Matusians first detected the approach of the *Antares* they had attempted to establish radio contact. Having failed, they then endeavored to speak to *Lunar Base* via a relay from one of Earth's lunar satellites. Again receiving no reply, it was deduced that the station must be occupied by a hostile force. Now that the nuclear blast had revealed belligerent intentions, it was realized that any further move to contact the base would only serve to announce that the alien outpost had not been destroyed. It could, in fact, promptly motivate another attack if their antagonists possessed a second atomic bomb. Having barely survived one blast, they most certainly did not want to push their luck by deliberately advertising their presence and inviting another.

On the other hand, it was logical to suspect that the invaders might eventually seek to compel the astronomy department to train the orbiting lunar telescope on the region of the Matusian base. Should it be discovered that the 30-meter mesa was still intact, they would know that their initial strike had been thwarted. From the alien's point of view, their immediate concern was to prevent the launching of a second bomb attack from *Lunar Base*. To accomplish this they would really have no choice but to quickly neutralize their opponent's capability to transport another bomb.

With overwhelming superiority of spacecraft, it would not be difficult to achieve their purpose. What was greatly feared, however, was a volley of nuclear missiles launched from Earth. Against such a threat they had no effective defense.

Yet another incentive to dispatch a mission to *Lunar Base* lay in a somewhat horrifying thought. Since it would be most illogical for the invaders to leave any witnesses who could testify as to the blatant unprovoked attack on the Matusian colony, it was feared that the staff of *Lunar Base* was currently in grave and imminent danger. Indeed, in order to place the blame on the aliens, it was necessary that the Earth outpost be destroyed! It was merely a question of when this diabolical act would be carried out.

Hastily equipping one of their saucer spacecraft with a portable laser cutting torch, of a type generally used to vaporize rock in their tunneling operations, the Matusians proposed to knock out the lunar shuttle while it was parked outside of *Lunar Base's* hangar entrance. The remaining serious threat would then be the *Antares* which, as far as they knew, would be residing inside the station's underground hangar bay. Upon disabling their opponent's shuttle craft, the plan was to lay in wait for the *Antares*, where it could be ambushed and quickly rendered inoperable with one good laser burst should it emerge. With the element of surprise on their side, the retaliatory strike was launched some four hours after the nuclear explosion.

As events turned out, the task proved somewhat easier than expected. Nearing their objective, the damaged *Antares* was soon spotted, leaning at a sharp angle against a boulder. With a broken landing leg, there was clearly no way that it could be made functional in the immediate future. Setting down alongside what was promptly identified as the *Moonbeam*, a dozen space-suited aliens emerged from their ship. Armed with stun guns, capable of paralyzing a man for at least one hour, at a distance of 400 meters, they took up positions around both the shuttle vehicle and the two

Lunar Base exits. Finding the *Moonbeam* deserted, they proceeded to set up their laser torch. With carefully designed bursts, they burned holes through both rocket engines, thus effectively rendering the craft useless. Having accomplished their primary mission, they returned to their ship and radioed a report to Kobar before commencing phase two: the storming of *Lunar Base* itself. To their surprise, he informed them that there had been a change of plans, and that they were to return for further instructions.

The change had come about following a discussion between Kobar and the astronauts, in which a scheme had been devised for the purpose of minimizing casualties. Suspecting that the invaders would never surrender, preferring instead to blow up the base in hopes of casting blame on the aliens, an attempt would be made to infiltrate the station and recapture it from within. To storm it directly would likely cause them to detonate a second bomb (which they were presumed to possess), thereby destroying both the base and the Matusian ship, with considerable loss of life.

The plan was for the three male astronauts to enter the station through the little used back door. Armed with silent Matusian stun guns, they would endeavor to catch the invaders by surprise. If plan "A" failed, and they got themselves involved in a gun fight against poor odds, they would surrender. Curiosity as to how they had managed to survive the atomic blast would almost certainly cause the invaders to take them prisoner, if for no other reason than to extract much needed information. The big gamble lay in counting on them to lock up their captives while they pondered certain options.

In this event, plan "B" called for them to resort to the use of miniature stun guns concealed in the heels of their shoes. Currently being fashioned by Jevad and his assistants, they would each carry one that was good for a single shot. With an effective range of some twelve feet, they could instantly knock one unconscious for at least forty minutes. It was expected that the secret weapon would be ready shortly after the Matusian spaceship had returned to base.

One hour later, equipped with the trick shoes and standard issue stun guns, the three volunteers donned their space suits and entered the waiting alien saucer ship. In minutes they were deposited close to the prescribed entrance to *Lunar Base*. By agreement, the Matusian ship would move a safe distance away, lest it be caught up in a sudden nuclear blast. Perched on a high elevation of nearby Iridium-A, it was in a position to receive a radio message directly from the base — assuming, of course, that communications could be captured intact.

With no need for locks on any doors, it was a simple matter to enter the air lock. Cycling through, with guns drawn, they entered a vacant compartment and removed their cumbersome pressure suits.

So far so good," whispered Frost, moving cautiously toward a closed door which led into a long passageway.

"We would seem to have made it unobserved," agreed Hamilton, his stun weapon in hand.

"Where do you suppose they are?" asked Baldwin.

"Another question might be, how many?" remarked Frost, as he stood ready to open the door.

....

Unbeknown to the trio of would-be-rescuers, at this very moment the invaders had just concluded a radio broadcast to Earth, falsely telling of an alien invasion and of their capture of *Lunar Base*. They told of a fictitious escape in the *Moonbeam*, amidst a hail of weapon fire which had knocked out their radio, and of their subsequent and quite retaliatory atom bombing of the Matusian base. At present, they said, they were engaged in a fierce battle to retake the station. Against a superior force they had risked much in seizing control of communications long enough to warn Earth society. It was doubtful, Tyson told the world, whether they could prevent the aliens from destroying the base. Before signing off he fired several shots from his automatic assault weapon, as a means of adding sound effects to embellish his story.

Certain that the alien outpost had been annihilated by the blast, Tyson had not bothered to compel the astronomy department to confirm its destruction. Nor had they yet discovered that the *Moonbeam*, their only hope of escape, had been sabotaged in a swift Matusian attack. Initial success of their mission had caused them to become careless by reason of overconfidence. They did, however, have one obvious problem to resolve if they were to make it back to Earth. In short, with Wallace dead, they needed a pilot with far greater navigational skills than those possessed by Tyson.

"Who are we going to get to fly the *Moonbeam*?" asked Flynn, as he stood beside Piazza and Tyson in the base's communications center.

"I'm sure that both Butler and Yashin can pilot the ship," Tyson responded. "We could always arrange a little accident for them just before docking at *Orion*."

"If they were to learn of the demise of the alien colony they might well react as Wallace and attempt to blast us all off into outer space," Piazza was quick to point out.

"They would be certain to do so if they were to suspect that we intend to blow up *Lunar Base* shortly after we leave," remarked Flynn.

"Then we must take steps to assure that they are kept in the dark, so to speak," said Tyson.

"What kind of a story do you propose to tell them to explain our military presence on the Moon?" Flynn wanted to know.

"I suppose the only excuse we can give is to say that there was concern that the aliens might try to capture *Lunar Base*, and that we were sent as a covert security force by a nameless group of worried nations— a force that is no longer needed now that we have talked with them in person and have come to believe that they are indeed a benevolent race meaning us no harm," replied Tyson.

"Sounds like a lot to swallow," said Flynn.

"Got a better idea?" retorted Tyson.

"What about the disappearance of Wallace? How can we account for his absence?" asked Piazza.

"I guess our best story would be to blame his accidental death on a fall off a high cliff, while sight-seeing— which was why Tyson had to fly the return segment of the expedition," suggested Flynn.

"Not a bad scenario. With a little practice, your imagination could take you far in politics," said Tyson.

"When do you plan to activate the bomb and leave?" asked Piazza, cradling an automatic weapon in his arms.

"First, I think that I should have a little chat with Butler and Yashin," stated Tyson. "Have one of our terrorist friends bring them, one at a time, to Bergman's office."

"I'll go, volunteered Piazza, moving toward the door.

....

"Cover me," said Frost, as he flung open the door to what was a main passageway leading to a number of compartments.

"It's empty! Our luck is still holding," voiced Hamilton, as he followed Baldwin through an airtight door.

"But for how long?" asked Frost, also stepping over the bulkhead threshold into the long corridor.

"Where do you suppose they're keeping the prisoners?" Baldwin inquired of his comrades.

"My guess would be the kitchen/dining/lavatory section," answered Hamilton. "It would make sense to keep them all together in one easily guarded area, as I have to believe that they are comparatively few when compared to the staff at the base."

"How many of them do you think there are?" Frost wondered aloud.

"Good question. Offhand, I shouldn't think less than half a

dozen," Hamilton responded, after some thought.

They had almost reached a cross junction with another lengthy passageway, leading to the section where the prisoners were most likely to be held, when Piazza suddenly appeared as if out of nowhere. More startled than anyone, he had barely time to move a muscle before Baldwin fired a blast from his alien stun gun. A purple light seemed to envelop the man and he slumped to the floor with a dull thud. They quickly dragged his unconscious body to a nearby storage locker and thrust him inside, having first relieved him of his weapon.

"Sleep it off in peace," said Frost, closing the door and slinging the captured machine gun over his shoulder.

"One down and heaven only knows how many more to go," remarked Baldwin, cautiously scanning the intersecting corridor for any of their first victim's associates.

"All clear," whispered Hamilton, finally convinced that no one was coming to investigate the muffled sound made by Piazza's falling body.

Turning to the left the three moved silently along the narrow passageway. Reaching another junction they stopped and carefully peered around the corner. A short distance from them, to their right, were two guards armed with machine guns. They stood in front of an open doorway which led directly into the area believed most likely to hold the staff of *Lunar Base*.

"I'll take the one on the right; while you two can fight over the one that's left," quipped Hamilton.

In quick succession, Hamilton and Frost fired from a distance of ten meters. Enclosed in a purple glow, both of the guards promptly crumpled to the ground.

"Good shooting! That makes one each, should you desire to keep score," said Baldwin.

Unfortunately, their elation was a little premature, as they had not counted on a third terrorist being inside the room. Seeing his two comrades taken out by what had to be an alien weapon of some sort, he quickly seized several hostages at gunpoint. Standing behind them, Akim Hussem lined the others up against a nearby wall. Threatening to shoot them all with his automatic weapon, if the attacking trio would not surrender, he proceeded to show that he meant business by taking deliberate aim and firing a single shot into the shoulder of Carlos Bial, the likeable Brazilian astronomer.

Definitely confronted with a plan "B" situation, the three would-be-rescuers permitted themselves to be captured, rather than allow further harm to come to their colleagues. Having heard the gunshot, Tyson and Flynn came racing to the scene. Dumbfounded by the presence of men who had been considered dead, Tyson eventually recovered sufficiently to issue a number of commands. Subjecting their new captives to a thorough search, he then herded two of them in with the other prisoners. In an act of compassion, he allowed Dr. Rita Mitchell to administer first aid to the wounded astronomer, before proceeding to personally escort Hamilton— at gunpoint— to Bergman's quarters for interrogation. As had been anticipated, curiosity and a need to know what was happening had gotten the better of him.

Covering the prisoner with his pistol, Tyson sat at the base commander's desk opposite Hamilton. Glaring at him for some time, he finally spoke: "Now, would you please tell me how you ever managed to survive the nuclear blast? You were on the Matusian base, with Frost and Baldwin, when the bomb exploded, were you not?" he asked, still visibly shaken by the unexpected turn of events.

Seeing no reason to lie or withhold such information, Hamilton simply told him that they had been able to push the device over the 400-meter cliff before it exploded.

"How much damage did it do?" Tyson demanded to know.

Again, Hamilton could see no point in concealing the truth.

"Two of the Matusians were killed and about a dozen injured," he answered.

"What about the base itself, and their two spaceships?"

"The spacecraft were unharmed and only the lowest levels of their underground complex suffered any real damage," replied Hamilton.

"Then I guess we'll just have to drop a second bomb on them," said Tyson, confirming that there was indeed another nuclear device.

"How do you propose doing that?"

"With the *Moonbeam*, of course," responded Tyson, not thinking clearly or asking one pertinent question.

Hamilton chose to rectify this oversight. "And how do you suppose we got here?" he asked.

"You came on one of the alien ships," replied Tyson, suddenly becoming quite apprehensive. "Is the ship outside, now?"

"Not at the moment," answered Hamilton. "But they were here long enough to disable the *Moonbeam*."

"What?"

"You heard me. You're trapped and may as well surrender before there's any more senseless bloodshed," said Hamilton, feeling that in at least one sense the good guys held the upper hand.

"You're bluffing!" exclaimed Tyson, with a reply that, in all honesty, he would have to concede posed a bluff in itself.

"If you don't believe me, you have only to take a look."

Speaking over the base's intercom system, Tyson summoned Flynn and instructed him to suit-up and check out the *Moonbeam* for signs of any damage. "We should have our answer shortly," he said.

Meanwhile, confined behind a closed door in a wing of the station, Frost and Baldwin had wasted no time in briefing the others with regard to current events. In seclusion, they quickly extracted the dual components of the alien's miniature stun gun from the heels of their shoes, one-half being concealed in each shoe. Assembling the two sections, they looked in distrust at the completed weapon, which resembled a short and somewhat oval ball point pen. It did not seem much with which to challenge a terrorist armed with a big machine gun.

"I sure hope these things work as well as the Matusians claim," commented Frost, seeking assurance from his similarly armed companion.

"Jevad seemed certain of his product," responded Baldwin. "He says that they tested it several times."

"Do you think there's just the one guard left outside?" asked Frost, gently fingering the trigger mechanism of the pen-gun in his hands.

"As near as we can determine there are six of them," Bergman informed them. "If you bagged three of the invaders that leaves just Tyson, Flynn and the one they call Akim. Assuming Tyson still has Hamilton in my office, and that Flynn has been called away from guard duty as per the intercom message, this leaves only one of them to contain us."

"That one fellow is a trigger-happy monster, judging by the way he gunned down poor Carlos," said Rita.

"How is he doing?" asked Butler, looking toward his wounded companion who lay in a corner of what was the communal dining room.

"Not too good, I'm afraid," replied the physician. "I've managed to control the hemorrhaging, but he needs to be operated on to remove the bullet."

"Well, if we're going to stage our big counterattack, I suggest we do so before they dispatch a second guard," said Frost.

With all in agreement, and realizing that they would have just this one chance to succeed, they took up their previously discussed positions. Since it was an airtight door that they would be opening, it could not be flung open in an instant. The guard outside would have plenty of time to level his machine gun and commence shooting long before anyone could reach him. He would not, however, have any reason to expect return fire, which was a point in their favor. Yet another peculiarity of the entrance was to be found in the threshold of the door, which was raised a good foot above the floor. The door itself extended to within a foot of the ceiling. Stacking some furniture behind the hinged side of the door, so as to allow one of the two armed captives to climb to the top, the plan was to give him an unexpected angle of fire. In contrast, the other armed captive would lie low on the floor behind the raised bulkhead door jamb. When the door was finally opened it was hoped to confuse the guard, who would likely have his weapon leveled at chest height. Even if worst came to worst, it was extremely doubtful that he could get them both before being zapped himself.

Taking up their positions, with Baldwin on high and Frost at the bottom, Yashin began to turn the handle that would open the door. Butler and Bergman stood ready to lead a charge to retrieve the fallen guard's weapon. If merely dazed or otherwise, they would attempt to subdue him in a desperate fight to the death.

Pulling the inwardly hinged door wide open, as swiftly as he could, Yashin fully expected to have to dodge a deluge of bullets ricocheting around the metallic walls of the compartment. Instead, the plan worked almost to perfection. Seeing nothing to shoot at for a split second, the terrorist held his fire until he spotted the twin targets. He lowered his weapon to shoot at Frost. But Baldwin was a trifle faster, firing his stun gun at a distance of close to ten feet. With only one target in sight, Frost also fired, just before a bullet creased the side of his head and he lost consciousness. Akim Hussem, encased in a purple aura, fell backwards in a heap, but not before squeezing off several shots. In an instant, Bergman had seized the dropped weapon and stood ready to defend his companions from any attack.

First to reach the stricken geologist was Dr. Rita Mitchell. Upon examining the wound, she sprayed it with a combination sealant and antiseptic. "Without an X-ray, I can't be certain that the skull hasn't been fractured, but there would seem to be a good chance that it's not too serious," she said.

Back in Bergman's office, Tyson rose immediately to his feet when he heard the gunshots, his weapon still pointed directly at Hamilton's chest.

"Whatever happened, I didn't do it," said Mark, in jest, inwardly wondering how his comrades were faring in their attempted breakout.

Seriously considering shooting the astronomer/philosopher on the spot, before rushing to see what was going on at the prison compound, Tyson had second thoughts. If trigger-happy Hussem had already killed Butler and Yashin, Hamilton might prove useful in navigating the *Moonbeam* back to Earth — assuming, of course, that the lunar shuttle was still functional.

"Your man Flynn should be back with his report any moment now," said Hamilton, endeavoring to buy time.

Suddenly recalling that he had one of the alien stun guns in his pocket, Tyson decided upon a compromise. Told that the weapon would render a person unconscious for at least an hour, he proposed to zap Hamilton with it and worry about eliminating him permanently at a later date.

"Looks like I'm about to be the victim of my own weapon," remarked Hamilton, recalling that it was Tyson himself who had confiscated his stun gun. What his captor did not know, however, was that before dropping the weapon he had twisted a dial, reducing the charge setting to minimum power. According to Jevad, this would knock one out for a period of only five minutes or so.

Just as Tyson was about to fire, the intercom system was activated by the returning Flynn. "He was telling us the truth, I'm afraid. The *Moonbeam* isn't going anywhere without engines," he reported.

"Damn!"

"If you will surrender peacefully, I could contact the Matusian spaceship and arrange for us all to be picked up and returned to Earth," said Hamilton, hoping that reason might prevail.

"That does it!" exclaimed Tyson, pulling a rather sophisticated electronic device from a jacket pocket. In seconds he had punched in a series of figures. A flashing red light signified that the bomb had been activated. Placing the device on a corner of Bergman's desk, he took his pistol and blew it apart with one shot.

"Why did you do that?" asked Hamilton, almost certain that he knew the answer before he spoke.

"In exactly forty minutes this base will be the scene of a huge mushroom cloud, and there is no way to stop it," Tyson informed his audience of one.

Hamilton cast a furtive glance at his watch.

"When the bomb goes off, Earth will think that the Matusians were responsible and will retaliate with a swarm of nuclear missiles," Tyson stated.

"But why?"

Without answering, the terrorist leader pointed the Matusian stun gun at the astronomer's chest and fired.

Opening Bergman's bottom desk draw, Tyson calmly removed two hand grenades and slipped them into a jacket pocket. Instead of racing to see why Hussem was shooting, he headed straight to the base's communications center. If, by chance, a prisoner should escape and radio the truth to Earth, all would have been in vain. President Harker — along with his reactionary associates— would surely incur the wrath of the world. With the fate of the expedition members now irrevocably sealed, his first priority must be to prevent this from happening.

Having a similar thought in mind, Bergman and a number of the liberated prisoners also converged on the same compartment. To their knowledge, there was only Tyson and Flynn left to deal with. On the other hand, they were still outgunned by a factor of two to one. The status of Hamilton was unknown to them, although the one gunshot that they had just heard was far from encouraging.

"I sure wish we could lay our hands on a few more weapons," Cooper remarked to Baldwin, as the pair followed behind an assault group that included Bergman, Butler, Yashin, Stromberg and Kovakov.

"Let's check Bergman's quarters. Tyson may have stashed our stun guns in the compartment," suggested Baldwin, anxious to discover what had become of Hamilton.

Branching off from the main force, the two made their way to the compartment which Tyson had been using as his own. Unarmed, they crept silently and cautiously toward the open doorway and peered inside. Appearing to be deserted, at first glance, they soon noticed Hamilton slumped on the floor.

"He's still breathing and I don't see any wound," announced Cooper, much relieved. "He appears to have been shot with one of the Matusian stun guns."

"If that's the case, he'll probably be unconscious for about an hour — unless it had been turned to a low energy setting," Baldwin said, bending down to examine his stricken companion.

"Nothing!" exclaimed Cooper, in disgust, after concluding a hasty search of the room for any kind of weapon.

"I do believe that Mark is coming out of it!" shouted Baldwin, observing eye and facial movement, which was soon followed by moaning sounds indicative of an attempt to speak.

Recovering his senses, Hamilton's first concern was to check his watch to see how long he had been unconscious. Somewhat relieved to find that it had been little more than five minutes since Tyson had armed the bomb, he conveyed this information to Baldwin and Cooper. In turn, he was briefed on essentials of the breakout and of Bergman's current endeavor to seize the communications center. Having hastily assembled the dual components of his concealed miniature stun gun, he was about to suggest a course of action when there was the sound of an explosion.

"What was that?" asked Cooper. "Unless I'm mistaken, it seemed to come from the direction of our communications compartment."

"I'm afraid that's exactly where it did come from," Hamilton was quick to respond. "Tyson could not afford to let us make a broadcast to Earth, and he must have set off a grenade or an explosive charge of some sort."

Further dialogue was soon interrupted by the noise of sporadic gunfire."It would seem that Bergman must have run into at least one of the terrorists," said Baldwin.

"We've got to get everybody to the hangar bay and into pressure suits as soon as possible. Our sole hope of escape is to get to the *Hercules* before Tyson or Flynn can reach it. It has the only radio with which to summon the Matusian spaceship," Hamilton informed them.

"I'll make the announcement over the intercom," said Cooper, as he reached for the microphone on Bergman's desk.

"Give me a couple of minutes, Paul, before doing so. I'm going to try to get there before they do, and if they should become aware of our intentions they will endeavor to block us. If Bergman is between the hangar bay and Tyson, as I suspect, he'll have to take the long way around and I stand a chance of beating him to the vehicle," stated Hamilton.

"I'll come with you," said Baldwin.

"When you make your speech, tell Bergman to get over there with his heavy artillery just as quickly as he can," requested Hamilton, exiting the compartment and moving swiftly down the corridor leading directly to the underground hangar.

Unfortunately, at this moment, Bergman was pinned down and

engaged in a shootout near the communications center, which Tyson had just demolished with a grenade. His opponent, however, was not Tyson but Flynn, as the two gunmen had joined forces shortly before Bergman had arrived upon the scene. Tyson was now en route — by a much more circuitous pathway — to the hangar bay, with the avowed intention of destroying both the *Hercules* and its radio.

Upon reaching the closed airtight hangar door, Baldwin and Hamilton wasted no time in gaining entry. Shutting the door behind them, they sprinted to the nearby *Hercules*.

"We're in time!" exclaimed Hamilton, with a sigh of relief, after casting a quick glance inside the craft.

"We'll have to set up an ambush. How about hiding behind the door and subjecting our quarry to a purple blast when he enters?" suggested Baldwin.

"Sounds like a good idea. Let's do it," said Hamilton, moving into a position which afforded concealment.

Seconds later the door was thrust open and Tyson stepped inside, confident that the grenade in his hand would soon put an end to any escape and possible rescue by the Matusians. Noticing little more than the *Hercules*, parked some ten meters away, he started forward with one thought in mind. In an instant he was completely enveloped in a purple aura.

"Good shooting! He never knew what hit him."

"At such close range, how could I miss?" said Hamilton, deriving a measure of satisfaction from observing the prostrate form now lying before him.

"We had better see if Bergman needs any help with Flynn," voiced Baldwin, picking up the unarmed grenade and removing Tyson's pistol from its holster.

"One of us should stay here to guard the *Hercules*," suggested Hamilton. Finding his confiscated stun gun in one of Tyson's pockets, he quickly set it for maximum power.

"You stay and I'll go," said Baldwin, listening to the sound of occasional gunfire. "Evidently, Bergman is still hung up with Flynn."

Taking the same roundabout route that Tyson had been forced to use to reach the *Hercules*, Baldwin's plan was to approach the terrorist from the rear. Bergman, meanwhile, had found himself caught up in a dilemma. Unable to get a clear shot at Flynn, who was hiding behind an intersecting corridor, he could not risk being cut down while attempting a frontal charge down a long and exposed passageway. On the other hand, if he left his position to go to the hanger bay, he would allow his enemy to massacre the stream of base personnel who were endeavoring to flee toward the *Hercules*. Thus it was that the arrival of Baldwin quickly turned the tide of battle. Rounding a bend in the tunnel system, he spotted Flynn crouched down and looking the other way. Raising the pistol and taking careful aim, Baldwin fired three shots into the surprised terrorist, killing his adversary almost instantly.

"I got him!" Baldwin shouted triumphantly to Bergman, who was at the other end of the corridor.

"Good work! But what about Tyson?" Bergman asked, concerned that he might still be at large.

"We bagged him just before he could sabotage the *Hercules*," said Baldwin, upon joining his companion and moving swiftly toward the hangar bay.

Reaching their destination, they were relieved to see that Frost was on his feet and preparing to slip a helmet over his bandaged head. Rita Mitchell and Gustov Stromberg were busy helping Carlos Bial, the wounded Brazilian astronomer, into a space suit. In less than ten minutes Bergman, clad in his protective suit, had depressurized the hanger and was leading a group of similarly clad personnel out into the bright lunar sunshine. Loaded with passengers, including the two wounded men, the *Hercules* was promptly driven from the hanger bay with Butler at the controls.

"I've established contact with the Matusian spaceship," Cooper announced. "They're on their way to pick us up."

"Tell them to make it fast!" shouted Hamilton, glancing at his watch.

"How much time do we have left?" Baldwin wanted to know, but was almost afraid to ask.

"About twelve minutes," Hamilton answered. "It's going to be rather close."

Stopping the *Hercules*, a scan hundred meters from the main entrance to *Lunar Base*, Butler ushered everyone outside to join Bergman's group of pedestrians.

"There it is!" exclaimed Yashin, looking up and to the north-west, where a tiny speck was growing larger before their very eyes.

Setting down a short distance away, the Matusian craft had its air lock door open and ramp extended by the time the first refugees had arrived. Climbing aboard, with all possible haste, the door was quickly closed and the craft shot up and away at a pace which thrust the group harshly to the floor of the air lock while it was still in the process of being pressurized. In spite of their highly advanced technology, there was no way in which to circumvent the firm laws of physics when it came to such an effect as acceleration.

Three minutes later, when they were at a safe distance from *Lunar Base*, a blinding flash illuminated the southern horizon. For the second time in less than a day a great mushroom cloud had erupted on the surface of the Moon, clearly portraying the violent nature of an Earth society which had failed to choose its leaders wisely.

Chapter 12
SECLUSION AND OPTIMISM

Following the destruction of *Lunar Base*, in the heat of an atomic fireball, the refugees were taken directly to the alien's underground complex. Forced to operate in the now rather cramped quarters that had been reserved for Earth guests, Dr. Mitchell endeavored to treat her two wounded patients. Assisted by a Matusian physician, wearing a protective isolation suit and utilizing alien equipment, the bullet was successfully removed from Bial's shoulder. In spite of losing a considerable amount of blood, he was expected to make a swift and full recovery. Likewise, Frost's head injury was revealed to be of a minor nature. It had been a really close call, as a fraction of an inch difference in Hussem's aim would have ended the geologist's life.

Although the Matusians were most anxious to return the refugees to Earth, it was also desirable to withhold news of their base's survival for as long as possible in order to buy time. As long as whoever was responsible for the nuclear strike could be made to believe that the alien base had been destroyed, so they would likely be safe from any fresh assault. Unable to withstand attack from a swarm of nuclear missiles, their immediate concern was to seek haven on the far side of the Moon, where they might be free to construct a new base hidden from their enemies— hopefully, until the arrival of their great starship.

Dispatching one of their saucer spacecraft to modify Earth's two orbiting lunar satellites, they succeeded in converting them into relay stations of their own—thereby preventing Earth factions from utilizing them as detection devices. Within hours the second Matusian ship, loaded with supplies and equipment, landed at the southeast corner of a large circular scar on the Moon's far side. Known as the Orientale Basin, this huge depression measured some 930 km in diameter and was about 7 km in depth. Lying just south of the equator, its rocky walls had been selected as the site for their new base.

Clad inprotective pressure suits, a group of Matusian technicians hastened to set up several powerful laser-type tunneling machines. Using the spaceship's fusion reactor as an energy source, it was not long before they were hard at work vaporizing great amounts of lunar rock. In a matter of hours they had succeeded in excavating a number of spacious chambers. Within four days an entire network of rooms and connecting passageways had been created deep inside the rock face. No sooner had they finished tunneling than the other ship arrived with a quantity of bulkhead/air lock doors and life support equipment, much of which had been cannibalized from their original complex.

In less than a week they had managed to pressurize the new base and were busily engaged in transferring supplies of food and water, followed shortly by a variety of sophisticated machinery — including their two smaller back-up fusion reactors. Some twelve days after the nuclear blast, which destroyed *Lunar Base*, the Orientale Basin outpost became functional in many essential respects. Already, slightly more than one-half of their personnel had been transported to the hastily constructed sanctuary. While considerably smaller than the Matusian's old base, and lacking many of its amenities, it was the best that could be done under the circumstances. Perhaps, at some future date, it might prove feasible to enlarge and improve their quarters— if only Harker and his associates would allow them to salvage sufficient material and equipment.

Utilizing a narrow laser-like electromagnetic beam, so as to avoid detection by Earth radio telescopes, Kobar transmitted an account of recent events to the great Matusian starship now en route to the Solar System. Currently about six light-years distant, and traveling at close to 20% light speed, the message was expected to reach them some five years from the present. Also included in his report were many suggestions for global reform— recommendations which had served to trigger a violent reaction on the part of certain religious fanatics and selfish multimillionaires.

Some twelve days after the destruction of *Lunar Base*, exactly what the aliens had expected did, in fact, occur. Unable to contact either party by radio, Earth had sent the *Lunik* to find out what had really happened. Entering into Moon orbit, the international crew subjected the two bases to a telescopic scan. The crater remains of mankind's treasured lunar outpost clearly told the fate of their station. In contrast, the Matusian complex was observed to have suffered only superficial damage; for while a substantial portion of the 400-meter plateau had vanished, the 30-meter upper mesa— which housed the base itself— seemed to be unscathed. Telemetry showing the extent of damage to both bases was promptly beamed back to Earth.

Realizing that there was no longer any reason to maintain silence, now that the status of their base had become known, the Matusians decided to establish contact with Earth the moment that *Lunik* blasted out of orbit. Although it was deemed unlikely that the craft carried another atomic bomb, there was no point in taking an unnecessary risk by opening a channel to the orbiting ship. Should the *Lunik* land at their base, then they would have no choice but to reveal themselves and trust that their rescued countrymen would be able to convince the crew of the alien's peaceful intentions. As it turned out, the *Lunik* was advised to return to *Space Station Orion* after a few more orbits.

With departure of the reconnaissance craft Kobar immediately swung into action. Beaming a prepared televised broadcast to Earth, in all of the world's major languages, he spoke of the treachery behind the unprovoked nuclear strike in which two of the Matusians had been killed and a dozen others injured. He then undertook to introduce the evacuated staff of *Lunar Base*, along with the Frosts, Baldwins and Hamiltons. In turn, they each told of their experiences at the hands of the six terrorists, led by Colonel Edward Tyson, a U.S. Marine officer who was known to be a minion of General Turnbull and President Adolph Harker.

In giving his account of their narrow escape and rescue by the aliens, who had risked their lives just moments before *Lunar Base* was destroyed, Bergman called for the impeachment of President Harker. Yashin and Hamilton went much further, requesting that the United Nations launch an immediate investigation, with the intention of bringing serious criminal charges against those responsible. Even Ron Harland, the CIA agent who had been deemed expendable in the plans of the terrorist conspirators, testified as to the involvement of the top echelons of the U.S. government— including President Harker!

Confident that this damaging testimony would serve to negate any hostility against his people, Kobar then went on to describe the history of the Matusian race, and of their inherited role as the "guardian angels" of emerging civilizations. Stressing that they sought only to help Earth society in its struggle to evolve a World Government that would provide peace and prosperity for all, the alien leader proceeded to offer the world a number of precious gifts as a token of their good faith. In addition to giving Earth the technology needed for a controlled fusion reactor, they had already supplied valuable insight into such realms as science and philosophy—via Hamilton's revolutionary treatise. In the years ahead, the

Matusians were prepared to give Earth an effective cure for virtually every form of cancer, along with the prescription to retard aging and extend the average human life span by at least threefold. All they would ask in return was that the world adopt certain basic reforms which, in the eyes of the Matusians, were long overdue and would greatly benefit the average citizen.

In outlining his proposals for reform, Kobar began with a censure of many supposedly democratic administrations which currently governed the nations of Earth. They were, he pointed out, little more than a farce — being best described as wealthy aristocratic dictatorships, invariably comprised either of rich individuals or their most obedient puppets. Without reasonable equality of wealth, in view of the great cost of obtaining favorable publicity, any election was highly biased in favor of those supported by the major news media. In essence, only those candidates sponsored by the rich could even afford to stand for an election! Thus the democratic process, he again emphasized, could never be expected to function properly unless steps were taken to distribute wealth in a more equitable manner.

Mincing few words, Kobar placed the blame for the world's unsavory history of wars and social injustices upon mankind's lack of common sense and inherent selfishness. He made special mention of the twin evils which had long plagued the human race: economic inequality and religious intolerance. Starting with an essay on the merits and deficiencies of capitalism, he went on to expound the many virtues of the proposals that had been made to Vice President Donovan's lunar delegation— proposals which, in all probability, had never been disclosed to the general public. He now proceeded to rectify such an omission by dwelling upon these suggestions, arguing at length for a redistribution of wealth in order to compensate for many years of unfair compensation and lack of opportunity for the masses.

Kobar next attacked the admittedly volatile issue of religious beliefs, stopping just short of ridiculing a number of the world's most popular dogmas. Depicting them as totally unfounded and highly illogical, he attempted to present a condensed version of Matusian philosophy. Upholding the basic idea of a *Cosmic God Principle*, he elaborated strongly upon the premise of *universal reincarnation*, declaring it to be a fundamental truth and the foundation upon which a viable religion must be based. Further criticism was directed at the manner in which many children are indoctrinated (or brainwashed) in the beliefs of their parents, without being given a chance to consider other views. He deplored this widely accepted practice as a violation of a child's inherent right to receive an unbiased education. In fact, he regarded it as the chief reason why mankind's moral and spiritual outlook had lagged so far behind advances in science and technology.

In addressing the problem of an overpopulated planet, Kobar decried the foolish objection to birth control that had long been advocated by certain religious leaders, whom he depicted as irresponsible charlatans. He then mentioned the threat posed by inherited defects upon successive generations of humanity. The Matusian leader strongly urged a system of genetic testing and even licensing of births, as an alternative to long-term destruction from within. To knowingly incur a serious risk of bringing a defective child into the world was, in his mind, a criminal act. By way of emphasizing his point he asked a very simple question: "Who, in all honesty, would care to be born into a defective body in preference to a healthy body?"

Under the auspices of a new and completely revised United Nations, Kobar proposed a number of drastic reforms. High on his list was the need for world disarmament, especially with regard to the profusion of nuclear weaponry which periodically threatened to explode into some global Armageddon. Concurrent with this abolition would be the formation of an International Police Force—one that would act to enforce a ban on all manner of military armaments. Moreover, it would strictly prohibit the drafting of individuals into armies. An attempt to do so would be considered an intolerable violation of one's duty to respect conscience, and would call for prompt intervention and removal from office of any government endeavoring to impose such a law upon its citizens. In short, sanctity of the human soul was to be regarded as something which had to be preserved at all cost. With very few willing to fight their battles for them, and faced with the prospect of being confronted by overwhelming force, any ambitious leader would be compelled to think twice before plotting an act of aggression.

Literally pleading with the nations of Earth to accept the logic of his proposals for what, in essence, was tantamount to establishment of a World Government, Kobar felt obliged to mention the serious consequences of just such a refusal. First, without intervention, there was a very real threat of the world destroying itself through the folly of warfare. Second, when the powerful Matusian starship arrived (some 30 years hence), they would be prepared to accomplish— by force, if need be— what Earth politicians had failed to do willingly. It would not bode well for those leaders who foolishly chose to ignore the glorious destiny in store for the world, by offering physical resistance to what was obviously a benevolent and more advanced humanoid society — whose only interest in the planet Earth was to assist its inhabitants to achieve a higher perspective and status in life.

Wishing his audience well, and trusting that common sense would be allowed to prevail over prejudice and ignorance, Kobar terminated the transmission.

....

The Matusians did not have long to wait for a response. Six hours after the momentous broadcast, no less than sixteen missiles were launched from a nuclear submarine in the Pacific Ocean. Unbeknown to the ship's commander, who thought it was just a test firing with dummy warheads, powerful hydrogen bombs had been substituted. By order of President Harker, the guidance systems of the missiles had recently been reprogrammed to send them on a trajectory which would destroy the alien base on the Moon. In little short of three days they were destined to strike their target.

Detected almost immediately by Earth orbiting satellites, designed to reveal missile launches, word was quickly flashed to diplomats at the United Nations. Called before this international body to explain his action, President Harker steadfastly maintained that he had acted in the best interests of the planet Earth. With all the guile of a skilled actor, Harker claimed that the aliens had destroyed *Lunar Base*, captured its staff, and either forced or brainwashed them into making the recent taped broadcast before probably killing them. It was a wild fabrication, which he never really expected many in the audience to believe, but since the missiles could not be recalled there was absolutly nothing that they could do about it. Moreover, when the alien base was obliterated there would not be any witnesses to prove otherwise.

Although Harker's lame excuse would never receive much credibility, in the eyes of any thinking individual, this was not to be the case when it came to the general public. With the vast resources of his rich and influential associates in crime on his side, it was not difficult to implant feelings of suspicion and animosity in the minds of many. Depicted as infidels by Bible-thumping evangelists and organized religion in general, and as evil space aliens bent solely on enslaving the human race by the large TV networks and great newspaper chains, lack of logic in some tended to offset common sense in others— to the point where opinion was divided and the average person simply did not know what to believe.

With their worst fears now a stark reality, the Matusians planned to continue salvage operations until the last possible moment. Thirty years of seclusion, with minimal resources and few amenities, would seem like an eternity. There was so much that they wanted to save, and so little time in which to transfer supplies and equipment to their new underground home in the Orientale Basin. Hasty calculations had shown that, barring any unforeseen calamity, they would probably have sufficient food, water and air to see them through this lengthy period of siege.

There was, regrettably, no provision for housing and feeding the two dozen or so refugees from Earth who were currently sharing guest quarters at their Teneriffe Mountains base. Without a doubt, they would have to be returned home at earliest convenience. Indeed, since their physical presence and testimony would be required, in order to refute Harker's wild claims of alien coercion, it had already been decided to send them back on one of the two saucer spaceships. The only question remaining was whether they should be returned to *Space Station Orion*, or to some location on Earth where they would be safe from assassination until they could testify in person.

After much debate, both amongst themselves and in conversation with their guests, it was finally decided to deposit the refugees at *Orion*. Not only would this save them precious fuel— which was likely to be of concern in the years to come— but a recent United Nations pronouncement appeared to offer a measure of optimism. By a majority vote, they had passed a resolution censuring President Harker for his hasty action, and had expressly warned him against launching further missile attacks against any target— real or imagined — without the consent of the Security Council. Yet another factor leading to this decision was completion of repairs to *Orion's* communications system, which would allow them to make a broadcast to Earth. Surely, when surrounded by their fellow beings, one would not dare to claim alien coercion.

Thus it came to pass that all of the refugees were transported, in secrecy and without fanfare, to the presumed safety of *Space*

Station Orion. Cautiously pulling to within a dozen meters of the station's central hub, a line was soon strung between two air locks. Clad in the same protective space suits with which they had earlier fled the destruction of *Lunar Base*, the transfer went smoothly and without incident.

As they later watched, through one of *Orion's* windows, the alien craft receded swiftly into the distance and was quickly lost to sight. More than a few of the new arrivals were overwhelmed by sadness. In a short time they had come to trust and admire this noble space-faring race, and were deeply humiliated by the despicable manner in which certain Earth factions had received them. Perhaps, in the foreseeable future of those now present, mankind would mature to the point where close rapport might be established— hopefully, before the arrival of their great starship. It was a sincere hope shared by all of the refugees.

One hour later, with no means to intercept a swarm of incoming missiles, the Matusian lunar complex inside the 30-meter mesa was destroyed in a series of sixteen blinding flashes. Although resulting in the loss of irreplaceable facilities and equipment, through good foresight they had managed to safely evacuate the base of all its personnel.

....

"You mean to tell me that the reason we couldn't establish radio contact, with the approaching Matusian spaceship, was because they were deliberately jamming and silencing communications?" asked Peter Hawkins, commander of the space station, to a small assemblage of refugees gathered in the station's lounge.

"Exactly!" exclaimed Bergman. "It was at our request, since we did not want Earth to learn of our presence until we are ready to make a most revealing broadcast."

"In case you hadn't heard, we're currently ranked quite high on President Harker's hit list," Hamilton informed the rather puzzled commander. "As a matter of fact, I shouldn't be surprised if he hasn't devised some back-up scheme to stop us from testifying in person."

"What do you mean?" inquired Hawkins.

"He must realize that there was always the possibility that we might escape the missile assault in one of their spacecraft. If so, and since the aliens would probably be reluctant to risk a landing on Earth, the most logical place to deposit us would be *Orion*," said Bergman.

"Do you really think that he would dare to attack an international establishment?" Hawkins asked, beginning to be concerned for the safety of close to forty regular base members— to say nothing of the recent influx of refugees.

"It would not be an open act of aggression, of course, but he could well be party to a covert plan to destroy the station by his favorite method— namely, a bomb!" explained Baldwin.

"Especially, of the nuclear variety," added Frost, who was now fully recovered from his gunfighting ordeal.

"Needless to say, any such explosion would be blamed on the Matusians," remarked Susan.

"If your fears are justified, then I believe we should make an immediate and thorough search of the station," concluded Hawkins. "I'll also see to it that a guard is posted at the communications center, to ensure that your arrival on *Orion* remains a secret to all on Earth."

"I've already recruited Butler and Yashin for the job, armed with Matusian stun guns," said Bergman. "After what we've been through, you tend to get a little paranoid when it comes to dealing with Harker."

"Good thinking! I'm sure we have several reporters on board who must be itching to send a news bulletin, informing the world of your presence on the station," responded Hawkins.

"Incidentally, when making your search, it might be wise to send a crew outside to make certain there are no surprise packages affixed to the exterior of the station," Bergman advised.

"Shall do," agreed Hawkins. Having already received a first-hand account of their terrifying moments, at the hands of Harker's minions, he was convinced that a potential danger did, in fact, exist.

"Perhaps it would be in order to issue a statement to your staff, explaining the situation to them," suggested Hamilton.

Hawkins hastened to comply.

Some four hours later, when the search had been completed, the station commander was thanking his lucky stars for having heeded the advice of his peers. Concealed inside what was ostensibly a large fuel canister, intended for one of the lunar shuttles, was a small low-yield atomic bomb! Evidently brought to the station a few days earlier, it now rested in the cargo bay where it had just been defused. The triggering mechanism was found to be via a radio signal, rather than any timing device. They had little doubt as to who might have ordered the coded impulse to be transmitted.

With the support of the entire station behind them, the *Lunar Base* refugees wasted no time in broadcasting a scathing condemnation of President Harker and his reactionary associates. Invariably, under normal circumstances, the overwhelming body of evidence — including video telemetry showing the defused nuclear bomb— would have resulted in cries for immediate impeachment. Instead, by reason of their control of all the major TV networks and newspaper chains, the average American citizen knew nothing about what had transpired. Should word ever leak out it could always be countered by fabricated claims that an alien invasion force had captured *Orion* and had, once again, either coerced or brainwashed their captives into speaking lies.

"It's beginning to look like nothing short of making a personal appearance will suffice," said Bergman, after watching a televised newscast from Washington, D.C. His audience, in *Orion's* lounge, was Peter Hawkins and Mark Hamilton, both of whom were appalled by the extent to which events had been distorted.

"When is the next shuttle craft due to arrive?" asked Hamilton, pacing the floor before finally stopping to glance through a window at the blue-white planet beneath them.

"Four days from now," answered Hawkins. "Do you suppose Harker will make an attempt to prevent us from returning to Earth?"

"I think we should presume that he will do his best to keep us from testifying in person," declared Bergman.

"For this very reason, I would strongly recommend a search of the shuttle before we allow it to dock," opined Hamilton.

"What if they plan a suicide mission, and simply refuse to permit inspection?" asked Hawkins.

"It's a definite possibility," conceded Hamilton. "If so, it sure wouldn't be the first time that they hijacked a spacecraft."

"Then how can we guard against such a scenario? Even if we took the *Lunik* and intercepted the Earth shuttle, we have no means with which to force compliance. A terrorist could still ignore our radio messages and continue on to *Orion*," stated Bergman.

"Obviously, what we need is a way to gain entry without arousing suspicion," concluded Hawkins. "Unfortunately, the very act of contacting them by radio and requesting a search is bound to alert any terrorist who might be aboard."

"Anyone care to offer a solution?" asked Bergman.

With all three engrossed in deep thought, it was several minutes before the silence was finally broken by Professor Hamilton. "I do believe I have a scheme that just might work," he said.

....

Four days later the *Rigel* lifted off from Florida's Cape Canaveral sprawling launch complex. Aboard the shuttle was a hasty substitute by the name of Karim Abdullah. Replacing an American technician, he was a religious zealot enlisted by Harker and his group of fanatics, in a last desperate attempt to preserve the status quo. Acting as pilots were Donald Prentice and Ivan Kuprin. The former was a veteran U.S. astronaut from Chicago; while the latter was a skilled Russian shuttle pilot and a native of the city of Kiev. Neither crew member was aware that their lone passenger was armed. Nor did they have any knowledge of the sinister nuclear bomb concealed within the shuttle's spacious cargo bay. The mission of the pilots was to ferry *Lunar Base* refugees to Earth. Their passenger's intention was to destroy *Space Station Orion*—even though it would mean his own death!

Some one hundred kilometers distant from their destination, and closing at a rate of 1,200 meters per minute, the *Rigel* received an unexpected radio communication. It was from the *Lunik*, informing them that they were searching for a lost scientist who had gone after a valuable piece of equipment with a jet pack. Somehow, it had either malfunctioned or a miscalculation had sent him drifting away from the station. According to their data, his most likely position lay almost directly in the path of the inbound shuttle. Would they please look for him on their radar and, if at all possible, pick him up and return him to *Orion*? At present, the *Lunik* was further away and in a less favorable position for interception.

Acknowledging the request, Kuprin commenced monitoring the ship's radar screen. Surprised, but not too concerned, Abdullah remained seated. A delay of mere minutes was of small consequence or threat to the fulfillment of his task — namely, to dock with Orion so that the bomb might be set off by a coded radio signal beamed from Earth. With his death he would become a martyr for his faith, and his name would go down in history forever.

To the utter astonishment of the two professional astronauts, who tended to view the request as little short of hopeless, they soon picked up a tiny blip on their radar.

"He's currently about four kilometers off to starboard and just a little below us," announced Kuprin, as his companion initiated a brief low-thrust burn, having previously oriented the craft in a direction that would facilitate a rendezvous.

"See if you can raise him on the radio," said Prentice, as he fired tiny maneuvering jets and swung closer to the solitary drifting figure. Approaching, it was soon perceived that he was clinging to a canister of some sort— an object which served to greatly enhance the radar echo.

Moments later, Kuprin's efforts proved to be successful. "I've managed to establish contact," he declared. "He wants to know if we can open the door to the cargo bay, so that he might bring in his illusive but extremely valuable container."

"What's so precious about it that he was willing to risk his life by chasing it through space?" asked Abdullah.

"He's evidently an astronomer and describes it as an electronic device used in gamma ray astronomy," responded Kuprin. "It would appear to be of immense importance to scientists."

"Ask him if he needs help to bring it into the shuttle bay. If so, one of us can suit-up and assist him with the use of a jet pack," said Prentice, pressing a button which would open the cargo door.

"He says that his controls seem to be functioning properly, and that he believes he can manage by himself," said Kuprin, as the *Rigel* slowly pulled alongside the space-suited figure sitting astride an alleged runaway canister.

With bursts of gas from his jet pack, the lone space-walker skillfully guided the fat cylinder inside the shuttle's open cargo bay. In moments he was able to secure it to a bulkhead wall with a length of nylon cord. Casting a glance about the interior, he soon spotted a suspicious looking object in one corner of the compartment. Upon noticing a surveillance camera, he approached it from behind and promptly deactivated it by cutting a connecting cable with a pair of wire cutters which he had removed from his utility belt. A quick examination with a geiger counter confirmed his fear that the object in question was indeed an atomic bomb. Unfastening it from the straps which held it, he proceeded to push it toward the open door, thankful for the weightless state of orbital freefall which allowed him to move hundreds of pounds with comparative ease. With a sharp burst of jet exhaust he accelerated the bomb through the opening and shoved it into space in a direction opposite to that of the *Rigel's* motion. Taking a small electronic device from his pocket, he flung it after the silver canister as it receded into the distance. By the time they docked at *Orion* the deadly bomb would be dozens of kilometers away.

Reentering the craft, the rescued figure signaled through his helmet radio that he was entering the air lock, and to please close the outer door to the cargo bay. Although puzzled as to why the surveillance camera no longer worked, Prentice complied.

Abdullah, becoming a little suspicious at the camera malfunction, rather nervously fingered the pistol in his jacket pocket. With his sworn duty to see that the *Rigel* reached the orbiting space station, he was prepared to shoot the new arrival if he showed the slightest sign of interfering with the flight. Upon observing a lone and apparently unarmed and harmless astronaut/scientist entering through the air lock, he relaxed his grip on the weapon.

"Thank you for picking me up. My name Mark Hamilton," said the newcomer, taking off his helmet and commencing the task of removing the cumbersome pressure suit and jet pack.

"You are the famous — albeit, controversial— Professor Mark Hamilton?" inquired Prentice.

"I'm afraid so. Incidentally, you are now cleared to dock at Orion at your earliest convenience."

"You say we're *cleared* to dock?" asked Kuprin.

"Yes. The nuclear bomb that you were carrying in your cargo

bay has been safely ejected into space. Already, it must be trailing us by more than a kilometer."

"My God! Who would put such a thing on board?" Prentice wanted to know.

"Try President Harker and his cronies," answered Hamilton. "He has evidently become so desperate that he cannot allow us to testify in person."

"You mean that he intended to blow us all up the moment that we reached *Orion*?" voiced an angry Kuprin.

"Affirmative!"

"You will go back and retrieve it!" Abdullah demanded, rather hysterically brandishing his pistol.

"Are you crazy? Why would we be so stupid as to do that?" asked Prentice, both astonished and appalled by the request.

"Because if you don't, I will shoot the lot of you!" shouted Abdullah, furious at himself for not having foreseen the ruse that had been used to gain access to the *Rigel's* cargo bay.

"Put the gun down!" ordered Kuprin. "We're hardly going to let ourselves get vaporized by a nuclear bomb."

His attention focused on the Russian pilot, Abdullah did not notice Hamilton reach inside his pocket for a small object resembling a ball point pen. Just as the terrorist was about to fire point blank at Kuprin, he was suddenly enveloped in a purple glow.

"I guess we can proceed to *Orion*," said Hamilton, removing the pistol from the rigid form which floated aimlessly in the cabin of the shuttle.

"We owe our lives to you," responded Prentice, exuding gratitude. "But tell me, what was really inside the canister which you brought aboard?"

"Another bomb of the same type that I cast into space."

"What!" exclaimed Prentice.

"Surely, you're joking?" voiced Kuprin.

"Not to worry. This one can't be exploded by a radio signal

from Earth. Only a specially coded impulse could detonate it. Had it not been possible to eject Harker's bomb, I was prepared to stop the *Rigel* from docking at *Orion*. With the electronic detonator no longer a needed item, I simply dumped it into space."

"What would you guys have done if we hadn't picked you up?" asked Prentice.

"In such an event, the *Lunik* would have intercepted you before reaching *Orion*. If you failed to back off and submit to an immediate search, then they would have deliberately rammed the *Rigel*."

"Who are they?" inquired Kuprin.

"Jerry Butler and Alexei Belinsky," replied Hamilton. "A bunch of us drew lots for the privilege of becoming potential martyrs."

"Don't you think we had better inform them that all is now well?" Prentice asked, noting that a blip on the radarscope, which he took to be the *Lunik*, was only 40 kilometers away.

"I'll speak to them," said Hamilton.

Within minutes of informing Earth that the *Rigel* had docked at *Orion*, a bright flash harmlessly lit the night sky.

....

Some four hours after it arrived, the *Rigel* departed *Space Station Orion* with fourteen passengers. (The others would follow a few days later in the *Polaris*.) En route to Earth were the Frosts, Baldwins, Hamiltons, Bergman, Butler, Yashin, Kovakov, Cooper, and ex-CIA agent Ron Harland. (In a recent televised broadcast, Harland had blasted the Harker administration, calling it most unprincipled and publicly tending his resignation.)

Deciding against a scheduled landing at Cape Canaveral, for fear of yet another attempt to silence them, Prentice and Kuprin piloted the *Rigel* to a Russian space launch facility some 2,000 kilometers to the southeast of Moscow. Promptly flown to that nation's capitol, they were given a hero's welcome and invited to present their account on national television. Yashin and Kovakov, in particular, were interviewed at length by the news media of several countries. It was not long before they succeeded in arousing the ire of the Soviet public, who demanded that the United Nations declare President Harker to be criminally insane.

The following day the entire group was flown to London, where they gave a repeat performance before a highly receptive audience. Again, there was strong resentment of the shameful treatment accorded the Matusians and a cry to impeach the U.S. President. British Prime Minister, Cecil Jameson, promised to bring the whole affair to the immediate attention of the United Nations. In fact, he had already arranged for the *Lunar Base* refugees to present their stories in person, in an emergency session to be held some two days hence.

Arriving under heavy guard and without incident at the United Nations headquarters in New York, the group testified before a global television audience. For the first time most American citizens were allowed to learn the real truth about the alien presence on the Moon, and of the nefarious role played by their President and his associates in attempting the destruction of this benevolent and highly advanced humanoid race. When informed of the many priceless gifts that they had proposed to give Earth, for merely the price of reforms which would greatly benefit the average individual, feelings of outrage quickly gripped the nation. Within hours of concluding the interview, an angry mob stormed the White House. Almost unopposed, and even supported by a number of security guards and military personnel, they proceeded to assassinate Harker and Vice President Donovan.

Nor was the U.S. Presidency the sole target of the people's fury. Upon learning from staff members of the infamous meeting of sixteen of the world's most wealthy and influential men, who were clearly just as guilty, an attempt was soon launched to bring all the plotters to swift justice. With their identities known, the United Nations passed a resolution to confiscate their wealth and to hunt them down and try them as dangerous terrorists. The pope acted immediately to distance himself from Cardinal Manzella, claiming that the devil must have inflicted him with some form of mental illness. Likewise, several Islamic leaders suddenly decided that Muhammed Bakr was no longer a true representative of their faith.

Over the course of the next few months considerable progress was made in achieving a number of much needed reforms on Earth. Realizing the necessity of having to eventually form a World Government, the United Nations voted to disarm and abolish the armies of all countries in favor of one International Police Force, comprised solely of highly principled volunteers dedicated to the preservation of peace and sworn to uphold the dignity of the human soul. Henceforth, any government seeking to violate the outlawed practice of military conscription, or of mistreating its citizens in any way, would be promptly removed from office and its leaders charged before a World Tribunal.

Motivated by advice proffered by the Matusians, other planned reforms included a more equitable distribution of wealth and a more realistic approach to the issue of religion. In the interest of reducing long-standing religious friction and prejudice, it was now decreed that the education of children should not be restricted to one specific religion. No longer would a child be obliged to follow in the footsteps of naive parents who had blindly embraced many outworn and archaic concepts handed down by their ancestors.

Thirty years would elapse before the advent of what would clearly be a momentous saga in the history of the planet Earth. Hopefully, in this interval, humanity could find within itself the fortitude and the wisdom to rise to new heights in a universe which was now slightly less mysterious by reason of its encounter with a superior and more highly evolved alien civilization. Perhaps, in a few generations, mankind might even be permitted to become a junior member in what the Matusians had described as a Galactic Federation of Planets.

Science Update

Since the writing of *Lunar Encounter* there have been a number of significant developments in the field of astronomy which deserve mention, as they afford convincing evidence in support of the "New Cosmology" presented in the text of this work. These scientific revelations may be stated as follows:

A "Cosmological Constant"

Impressive evidence against any form of Big Bang cosmology is inherent in a study of type Ia supernovae. To the astonishment and consternation of many scientists, it has now become necessary to postulate a negative side to gravitation in order to account for observation. (The highly respected journal, *Science*, cites the discovery of a *cosmological constant* as "the most important scientific advance of 1998.") What has caused this sudden conundrum among certain members of the scientific community? As reported in a number of astronomy journals, studies of distant type Ia supernovae (which are of remarkably similar luminosity) have revealed that expansion of the universe is not slowing down with the passage of time. (This slowing of cosmic expansion is a firm requirement of traditional viewpoint, which would consider gravitation to be solely an attractive force propagated indefinitely into space.) Instead, supernovae research has disclosed that the universe is expanding at a rate consistent with the premise that if you double the distance you also double the speed of recession. In turn, this must indicate a steady repulsive factor and rule out any form of Big Bang cosmology, leaving us with only one alternative — an Eternal or Steady-state universe featuring the principle of renewal through continuous creation.

The "Principle of Equivalence" Law

An interesting observation has come to light with regard to NASA's Pioneer space probes. (See: "A Space Mystery," *Newsweek*, October 4, 1999.) Contrary to expectation, the two probes (moving outward in nearly opposite directions) are slowing down at a rate which cannot be explained upon the basis of current laws of gravitation. Although this discrepancy would appear to be only one part in ten billion, at the distance of the Pioneer probes the actual modification of gravity needed is likely of the order of one part in 170,000. The additional ingredient may be ascribed to the inferred distance/repulsion aspect of gravitation. The big question which arises is why the probes are slowing down instead of accelerating. To grasp why this is so we must consider the *cumulative* effects of what might be termed a fourth expression of gravitation — namely, a *time lapse* factor in which it is conceded that no physical reaction can take place in zero time. Since the force of gravitation is believed to propagate — at close to the speed of light — from atom to atom, it follows that a massive body will resist acceleration more than a tiny object. Invariably, it will be slightly more efficient with respect to the smaller object, and the "principle of equivalence" law, long cherished by physicists, will have to be modified accordingly.

A "Small Bang" Creation Site

What must be considered to be crushing new evidence against the Big Bang has surfaced in observation by NASA's orbiting Chandra X-ray Observatory. Revealed in an image of the distant galaxy 3C295 (about 5 billion light-years away), the intense X-ray flux is ascribed to the presence of a supermassive central black hole. It is reported that within a radius of a million light-years from

3C295 there are "more than 100 galaxies and enough material to make 1,000 more." (*Astronomy News* Web site announcement, November 23, 1999.) What does such incredible celestial density signify? *Quite simply, it displays all the characteristics of a "Small Bang" creation site!* This object is totally against the dictates of Big Bang cosmology, since any concentration of gas and dust of this magnitude would surely have been among the very first to have condensed completely into stars and galaxies. Instead, we have before us matter of incredible density which has failed to condense even after roughly 10 billion years following a supposed Big Bang explosion! Clearly, we are most likely viewing a "Small Bang" creation site which may possibly have an antiquity as recent as a hundred million years or so. It may be predicted that many more such primordial creation sites will be found with future observation.